D0529522

The Last Words We Said

The Last Words We Said

LEAH SCHEIER

SIMON & SCHUSTER BFYR
NEW YORK | LONDON | TORONTO | SYDNEY | NEW DELHI

An imprint of Simon & Schuster Children's Publishing Division
1230 Avenue of the Americas, New York, New York 10020

This book is a work of fiction. Any references to historical events, real people, or real places are used fictitiously. Other names, characters, places, and events are products of the author's imagination, and any resemblance to actual events or places or persons, living or dead, is entirely coincidental.

For information about special discounts for bulk purchases, please contact
Simon & Schuster Special Sales at 1-866-506-1949 or business@simonandschuster.com.
The Simon & Schuster Speakers Bureau can bring authors to your live event.
For more information or to book an event, contact the Simon & Schuster Speakers Bureau at
1-866-248-3049 or visit our website at www.simonspeakers.com.
Interior design by Hilary Zarycky
The text for this book was set in Perpetua.
Manufactured in the United States of America
First Edition
2 4 6 8 10 9 7 5 3 1
Library of Congress Cataloging-in-Publication Data
Names: Scheier, Leah, author.
Title: The last words we said / Leah Scheier.
Description: First edition. | New York : Simon & Schuster Books for Young Readers, [2021] |
Audience: Ages 12 up. | Audience: Grades 10-12.
Summary: Nine months after Danny disappeared, his closest friends, Ellie, Rae, and Deenie, deal with their loss very differently but will have to share secrets about the night he disappeared to uncover the truth. Chapters alternate between past and present.
Identifiers: LCCN 2020055971 | ISBN 9781534469396 (hardcover)
| ISBN 9781534469419 (eBook)
Subjects: CYAC: Missing persons—Fiction. | Friendship—Fiction. | Secrets—Fiction. |
Jews—United States—Fiction. | Loss (Psychology)—Fiction.
| Dating (Social customs)—Fiction.
Classification: LCC PZ7.S34313 Las 2021 | DDC [Fic]—dc23
LC record available at https://lccn.loc.gov/2020055971

For Ms. Fowler,
my English teacher,
and all teachers
who inspire their students every day

Prologue

The last time I hugged Danny was nine months ago, on January 1st at six a.m.

I'm absolutely sure of the date and time. I won't change my story, no matter how many times the cops repeat the question.

I hugged Danny for the last time on January 1st, early in the morning before the sun rose.

It was seven days after our big fight.

Six hours after he left my best friend's party.

And five hours after they claim he disappeared into Lake Lanier forever.

Chapter 1

"So basically we've narrowed our choices for movie night to *PAW Patrol* or a National Geographic show about gorillas?"

Rae is trying to keep the irritated judgment out of her voice and failing—again. She and I had agreed to treat Deenie's new convictions with respect, but recently our best friend's spiritual growth had begun to interfere with pretty much everything fun. Parties. Concerts. Even ice cream.

But Ben & Jerry's is totally kosher! I'd argued when she gave it up last month. *Your father eats it—and he's a rabbi!*

Deenie had ducked her head contritely as she always did when forced to assert herself on matters of religion. *I'm sorry,* she'd murmured into her lap. *You guys can totally go ahead. I'll just drink a soda.* She hated this part, the explanations why she couldn't eat something, or wear open-toed sandals in the summer, or swim if there were boys within a ten-mile radius of the pool. She hated being different, especially when her choices affected Rae and me.

Today, though, Deenie doesn't seem to mind the argument. "You know I'm right about this one," she says softly. "They've done studies about this. Watching that stuff changes how you think."

"What stuff?" Rae challenges. "Movies with a plot?"

Deenie sighs and plucks at her long black braid. "Movies that exploit women. That portray them as objects." Her face flushes. "You know what I mean."

Rae rolls her eyes. "Right. Then I guess the documentary is out too. I hear one of the gorillas flashes a tit at the end."

"All right, stop it, Rae," I say. "We don't have to watch a movie. Why don't we make something instead? I think we have brownie mix and that vegan ice cream Deenie can eat. I'd love a brownie hot fudge sundae."

Rae shrugs and agrees with a reluctant smile.

"I've been taking a crocheting class," Deenie remarks as we head to the kitchen. "I can show you guys how to embroider designs into a kippah if you want."

"I'll pass," Rae replies. "Baking is one thing, but I'm not trying to be a seventeen-year-old grandmother. Besides, who are you making kippahs for? You don't speak to boys anymore."

"I speak to them," Deenie protests.

"And none of the boys I'd date would wear a kippah anyway." Rae winks at us. "At least, not after I'm done with them." She knocks over the box I've placed on the counter. "Come on, what is this crap? Why would you use a mix when you can make real brownies?" She nudges me with her butt. "Move aside. I've got this."

Deenie and I exchange a smile. We both knew this would happen. You wouldn't know it to look at her, but Rae has a serious baking obsession. She's stick thin, with deep-maroon hair—half spiky, half buzzed—and a collection of colorful helix ear piercings. But once she's in the kitchen, her shiny RESIST bracelets come off and her battered oven mitts become her badge of honor. Rae's rosemary macarons make our local bakery's taste like sugar paper in comparison. My dad once rebooked a flight when I told him she was making her famous chocolate lava cakes that evening. Seriously. They're that good.

Sometimes I wonder if her pastries are the only reason my parents have put off having "the talk" with me about my wayward friend.

"The talk" for religious Jewish parents is a little different from the "facts of life" that most adolescents get. We get a modified version of that, too, but there's a special edition for the religious Jewish teen. It usually concerns the friend that has gone *off the derech*, or strayed from the "straight and narrow" path of our religion.

Only Rae didn't just go *off the derech*—she took a blowtorch to it.

Rae's parents are much like mine: They all went to the same Jewish high school, they keep a Sabbath-observant, kosher home. They attend the same synagogue and contribute to the same charities. Our families fit into the category of the "modern" Orthodox Jew. In our parents' view, anyone to the left of us is probably a little lost and still searching for God, and anyone to the right is slightly medieval and possibly a fanatic. Basically, we follow all the rules but also enjoy sampling from the secular (read: goyish) world. We go to the movies, keep up with the Kardashians, and follow the latest fashions, with modifications for modesty, of course.

I don't think the non-Jewish world realizes how many flavors of religiosity there are within our people. The term "Orthodox" immediately conjures up an image of swaying bearded men in fur shtreimels and curly sidelocks. But my community is as different from theirs as we are from the Amish. The ultra-Orthodox shun the secular world completely for fear that outsiders will burst their insular bubble. They dress to stand apart while we dress to fit in. If it weren't for the small knit kippah on my dad's head or the loose skirt covering my mother's workout leggings, no one would even guess that we were Jewish.

Deenie's long dress tangles around her legs as she climbs down from the counter, clutching a bag of marshmallows. She's singing softly to herself, like she always does when she's distracted, but she stops abruptly when my dad sidles into the kitchen.

"What are we baking today?" he asks with an eager smile.

"Hey, Dr. Merlis." Rae hands him a spoon covered in batter. "I'm making brownies topped with marshmallow and peanut butter crunch."

"Elisheva, you are a genius," he says. He still calls her that, even though she dumped her Hebrew name when she started dumping everything else. It used to drive me crazy how wrong "Elisheva Temima" was for her. (It literally means "God's oath of innocence.") For me it was a relief when Elisheva declared that she wanted us to call her Rae. She insisted that "Rae" sounded celestial and limitless.

"Wait until you taste the fudge that's going on top," she says with a grin.

"I hold you personally responsible for my cholesterol, young lady," Dad replies. "And for this," he says, grabbing the chunk of gut hanging over his belt.

Rae shrugs and reaches for the vanilla. "Life's too short to be on a diet."

That's how Rae relates to most things: life's too short to date one guy at a time, to obey a midnight curfew, to never eat ham.

"I guess." Dad gives me an uneasy look. "Still, all things in moderation, right?"

Rae doesn't answer, because I'm pretty sure that's the opposite of her life mantra. But she'd never contradict my parents. Not to their faces, anyway.

"Hey, Dad, why don't I call you when the brownies are ready?" I hint.

He blinks and shoots me a bashful smile. "Right. No problem. Message received." He turns to Rae and gives her a thumbs-up. "Keep up the good work!"

She rolls her eyes as he slinks out of the room. I know what she's thinking. My dad means well, but he and my mother have been walking on eggshells around Rae since the day she began her full-body rejection of everything they believe in. Deenie, Rae, and I have been friends since elementary school and my parents love them both. But around Rae, they're super chipper and supportive, as if they're afraid that the slightest ripple of disapproval will drive her to get a giant face tattoo or something.

My father is barely out of the room before Deenie looks up from sifting the flour. "I do so talk to boys!" she exclaims, as if there's been no break in the conversation.

We both stare at her.

"I talk to Danny."

Rae glowers at her. "Talked. You talked to him. Ellie is the only one who still does."

"Stop it," Deenie reproaches her. "That isn't nice."

Rae turns to me, and her sharp blue eyes soften. "You know what I mean. I wasn't trying to be—"

I cut her off with a wave. "I know what you meant. It's okay."

Deenie and Rae exchange the same look they've been exchanging since Danny disappeared. The *How close is Ellie to the edge?* look.

"So—where *is* Danny right now?" Deenie asks, in the same tentative, diplomatic voice she's used since she discovered my secret.

"In his favorite spot." I point to the window seat in the dining room behind us. He's half buried in pillow cushions, but he looks up from his comic book when Deenie says his name.

Deenie turns around immediately and beams in his direction. She doesn't say anything; I think my friends have a secret agreement never to acknowledge him with words. "I didn't see him there," she murmurs to me.

Rae doesn't turn to look; she's beating the brownie batter with vicious energy. "So—should I add white chocolate chips, then?" she asks me. Her voice is neutral, innocent.

But I see Deenie flinch and stiffen. "Rae—" she whispers.

"No. You don't need to do that," I reply. From the corner Danny shoots me a wounded look. White chocolate is his favorite. "We ran out of it last week, anyway."

And my mother wouldn't let me buy more, even when I'd insisted. *We don't eat white chocolate, Eliana. Nobody in our house eats it.*

I hadn't argued. A few months ago I would have shouted at her: *Danny eats it; Danny loves white chocolate!* I know better now.

"So, I found the brochure for Derech HaEmes sitting on my dresser again," Rae says in the same light voice. "I put it right back on the dining room table." Danny shakes his head and chuckles quietly to himself.

Deenie is also laughing. "How many times has that brochure made that trip?"

"Six." Rae pours half the batter into the pan and pats it down. "This time, though, I drew mustaches on all the girls. So my parents will know I saw it. Hopefully, that'll send them the message." She gives Deenie a Cheshire cat grin. "But if it comes back again, I'm afraid those sweet girls are getting penis hats."

Deenie chokes a little and takes a gulp of water.

"That's a summer camp for 'at-risk' girls, right?" I ask. "Is this one at least near Atlanta?"

Rae shakes her head. "Not even close."

"Then I'm glad you're not going," I declare. "It really sucked when they sent you to that uber-religious yeshiva in New York."

"Yeah, that was intense." She sighs and tears open a bag of marshmallows. "I can't believe I stayed as long as I did."

"Well, you did say they were really nice," Deenie reminds her. "Except for all the conversion stuff."

Rae looks up suddenly, and her eyes narrow. She studies Deenie's expression for a moment before replying. "It wasn't like that. Just lots and lots of learning. I bet *you* would have loved it."

Deenie smiles. "I wish I could have gone with you."

Rae looks away. "Yeah, but then you wouldn't have met Danny," she points out softly.

They both glance over at the window seat where Danny's sitting. He waves at them, but neither of them wave back. He seems disappointed and slumps back against the pillow.

"I'd have met him eventually," Deenie says.

"Yeah, but Ellie would have claimed him all to herself before we got back." There's a bitter ring to Rae's voice. "Neither of us would have stood a chance."

I want to protest, want to insist that I never would have been that selfish, but a look from Danny stops me. Reminds me of just how selfish I can be.

But I can't think about that now, not in front of them. "Your parents are really still hoping that you'll find religion at a summer camp?" I ask, mostly to change the subject. "I thought they've accepted by now that you're—"

I pause and consider how to finish the sentence. It's hard to describe Rae sometimes. She doesn't really fit into a category.

"Our favorite RAWR," Deenie suggests.

Rae sighs and flicks a marshmallow at Deenie. "I wish you'd stop calling me that."

I steal another look at Danny; he's glanced up from his comic book and is watching Rae intently. He was the one who'd coined the term RAWR to describe our friend. It stands for Respectfully Awesome Wannabe Rebel, l and it describes Rae better than her real name ever has.

I don't hang around a lot of rebels, but I'm pretty sure that most of them don't text sweet messages to their parents while blatantly breaking curfew. (*Staying out later, love you, Will text again in an hour.*)

Danny once teased her about her unorthodox rebellion. *Seriously, Rae, have you ever told them off, or at least slammed a door in their face?*

She'd turned on him so fiercely that he'd stepped back a pace. *This is about* me, she snapped. *And the life I want to live. It has nothing to do with being a bitch to the people who love me.*

That was when Danny came up with the term RAWR to describe her. She pretended to hate it.

"You're a total RAWR," I insist. "And it's not like it's a bad thing."

"Among rebels it is," she replies. She smiles, though, and I know that she secretly doesn't mind. "But, yeah, to answer your question, I think my parents have accepted that I'm never going to be *frum*. But they can't help hoping, you know?"

From the corner Danny sends me an urgent look. "I need to talk to you," he mouths, pointing to the stairs. I slide off the kitchen stool, taking care that my face is neutral and turned away from Danny. "Be right back," I say lightly. Deenie watches me as I leave; I can feel her dark eyes following my every move. Rae is completely absorbed in some marshmallow-related activity.

Danny hops off the window seat and follows me up the stairs to my room. I wait until the door is closed behind us.

"What is it?" I ask him. "Is something wrong?"

He nods and sinks onto the rug. I settle down next to him and cross my hands on my lap. I want so badly to reach out and take his hand, the way I used to when we were alone together. But I know that I can't do that anymore. Danny will only stay if I obey the rules.

"Something is bothering Rae," he tells me. "I think she's really worried about someone."

I shrug. "Yeah, she's worried about me, as always. What else is new?"

He shakes his head. "This isn't about us, Ellie. Didn't you see how distracted she was just now? She actually forgot to add the sugar."

"Seriously?" I say with a laugh. "You picked up on that?"

I'm not surprised, though. That's Danny for you. People naturally confided in him—but even if they hadn't, I think he would have magically discovered all of his friends' secrets.

"Didn't you notice?"

"Of course not."

Over the years, Danny had tried to teach me how to spot little signs, to work out what people were thinking. I was never very good at it, and I'd gotten rusty since he went away. Now I spend all of my time straining to hear his voice. I don't have the energy to worry about sugarless brownies and what they mean.

"I'll talk to her," I assure him.

He scrambles up from the mat and looks at the clock. "Well, I'd better go."

Eight p.m. It was one of the rules, the one I hated most, the one I'd negotiated and bargained for. So far we'd never broken it.

"Just five more minutes," I beg, like a little kid on the swings. He hesitates and I'm so grateful. I take a slow, tentative step toward him. He tenses, stops breathing for a moment; I can see the struggle in his eyes. He knows my instructions, the promises I made so that I could keep him with me. I sigh and back away.

"Can you come over tomorrow morning?" I ask him.

"Of course. I always come with you to Nina's. But isn't therapy after school?"

"Actually, I was hoping you'd come with me on my morning jog. It's really boring to run alone."

He wrinkles his nose. "I hate running."

"Please? You owe me a story, remember?"

His face glows the way it always does when I remind him of our game. "I'm working on a good one for you."

"Awesome. Truth or fiction?"

He crosses his arms. "You know I can't tell you that."

That's fine with me. It's actually what I love most about him. I'm never quite sure which of his stories are true or pure imagination. Sometimes I'm sure I've guessed correctly, but he never tells me if I'm right.

I don't think I want to know.

"I guess I'll see you tomorrow?" he says. He turns toward the window and then pauses, remembering. "I have to use the door, don't I?"

I nod. "One of the rules. No magical entrances or exits."

"If your parents hadn't cut down our tree, it wouldn't be an issue," he points out.

I walk over to the window and gaze down at the spot where my beautiful oak once stood. In its place is a miserable stump covered in weeds. "We didn't really leave them much choice, did we?"

He doesn't answer me, and after a moment I look back to find that he's gone.

Chapter 2

The next morning, Danny shows up on my front lawn just as I finish stretching. He's wearing a black polo shirt that billows like a tent around his thin frame.

"So, when did you take up running?" he asks me, glancing up the empty street. It's just after dawn, and the road is eerily quiet. A heavy mist still shrouds the horizon; the red-roofed homes bordering our cul-de-sac are blurred, like ghosts.

I shrug and sink into a lunge. "It was a therapy suggestion from Nina. It's supposed to release endorphins or something. Raise my mood. Clear my mind."

He grins. "Clear me from your mind, you mean."

I smile. Maybe inviting him on my run was the exact opposite of what Nina intended.

"Well, I'm ready when you are," he says.

"But you haven't stretched."

He gives me a wry smile. "I haven't pulled a muscle in nine months, Ellie."

I smother a pang of guilt. He didn't mean it as an accusation, I tell myself. He was just joking around. "Nice one," I reply, trying to match his lighthearted tone. "You're hilarious."

He throws his arms out. "Well, that's why I'm here, aren't I? For your entertainment."

"Are you in one of your sarcastic moods again?"

"Now, why would you say that?" He's bouncing on his heels like a kid holding his pee. "All right, Ellie. Ready or not—"

"Danny!"

"Catch me if you can!" He takes off in a sudden sprint, kicking dust into my face. I drop my water bottle and race after him, but he's too fast. His feet barely touch the ground as he runs.

"Danny, slow down!" I shout.

He obeys, and I race to his side. "Don't yell my name like that," he warns, pointing to another jogger down the road. "Someone will hear you."

"She's far away," I assure him. "It's fine."

"Whatever you say, m'lady."

"M'lady? Really?" I sigh and shake my head. "You are in one of your moods."

"My moods are your moods. I don't have my own moods anymore."

Again, the jab of guilt. I frown and try to ignore it. "I hate it when you say that."

"It's true." He speeds up a little, and I struggle to keep up. There's a stitch in my side that is stabbing me with each breath. We've zipped past the squat, comfortable ranchers on my street and are pounding toward the nature trail before I manage to catch up with him.

"Wait up. You promised me a story, remember?"

He nods but doesn't break his sprint. "As you wish, Princess Buttercup."

"Jeez," I exhale. "This is definitely all you. I would not have come up with that."

He doesn't answer right away; his lips are twitching, and his eyes get the faraway, dreaming look I love.

After a couple of minutes, he settles into a comfortable jog and glances over at me. "There once was a young man who fell in love with a girl he could never have." He pauses, and I wonder if this is just an idea, if he's working out the details while we run. The best stories are the ones he makes up on the spot.

"Why couldn't he be with her?" I prompt. My breathing is more regular now that we've slowed our pace.

"Because he came from a cursed tribe," he replies. "A tribe of men doomed to eternal sadness. The villagers of the town had exiled much of the tribe years before, so they wouldn't be tainted by their pain. But the man managed to keep his job as town treasurer, and he sometimes saw the girl when she came to inspect the city's coffers. He was forbidden from speaking with anyone for fear of contamination, so he'd hand her the ledgers and step back, his head low, so that she wouldn't have to see the sadness in his eyes."

"She never spoke to him? Not once?" I'm breathless with anticipation, like a child at a candy store.

"Never. Until one day he learned her secret, and he understood the key to her heart."

We pass by the entrance to my running trail and head up the main road toward the elementary school; I normally prefer to run on small streets, but I have no choice but to follow him.

"What was her secret?"

"Well, it turns out that the young lady was also in pain, though she pretended happiness so that the villagers would accept her. Her first husband had died young, leaving her alone. And she wanted a baby more than anything in the world. But the doctor had told her she would never be able to have children. She lived in terror that the others would learn of her sadness and exile her, too."

I've heard this story before. He'd told variations of it for years. I already know where it's headed.

"So what could the man do?" I ask him.

"He couldn't do much while they were both surrounded by judging eyes," Danny says. "So he packed up his bags and went searching for a way to make her happy. Years later, when he finally returned to the village, he was carrying an abandoned orphan in his arms. The lady was so excited by the baby that she convinced herself that she'd fallen in love with the man. She agreed to marry him even though he was cursed."

"But if he got everything he wanted, the curse would have been broken," I point out.

Danny stops by the entry of the local elementary school and looks toward the parking lot. A couple of teachers are unloading books from their car, but the area is otherwise deserted.

"The curse doesn't work that way, Ellie," he says, switching abruptly to present tense and dropping the singsong voice.

"Curses in fairy tales do," I argue. "And that was obviously a fairy tale."

As usual, he doesn't tell me if I'm right.

"Those teachers are staring at us," he remarks, pointing to the two ladies in the parking lot. "I should probably go." One of the women lays down her bundle of books and heads toward me.

"Hey there," she calls out. "Are you lost, my dear?"

I shake my head and wipe the sweat from my flushed face. "Nope, just jogging."

She stares at my loose skirt in confusion.

"Oh, that's a religious thing," I explain. "I always wear skirts. Even when I jog."

"Ah." She nods but doesn't appear satisfied. "I thought I heard you talking to someone," she observes, scanning me up and down.

I reach into my pocket for my cellphone and realize I've left it behind. There's no easy explanation I can offer this nosy woman.

I glance at Danny for help, but he just gives me a toothy grin.

"Yeah, that was also a religious thing," I declare. "I was chatting with God."

Chapter 3

I'm late to my appointment at Nina's because Ms. Baker, my English teacher, wants to have a chat after school. Something about the creative writing assignment I handed in and how it relates to my future. I'm not really listening, though. The woman likes me for whatever reason and is convinced that I have a knack for something.

I don't really have time for writing, I tell her. I'm going to major in biology and then go to med school, like my parents and my grandparents. (Dad says that practicing medicine is the best way to give back, a way to pay the miracle forward. He likes to remind me that modern medicine is the reason I exist.)

"Okay," she says slowly. A strand of gray hair falls over her eyes, and she brushes it back absentmindedly. "You can still participate in the contest, though. Broaden your horizons a little." She pushes a folded piece of paper into my hand. "Ellie, I really think you have a shot."

"A shot at what?" I ask, glancing at the announcement in my hand. "This is for a short story contest. I have no ideas for a short story."

She blinks at me. "But you just handed in one of the best writing samples I've ever read. And I've been teaching for twenty years."

"It's not a story, though. I don't tell stories."

"The building blocks are all there. The character sketch. The vivid descriptions—"

"I don't tell stories," I repeat. "I think you have me confused with someone else."

She gives me that pitying look. The cocked head, the narrowed, understanding eyes, the puckered lips. I hate that look more than anything. It makes me vicious.

"And if you think that writing a stupid story about elves or fairies is going to be some kind of therapy for me, you can just forget it, okay?" I continue, my voice rising. "I'm getting enough therapy."

"Ellie, I just think that it would help—"

"I'm getting plenty of help, thanks."

"Okay, but this isn't about Danny—"

Except that it's always about Danny. "Look, if you want someone to write for your story contest, why don't you ask Danny to do it?"

That shuts her up, and I make my exit with a little more noise and door-slamming than is really necessary.

I realize that she was just doing her job. If Danny had been there with me, I would've been nicer to her, I know it. He would have calmed me down, showed me the humor in the whole thing. But the rules say that he's not allowed in our school anymore. The closest we can get to each other during class is in English. It's the only period where I sit next to the window. Sometimes he's on the soccer field outside, kicking a ball around. He makes that hour tolerable, at least.

My mom is tapping impatiently on the steering wheel when I run out to the parking lot. "Are you okay?" she asks, scanning me anxiously. "We're late to Nina's." Everything seems to make her nervous now; the final school bell rang less than ten minutes ago, and she's already short of breath.

"I'm fine, Mom," I say, sliding into the passenger seat and tossing my bag aside. "Ms. Baker wanted to congratulate me on my last project."

The tension in her shoulders eases a little. "Oh." She exhales. "Great. That's wonderful, honey."

"She wants me to enter some kind of story contest."

She nods and puts the car into drive. "Well, I think that's a great idea. Don't you?" She glances at my doubtful expression, and her face gets all maternal and wise. "Creative writing is an important skill. How else are you going to put together a coherent research paper?"

"It's not really the same thing." I pretend to consider the idea for a moment. "But I guess I could write something inspirational about medicine," I suggest. "Some medical miracle story or whatever."

"That's what I was thinking!" The nervousness is completely gone; she's practically radiating approval and encouragement. "What's that saying again? Write what you know."

"Exactly! I can tell the story of a boy who drowned, but as he was sinking to the bottom of the lake, he was bitten by a radioactive eel."

Her brightness blinks out in an instant. She stares at me, open-mouthed, but I barrel ahead.

"And then the boy becomes Eel Man. His superpower is electricity—obviously. Except humans already have electricity, so he goes around fixing broken fuse boxes."

"That's not—" She pauses and gives me the same pitying look I'd just gotten from Ms. Baker. "Ellie, that's not okay."

"Yeah, I know," I say flippantly. "Like I said to my teacher. I don't have any good ideas."

The tension returns to her lips. “Maybe we should ask Nina what she thinks.”

“Right, because Nina will have all the answers. Maybe she can even give me some plot suggestions for Eel Man.” I am all snarky bitch today for some reason. Mom doesn’t look sorry when we pull up to my therapist’s home.

Nina practices out of a converted garage attached to her little ranch. The entire place (including the garage) is decorated like an episode of *Antiques Roadshow*, complete with ceramic milk-maids and walls of butterfly wing art. As Dad puts it, Nina is a fully accredited psychologist who marches to the beat of her own drum. (Speaking of drums—she has a set of aqua flame bongos from the sixties that hang directly over her desk.) According to my mom, Nina is a fully accredited kook whom we have entrusted with my mental health. During our sessions Mom sits alone in the living room on the carved oak rocking chair. She doesn’t rock or even move; she waits the hour until Nina finishes plumbing the depths of my psyche, and then she dutifully drives me home. Mom doesn’t sample the plate of home-baked oatmeal cookies Nina sets out for her (they’re not kosher) and doesn’t read the alternative healing magazines on the ottoman next to her (she doesn’t believe in alternative medicine). Mom listens politely to Nina’s advice at the end of each session and breathes deeply throughout the entire ordeal.

The only reason she’s agreed to pay for this is that Nina is the last in a long line of therapists. And so far, she’s the only one I haven’t torpedoed.

The first two psychiatrists didn’t even get a word out of me. It’s not their fault; I’m sure they were decent doctors. But I was not the problem then, no matter what they said. I wasn't delusional or depressed. I was simply waiting, like everyone else, for the police to do their job. I didn't need a psychiatrist; I needed a competent detective.

Danny is bouncing on his heels outside the garage door as I follow Nina into her office. I smile at him, and he gives me a nervous grin. He doesn't look pleased to be here; this whole therapy thing has made Danny uncomfortable from the beginning.

I really can't blame him. He's the reason I'm here.

Nina acknowledges Danny as she always does at the start of each session. (That's one reason that I agreed to talk to her. She was the only therapist who did.)

"You've come with Danny again, I see," she says, as we settle in. Nina and I sit on chairs. Danny perches on top of the bookcase and stretches out his long limbs. His heels knock lazily against the wood.

"Yep." I steal a glance at him. He waves at us and rolls his eyes.

She turns in his direction. "Ellie, how did he get up there?" Her voice is a bit sterner; the lines around her gray eyes deepen.

"I—I don't know."

"Did he climb?"

"I guess." Danny's always been a good climber; he could scale the tree outside my window in two minutes.

She sighs and looks back up at the bookcase. "Danny, you're breaking rule number two," she calls out. "No magical powers."

He gives her a grudging nod and drops down from his perch—a touch magically, as he doesn't grunt or stagger when he lands. But he's on the ground with us, and she seems satisfied with that.

Nina struggles out of her chair and pushes a dusty ottoman

out from under her desk. The movement seems to give her pain; she rubs her knee and exhales deeply as she sinks back into her armchair. "You can sit on that," she tells him.

"Are you okay?" I ask.

"I'm great—just great." She pushes back a strand of damp white hair with a swollen, knobby finger. "For a seventy-year-old with rheumatic joints, I'm the picture of health."

"I'm sorry, I could have gotten my own chair," Danny tells her. "You didn't have to do that."

She ignores his apology and focuses on me. "So, tell me about the last few days, Ellie. Anything new?"

Nina is a big fan of open-ended questions. I'm not. The way I see it, I'm here to report my "progress," not chat about school gossip.

"We've been following your rules," I assure her. Danny's acrobatics on the bookcase notwithstanding, we really have. "Home by eight p.m., no magical entrances or exits." I tick them off on my fingers. "No public discussions. No meetings on school grounds." I pause and look at Danny before I continue. He's sitting cross-legged on the ottoman, his face turned away from me so that I can't see his expression. "No touching," I conclude. He flinches but doesn't speak.

Nina appears surprised. "Really? No touching?" she asks.

Danny and I both shake our heads.

"Look, it's a good idea, Ellie. I was going to suggest it down the road a bit. But I just assumed that it would be too harsh for you at this time."

I look down at my lap. "The no-touching thing was Danny's rule. He doesn't—"

I'm struggling to find the words to explain. It's not that I don't want to touch him. More than anything, I wish I could feel the comfort of his arms again. But Danny breaks apart when I get too close. There's so much pent-up guilt now that even the brush of my hand can shatter him.

"We haven't touched since—not since that night—"

"The night Danny disappeared?"

I'm grateful she still uses that word. No one else does. "Yes."

"I see."

I'm betting that she doesn't see. In her mind, I'm sure she has some picture of two horny teenagers who just can't let go of each other. She really doesn't get it. But so far, she's come the closest.

"It's a healthy rule, Ellie. I'm proud of you."

Yeah, she really doesn't get it. It has nothing to do with health. But I'm not going to try to enlighten her. She's been friendly to Danny so far, and the two of us can use all the friends we can get.

"You understand the need for all the rules, don't you?" she persists. "Why I established them?"

I nod, my eyes still cast down. Is she going to make me review the reasons for her rules? Again?

"It's about boundaries, Ellie. You can't let Danny take over your life."

My head shoots up. "He doesn't! He would *never*—"

The protest bursts from me, involuntarily, before I have a chance to check myself. Next to me, Danny is watching us quietly, waiting for me to defend him. I swallow and consider my options. Fighting for Danny has never ended well for me, not since the accident nine months ago. My parents were all sympathy and understanding at first—until the day Danny reappeared in my life. That's when they totally lost it and the intensive therapy merry-go-round began. Rae and Deenie were also supportive, but like my parents, only at first. When Danny came back, Rae went totally cold. She wouldn't even look at him. Deenie's reaction was milder, more accepting, but she vibrated concern whenever he joined us. I could feel it every time she asked, "*Where is he today, Ellie?*"

"Maybe just go over the rules again," Danny suggests after a long silence. "I think that's what Dr. Nina is getting at."

"Okay." I take a deep breath. "Here goes: the eight p.m. curfew is so I can spend time on my own, without my boyfriend. It's the harshest rule, I think. But I understand it."

"Good."

"Besides, I'm used to curfews. When we started to date, my parents insisted that Danny had to go home by eleven p.m. Your curfew is tougher than theirs."

She nods and crosses her hands placidly on her lap. "The situation is different now."

"I never really obeyed her parents' curfew anyway," Danny interjects. "There was this tree outside Ellie's window—"

"And the rule against magical powers?" Nina continues. "What about that?"

It kind of pisses me off that she's interrupted him, even though I know she didn't mean to. "Danny doesn't actually have any magical abilities," I say shortly. "I'm not sure why it has to be a rule. My boyfriend isn't some mythical creature from a fantasy novel. He's just a boy, okay?" My voice shakes, and I struggle to steady it. I need to sound reasonable and sane so she'll just leave me alone. All I want is to be left alone with him. I take another deep breath and look into Nina's sympathetic eyes. "Danny is just a boy. Not a ghost or an angel." Next to me, Danny puffs out his cheeks and makes a flapping motion with his arms. I can always count on him to make light of an honest confession. "He's just a silly, irreverent, completely impossible boy," I conclude. "He didn't die on New Year's. He just went *missing*. They *will* find him."

Nina sighs and shifts in her seat. She's clearly not satisfied with my statement. I've stopped short of giving her what she wants, what they all want. I know my parents have been pressuring her for a "breakthrough." In their view, I'm not progressing fast enough in therapy. Before she'd led me to the garage, I'd sensed the static between Nina and my mother. *Get her to disown him already*, my mother had screamed at her through desperate, narrowed eyes. *Come on. It's been nine months!* It's the same thing Mom has hissed at my father every single night. The walls in our home are pretty darn thin.

Nina doesn't go straight for the throat, though. She's far too diplomatic for that. Instead, she sticks to the rules. "Let's move on to the next one?" she suggests mildly. "No public discussions with Danny. What do you think of that?"

"What do I think?"

"Well, you said you've been following that one?"

"Not really," Danny remarks.

"We have," I insist.

She raises her eyebrows. "You're sure?"

"Look, I know what you want me to say." My voice rises again, but this time I don't try to check myself. I'm getting angrier by the minute. This is not good therapy. Therapy is supposed to make you feel better. And Nina's did—at first. She was the only one who'd never tried to label me, never judged my relationship with Danny. I should have known that it was too good to last. "You want me to say the obvious out loud."

"Is it really obvious to you?" Her voice is so mild, she might be inquiring about the weather. *Is it really raining outside? Have you lost touch with reality? Are you really still seeing people who aren't there?*

I'm tired of playing this game. I'm tired of admitting over and over what other people need to hear. That I haven't lost my mind. That I know the difference between fantasy and reality.

"Danny never really left," I say, my voice trembling with frustration. "I don't know how else to explain it. I'm not imagining him. He's here, he's with me now because he wants us to find him and bring him home."

She nods but doesn't respond. I'm afraid to look at Danny, afraid to see the expression on his face. He's the only one who knows that I'm lying, and I can't bear to see the accusing look in his eyes. It's bad enough that I can hear what he's thinking. *Why haven't you told her why I'm gone, Ellie? When are you finally going to tell her?*

I shake his thoughts from my head. "You don't believe me?" I ask her.

"I believe that *you* think that's true."

I roll my eyes. "That's psychiatrist doublespeak. It doesn't mean anything. You can say the same thing about a psychotic person."

"But you're not psychotic, Ellie." A statement, not a question. It's strange that I find it comforting.

"I know I'm not. What's your point?"

"My point is that you believe that you need to hold on to Danny. Ellie, you're more self-aware than most of my teen patients, even many of my adult ones. What do you think would happen if you let him go?"

I'm gripping my armrest so tightly, my fingers have gone numb. She has no idea what would happen to me if I let him go. She's probably scribbled "depression/possibly suicidal after boyfriend's disappearance" on the top of my file to remind herself that I'm always near the edge—literally. But that's not even close to the whole picture. My lack of faith almost killed Danny—almost killed both of us. I'm never going to make that mistake again. "I'm not letting him go," I tell her, "because it would be wrong to give up on him. Not because I can't live without him."

And yet—even as I say it, I know that's also a lie. I can't live without Danny because I can't live with what I did to him.

"Do you think you're in the same place as you were after Danny disappeared?" she asks.

"How would I know?"

"Well, do you ever think about hurting yourself?"

I finally turn to look at Danny. He's moved closer to me, balancing himself on the very edge of the ottoman, so close that I can almost touch him. "Do you, Ellie?" he asks me.

"No," I tell him. "I promised you."

I don't care that I've broken the third rule, the one that's supposed to give me the appearance of sanity. Danny is sitting here, just inches from me, his gray-flecked green eyes drawing me in, his thin lips slightly open, waiting for mine. Each curve and hollow of his face, every familiar freckle on his nose, the little diamond-shaped birthmark at the angle of his jaw—they're more real to me than my therapist's round and wrinkled face.

"You promised?"

I barely hear her question; Danny is shaking his head and putting a finger to his lips. He's better at following the rules than I am, and he's reminding me that I'm not supposed to be speaking to him here. Not in front of the woman evaluating my mental health. He gestures toward Nina, and I know that he wants me to address my therapist instead of him. But I'm not interested in talking to her anymore.

"I promised you I'd wait," I assure him. "That I wouldn't give up hope again, like I did after you disappeared. And I won't, no matter how long it takes."

"How long what takes?" Nina says.

"They're going to find me," Danny replies. "It's just a matter of time." He's so confident, so certain; he gives me the strength to face my worried psychologist.

"I made a mistake once," I tell her. "But I promised him I would never make it again. The night I hurt myself, I believed what the police were telling us—I believed statistics and probabilities and predictions. But they only have theories about what happened the night he disappeared. They have no proof."

"The police say that Danny drowned, Ellie."

I nod. Her calm statement doesn't bother me. I've heard it dozens of times over the last nine months; I've read it hundreds of times in print.

"Yes, that's what they say. In Lake Lanier, after the accident."

"But you think they're wrong."

I look over at Danny. He's sitting cross-legged on the ottoman again, his thin arms folded across his chest. There's a shadow of a smile on his face.

"I *know* that they're wrong." My voice is calm and steady; I'm speaking for him now, and I need to be as confident as he is. "They never found a body," I inform her. "The divers searched the lake for days, and they never found him."

"And you think that must mean—"

"It means that he isn't there. He never drowned in that lake."

She just sits there after I say it. She doesn't contradict me—not even with a flicker of doubt in her eyes. I'm grateful for her silence, and scared that it will end, that she will say something that will make me hate her.

I have to give her something else to chew on, to distract her from pulling me down into her favorite rabbit hole. So, on an impulse, I tell her about my conversation with my English teacher. Just to show her that I'm still doing well in school, so she can write something positive in her notebook.

Thankfully, she takes the bait. "A story competition? That actually sounds like a great idea!"

"Oh—" I hesitate and glance over at Danny. He's gotten up from the ottoman and is studying the ceramic gargoyle on her bookcase.

"I say, give it a shot," Nina persists. "Even if you don't hand it in. I think writing would be good for you."

I'm so grateful for the change of topic that I actually consider it. "A story?" I ask her. "Don't you all think that my imagination is overactive as it is? You really want to encourage more of that?"

She laughs, and the wrinkles around her eyes deepen. I catch a glimpse of a dozen silver fillings. "You don't have to make it up," she suggests. "Start with something true. Life can be stranger than fiction, right?"

I smother a smile. She doesn't realize it, but she's just referred to the game that Danny and I have played for years. An idea springs into my mind, an idea that is the exact opposite of what Nina intended.

They want me to write a story? No problem. I'll give them a story. I'll give them an entire collection. But it will be the ones that I want to tell.

I already have a title for the first one: "The First Time I Hugged a Boy."

"You're brilliant," I say to Nina. Her smile fades, and her eyes narrow suspiciously.

"Excuse me?"

"No, really. It's perfect. I'm going to do it. I can't wait to get started."

She looks downright frightened. I suppose that sudden bright enthusiasm can be a little scary, especially coming from a disturbed individual like myself.

"May I ask what you're planning to write—" she begins.

"Oh, I'll show you when I'm done," I interrupt. "I have to go now. I can't wait to get started."

TRUTH OR FICTION by Eliana Merlis

A collection of love stories they want me to forget

(working title)

THE FIRST TIME I HUGGED A BOY

"Is this your first time flying alone?"

I nodded and gripped my passport so tightly, it bit into the tips of my fingers.

"But not your first time on a plane?"

I shook my head and swallowed. "I didn't mean to push the button. I'm just really really—"

The rest of the thought disappeared into a moan as the floor beneath us dropped and shook. The flight attendant lurched forward and grabbed the seat in front of me.

"Oh God, what's happening?" I gasped.

"Totally normal," she assured me. "Just keep your seat belt fastened, and everything will be fine." But her voice cracked at the end, and there were beads of sweat above her painted lips.

My father told me once to always look at the faces of the crew. *If they're handing out drinks and smiling, there's nothing to worry about.*

They had been serving coffee before this started, but most of the cups had flown off the cart; there were still pink sweetener packets littering the aisle like confetti. And the cheery attendant assigned to watch over the flight's unaccompanied minors definitely wasn't smiling anymore.

The pilot's voice came over the intercom again, urging passengers to stay in their seats until we'd passed through the "choppy air."

"I should get back," she muttered, and then gestured to the kid sitting beside me. "Hey, why don't you talk to him? He seems to be doing okay."

As she staggered back to her station, I turned to the boy next to me. I'd noticed him when we boarded; he was the only other unaccompanied minor on the plane, his plastic-wrapped passport dangling from his neck, like an oversized dog tag.

I hadn't planned on speaking to a random stranger; besides, he'd put in his earbuds, which is the universal signal for *leave me alone*. But as the plane rattled and dove, I grabbed the armrest to steady myself, accidentally dislodging his cord. He looked up at me, surprised. "Are you okay?"

I obviously wasn't. I could feel cold sweat streaming down my back and pooling in a gross puddle around the tag of my skirt. But if he could see the darkening shadow soaking through my shirt, he didn't let on. He smiled and held out a half-eaten candy bar. "Kit Kat?"

I shook my head and clapped my hand over my mouth. "How are you not scared?" I moaned through my fingers.

He shrugged and popped a piece of chocolate into his mouth. "My dad's a pilot. I know when to be scared. We're not even close."

It was a bold statement to make. All around us, full-grown adults were squeezing airsick bags and glancing frantically around the cabin. Even our flight attendant looked queasy, strapped into her little fold-out seat. And yet here was this skinny, pale kid, munching on candy and fiddling with his phone like we were on a merry-go-round.

"How do you know that it's okay?" I demanded.

He leaned forward—or pitched—toward me, as the plane dipped and lurched through the sky. "I'll tell you. Have you ever seen a scared horse go crazy?"

"No."

He grinned. "Well, just imagine what would happen if that wild horse was trapped on a plane with you. Terror at thirty thousand feet."

I'm not sure why I believed him, but I did. "You were on a plane with a wild horse? Really?"

He blew a strand of sandy brown hair out of his eyes. "My dad used to work for a transport company that flies racehorses across the country."

"What happened to the horse?" I was so grateful for the distraction, it didn't matter what he said; I was his captive audience until this hurricane was over.

"Tranquilizers didn't work for some reason. They were talking about shooting the horse. But then my dad had this idea to play this new agey music over the intercom. Calmed the horse right down. Plane was a wreck, though."

"Wow." I was gripping the armrests a little less forcefully. "So if everything's okay, why does our flight attendant look so scared?"

"Bernadette?" He waved at her and gave her a thumbs-up sign. "Maybe she's new. Not the bravest, is she?"

We'd finally leveled out a little, and I slowly sank back in my seat. "That's funny," I remarked. "Because her name literally means 'brave like a bear.'"

He wrinkled his nose and shoved the rest of the candy into his mouth. "Brave like—what?"

I looked down, embarrassed. "Nothing. Doesn't matter. I just—I just like names, that's all."

I knew it sounded weird, but I was so relieved that the plane had finally stopped pitching that I didn't care. I was starting to breathe normally again.

And then the floor beneath me shuddered, and the cabin lights went out.

I don't know who grabbed whose hand first (Danny swears that I was the grabber), but he didn't flinch as I squeezed his fingers. "Should I be scared now?" I gasped. There were sobs and moans echoing throughout the cabin. A couple near me had started praying loudly in a language I didn't recognize.

Danny shook his head. "I'll tell you when to be scared." His voice was so light, it slowed my hammering heart.

"Okay."

"Want to hear more weird airplane stories?" he asked.

If the tales he told me were to be believed, Danny had been on hundreds of flights, possibly thousands. Or maybe he simply attracted madness. My favorite was the one about the British gentleman who'd left the bathroom stall completely naked, angrily demanding to speak to the person who had stolen his trousers. ("And they really couldn't find his clothes anywhere on that plane," Danny insisted. "Had to wrap blankets around him in the end.") As we bobbed toward Hartsfield-Jackson, Danny actually made me laugh out loud, while the rest of the plane was panicking.

When we touched down in Atlanta, he plugged his earphones back into his ears and slipped his phone out of his pocket.

I was still a little unsteady as the flight attendant escorted the two of us off the plane to arrivals. Danny hadn't said anything since we landed, but I noticed that he wasn't searching for a familiar face in the waiting crowd. "My father's probably going to be late," he muttered to our escort.

"Aren't pilots supposed to be punctual?" I asked.

He shot me an enigmatic smile. "I guess. Except he isn't a pilot."

I blinked stupidly at him. "He's isn't? But you just told me he was. All those amazing stories—"

He looked away, his smile still lingering. "They were pretty good stories, weren't they?"

The flight attendant touched my arm. "I think I see your mom, dear." I had already spotted her; she was waving her arms wildly and calling to me. "Eliana! I'm over here! Eliana Tikva!"

"That's a cool name," Danny remarked. There was a hint of teasing in his green eyes. "It means 'God answered my hope,' right?"

My jaw dropped. Like, all the way open. He got a full view of my braces and a couple of silver crowns.

No one, not even my Hebrew teachers, had picked up on the meaning of my name. Who was this kid?

I didn't want to say goodbye to him yet, but my mom was pushing her way through the crowd toward us, so I didn't have much time. This boy was all kinds of awesome, with his crazy intuition and magnificent lies. He'd saved me on that plane. I had to thank him.

So I stepped forward and hugged him—hard. It was the first time I'd ever hugged a boy, and it was the stiffest, shortest, weirdest two seconds in the history of hugging. I managed to poke him in the ribs somehow. He made a pained "oof" sound.

Over the years, Danny and I would get better at hugging. We got better at other things too. Spinning stories. Collecting secrets.

Telling lies.

Chapter 4

I drop by Rae's house after my session with Nina, and as I walk up to the door, Danny suggests that I go in without him. "But you were the one who said I should speak to her," I protest.

"You don't really think she wants me there, do you?" he replies.

I can't argue with that.

So I'm alone when Rae's mom invites me in. She seems happy to see me; Mrs. Klein has always been kind and welcoming, though recently she's adopted an anxious pucker between her eyes when she speaks to me. "How are you, Ellie?" she inquires. "Rae's in the shower, but she should be down soon. We just made popovers, and she was covered in flour."

There isn't a speck on Mrs. Klein's business suit; she looks as immaculate as if she's just come home from her pharmacy rep job. "I'm doing great," I tell her. "Those popovers smell amazing."

"That's the Parmesan," she says, placing a plate in front of me.

Rae bounces into the kitchen, her hair plastered to her cheeks, a towel around her shoulders. "Hey, Ellie." She glances around the kitchen warily. "You came alone?"

I know what she's asking, but I'm not going to take the bait. "Yeah," I say, looking down at the steaming platter Mrs. Klein slides onto the counter. "It's just me today."

She nods, and the shadow rises from her face. "Great," she says brightly. "Have a popover."

I've been regretting the chicken salad I'd had for lunch ever since I walked in the door. It isn't kosher to eat meat and milk in the same meal, or even within several hours of each other.

"Thanks, maybe later. I just had meat."

She rolls her eyes. "Sucks to be you. Want to come upstairs?"

I didn't expect her to invite me to her room. Over the last few months she'd always found one excuse or another to keep me in the kitchen or in the basement. I didn't even realize what was going on, until I overheard Deenie and Rae arguing one day. *Look, I don't want that voodoo mojo in my space,* Rae snapped. *My bedroom is a ghost-free zone.* I'd never heard Deenie yell at anyone before, but she really ripped into her then.

"Sure," I said, as if it were nothing. "I wanted to talk to you."

Mrs. Klein picks up her keys from the counter. "I have to head back to work, honey," she tells her daughter. "But your brother and his wife are coming by later for dinner. You'll be home, right?"

"Of course."

Her mom gives her a warm kiss on the cheek, and Rae pretends to be embarrassed, mostly to keep up appearances. But we both know she's not.

I'm still confused by my friend's relationship with her parents. Most of the kids who rebelled in our community (and there had been a few) had focused their fury on the families who raised them. Rae had somehow managed to reject everything her parents believed in, without actually rejecting them. I didn't understand how that was possible. Maybe the Kleins knew something about unconditional love that the rest of us didn't.

"Everything looks pretty much the same," I remark as we settle onto her bed. "It's been a long time since I've been here."

"Yeah," she replies. "It has." There's a tense elephant-in-the-room silence. I can practically hear her thinking, *And whose fault is that?*

"So I came because I wanted to talk to you," I tell her. A look of fear springs into her eyes. "*Not* about Danny," I add quickly.

"Oh." The tension drains from her face. "What about, then?"

"I don't know. Maybe you can tell me."

"Excuse me?"

I'm struggling to find some way over the walls she's built. Lately it seems like every time I try to talk to Rae, she manages to erect a new one to shut me out. Maybe it is my fault. Or all of my voodoo mojo.

"It's just that you seem kind of worried—or preoccupied recently."

"I do." There's no question mark; it sounds more like an accusation.

"Yes, you do," I persist. "And I understand if it's about me and you'd rather talk to Deenie—or pretty much anyone except me. But—"

"It's not about you." She's watching me through narrowed eyes, her arms crossed over her chest. "And it's nice of you to notice."

It was actually Danny who'd noticed, but I decide it's better not to mention that. I don't want her to throw me down the stairs.

"So what's going on?"

She sighs and sags deeper into her pillow. "I don't know why I'm the only one who's worried," she muses. "Everyone else is seeing it. But I'm the only one who's worried about her."

"Are you talking about Deenie?"

"Who else?" Rae throws her hands up in frustration and leans forward. "She's *losing* it, Ellie. Haven't you noticed?"

Honestly, I thought everything was great between Deenie and

Rae. In fact, I was still convinced that Rae was angry at me and was trying to find a roundabout way to tell me. "I had no idea you were worried about her."

"Can't you see that Deenie is going off the deep end?" she demands. "It's terrifying! But nobody seems to care. They're all just standing on the edge clapping."

"Are you talking about religion?"

"No, I'm worried about her raging heroin addiction. Of *course* I'm talking about religion."

"Oh, Rae, you've been making cracks about that for years. Deenie's always been more religious than us. So she's recently decided to take on some extra rules. Lots of people do that."

"Yeah, but this isn't just a phase. She's taking it to a totally different level."

"What do you mean?"

"Well, take her clothing, for example. Remember that school shopping trip?"

That had annoyed me, too, actually. It was the longest, most painful two hours I'd ever spent in a mall. I'd picked out a variety of attractive new skirts and tops for myself while Deenie rejected whatever I suggested; everything was too tight, too bright, too short, too sheer. Even when the item fit the most stringent modesty standards, if it complemented her at all, she shook her head and returned it to the rack. She began senior year in a dress that was so loose, it was practically a muumuu, and so heavy, she sweated through it before first period.

"Deenie's so pretty," Rae says mournfully. "But now she seems to be hiding herself from the world. Like she's embarrassed if anyone notices her."

"Okay, but what are we supposed to do about it? If we tell her what we think, she'll just say that beauty is on the inside."

Rae grunts and shakes her head. "I have told her what I think. And that's exactly what she said. I know I'm not allowed to say anything about it at this point. She automatically shuts down if I try to bring it up."

"Of course she does. What do you expect?"

"Well, I suppose you have a better idea?"

"No, I don't. But I know she's not going to listen to you. Not about this, anyway."

She opens her mouth to argue, but I push on before she can protest.

"Rae, you can't take potshots at someone's religion for years and then expect them to respect your opinion on the subject. You've always been hostile about her faith, so of course she's going to protect herself."

"This isn't faith! It's fanaticism!"

"And Deenie will say that you don't know the difference. That everyone is a fanatic to you."

"Come on, Ellie, that's ridiculous."

"Is it? Then answer this: Would you call *me* a fanatic?"

"No! Of course not."

"And yet you still took a shot at me earlier. I bet you didn't even notice."

"What are you talking about?"

"When you offered me the cheese popovers and I told you I couldn't because I'd had meat. You said—"

She raises her hands in surrender. "I said *sucks to be you*. I know, I know." She rubs her palms against her forehead. "I didn't think you cared. You never seemed to be bothered by it."

"I'm not, really," I admit. "I don't take it personally. But Deenie does. To her, when you say stuff like that, it's like you're calling her newborn baby a troll. Over and over and over."

Rae sighs, and her shoulders sag in defeat. "We need to do something, though. Before there's nothing left for her to give up."

"What do you mean?"

"There's a new thing almost every week now. This week it was movies. Last week—makeup, even nail polish, I think. What's next?"

I shake my head.

"People," she says. She taps a hand to her chest. "And who do you think will be first on the chopping block?"

"Rae—"

"I'm a bad influence, Ellie. Why do you think your parents are so nervous around me? I don't do drugs, I barely drink, and I always wear my seat belt. In the real world, I'm a model citizen. But I ooze heresy. So, in the religious world, I'm kind of like a tumor."

I laugh. "Yeah. You're a melodramatic tumor. And we all love you. No one is cutting you out of their life."

"I'm serious," she says, with the doleful tone of a prophet predicting doom. "This is how Deenie is coping with the accident."

I flinch and look away. "I thought you didn't want to talk about that."

"I don't. I'm not trying to trigger you or whatever. I've actually enjoyed this time alone without—anyway, all I'm saying is that you have your way of dealing with it, and so does Deenie.

My question is—what is she going to do when there's nothing left to give up? How will she punish herself then?"

GOD ANSWERS MY HOPE

I never expected to see Danny again after that wild plane ride, though I spent a lot of time imagining unlikely meetings. On a trip to pick up my grandmother at Hartsfield-Jackson airport, I found myself looking for him in the crowds, as if his spirit somehow inhabited the airport and was waiting for me to find him.

But I didn't suspect that our paths would cross again in my own little suburban community, just a few months later. So when Deenie told me one morning that there was a new boy moving in on her street, I wasn't particularly interested in hearing details.

"I thought we could bring him some muffins," she suggested. "As a welcome to the neighborhood."

I just wanted to keep watching videos on my new phone. "Isn't that something our moms should do?" I said, without looking up. "They're the heads of the *shul's* welcoming committee. It's kind of weird for two ninth graders to just—"

She shook her head. "No, the boy is the new one. His dad has lived here for a few years—just around the corner from my house. If he's going to be my neighbor, I want to be friendly."

We argued about it for a little while, but the conversation ended with us trekking across our neighborhood hauling a giant basket of chocolate chip muffins.

I recognized the address as we rounded the corner. "Mr. Edelstein? I didn't realize he had a son."

She nodded. "I've seen the boy visit before. But I think he must be here to stay for good. He was hauling in a lot of suitcases. And some furniture."

"I wonder if he'll go to our school."

"Maybe. He wasn't wearing a kippah, though. So probably not."

He was wearing one when he answered the door. It was perched awkwardly over the part in his mop of sandy brown hair. He stared at Deenie, then at the basket, and then at me.

His eyes widened as they met mine. Before I could wonder if he recognized me, a smile lit up his face and he stepped forward.

"Hey, look at that," he said. "God has answered my hope."

"Mine too," I blurted out, before realizing that he was referencing my name, not professing a hidden crush. And yet, strangely, I didn't feel embarrassed or exposed. Something about his smile hinted at a double meaning.

Deenie frowned at us. "What are you talking about?"

"Well, I was pretty hungry," he explained. "And then you two show up with a buttload of muffins. I don't know what you'd call that, but to me this feels like a miracle." He was still staring at me.

Deenie looked like someone trying to work out the punch line of a joke. "It's really no big deal," she told him. "Our friend Rae over-baked before she left for boarding school, so Ellie's freezer was overloaded with muffins."

He took the basket from her hands. "You want to help me eat them?"

"Sure!" I said. "Can we come in?"

He hesitated. "Got somewhere else that we can go? It's a mess in there." His eyes shifted to the window. "There are—just—boxes everywhere."

As he shut the door behind him, I caught a glimpse of the living room before he blocked our view. It was stark and sparsely furnished and—totally clean. There wasn't a box in sight.

Deenie didn't notice anything odd, though, and I didn't want to mar their first meeting by pointing out the lie. I was actually a bit surprised by how quickly Deenie warmed up to Danny. She had always been shy around boys, even before she started "*frumming* out" (becoming increasingly observant—or as Rae would put it, trying to be more religious than God). I think I even felt a pang of jealousy as I watched them joke and laugh, because Deenie was the natural beauty in our little group, while I was still working through my messy red hair, zits, and braces stage.

I told myself that I was being silly. At the time, Danny was still reaching for puberty, while Deenie had already developed her curves and stood over a head taller than both of us. Danny looked like her little brother rather than a boy her age, so I knew she must have friend-zoned him at first sight. I had nothing to worry about.

"So what is Deenie short for?" he asked her as we headed over to my house.

"Adina Shira."

"It means 'gentle song,'" I put in. "And it's so perfect for her that it's embarrassing."

"It's not that perfect," she protested. "Lots of people sing."

"Lots of people don't land the lead every time they audition for a play."

Deenie blushed but didn't contradict me. Her talent was a fact, and despite her modesty, there was no way she could argue with that.

"Gentle song, huh?" Danny smiled at her. "So do you sing—very, very gently?"

She laughed and punched my shoulder. "Hilarious."

"Hey!" I rubbed my arm and punched her back. "He was the one who said it!"

"He's a boy. I can't hit him."

Danny gave her a confused look. "I'm pretty sure it's the other way around."

"No, she's *shomer*," I explained. "It means she doesn't touch boys."

"Really?" He bounced ahead and threw his arms out. "Not even a friendly hug?"

She shook her head and stared at the ground.

"Her father is a rabbi," I continued. "You should hear his sermons about being *shomer*. They'll blow you away." I could see I was just making things worse. Her cheeks were the color of wild cherries. I should never have mentioned the *shomer* thing. I'd forgotten how uncomfortable these explanations made her.

Danny's expression didn't change. "Hey, that's cool."

"Yeah, sure it is," she muttered. Worse than explaining the religion thing was the patronizing looks she got after she did. People saying, "That's so interesting!" when they were actually thinking "Freak!"

I cast about for a topic change but came up totally blank.

Danny was on top of it, though. "No, I'm serious!" he assured her. "That means I can get away with saying anything! And Ellie will take the hit for me. God, this is fantastic!"

Deenie's guarded frown melted a little. "You're not serious."

"I totally am! I've got a Jewish force field protecting me! So I can say—dildo face!"

"What are you—like, five?"

"Boob juice! Poodle sex! Butt plugs!"

"We could just not be friends with you," Deenie suggested. But her shoulders shook with suppressed laughter.

He held out the basket. "Yeah, but I've got the muffins. So—penis."

Chapter 5

A couple of days after our conversation about Deenie, Rae sends a text to our friend group demanding a trip to the mall. It's a little unusual for her, as she tends to prefer small shops, but it doesn't occur to me to question her motives until she plugs Perimeter Mall into her phone's GPS.

"But Phipps is closer," I point out. "Why Perimeter?"

"We always go to Phipps," Deenie says from the back seat. "I want to try something new."

I have to admit that it's a nice change from our usual crowded plaza. I'm enjoying our stroll down the large, gleaming corridors when Rae stops in front of a hair salon and stares at the ornate sign. "Hey, look at that!" she says. "I wonder if they take walk-ins."

I suppress a sigh. Not the hair thing again. "Why?" I ask, pretending innocence. "Are you thinking of going back to blond?"

"Never." She tilts her head to the side and studies my head. "I'd consider red, though."

"Ah, thanks for the compliment."

"Yeah, but *I'd* make it look good."

"Hey!"

"Maybe I'll ask for a cut too," Deenie muses, swinging her shiny black braid over her shoulder. "It's gotten so long."

Rae seems suddenly alarmed. She shoots Deenie a warning look, but Deenie continues on, unruffled. "Just below my ears would be perfect," she says. "Then I don't have to wear it in a braid all the time."

"But it's so pretty," I protest. "When you leave it down, you look like a Pantene commercial model. Why would you cut it off?"

She stiffens and wraps her fingers around her ponytail. "I could use a change. I think we all could."

Rae is shooting darts out of her eyes, but they keep falling just short of her target.

And then my mother materializes in front of us. She claps her hands together in a horribly fake show of surprise. "Well, hello, girls! I guess great minds do think alike!"

"Nice try, everyone," I say as I survey their bright, hopeful faces. Even my mother is in on the conspiracy. It's obvious suddenly why we're here; Perimeter Mall has a hair salon while Phipps does not. This spontaneous "expedition" had been planned, and their motives are clear.

"I'm not cutting my hair, you guys," I insist, covering the puffy mass behind my ears.

They all just look at each other. There's an awkward silence while my mother pretends to blow her nose. (She can't even do that convincingly.) Someone has obviously forgotten their lines. Or maybe I just jumped forward in their script.

"I'll go first, okay?" Deenie suggests mildly. "Maybe you'll like my hair short and get a similar style?"

It's no secret that my family and friends have been lobbying hard to get me to fix my hair. And I'll be the first to admit that it's horrible in its current state. In the past, I've worn it long and I've worn it short, but I've never worn it puffy-pyramid style—which is how it's been for the last nine months. In awful haircut limbo.

A couple of days before New Year's I'd decided to try a new salon; I wanted to surprise Danny with a sexy new do. The hairdresser styled and moussed and snipped for half an hour. The result was a multilayered disaster. My already thick red curls had somehow doubled in volume, and instead of the sleek cute bob that I'd envisioned, I looked like Little Orphan Annie after an electric storm.

I'd intended to get it fixed as soon as possible, but I never got the chance. Danny's disappearance after the New Year's party ended all trivial plans; I had other things to worry about. Since then, any time someone has mentioned my hair, I've dug my heels in deeper and shut them down. This was how my hair was when Danny went missing, so I've only trimmed it to keep it from changing, and hidden the mess with a thick hair band and tight ponytail. Time stopped for me when Danny went away; I wanted him to see that when he came back. I needed to keep everything exactly the same.

"Well, I'm going in," Deenie declares when I shake my head. "You can at least keep me company."

"You're here to keep Ellie company," Rae protests. "We all are. This wasn't supposed to be about—"

She freezes midsentence, and her breath catches; her eyes have fixed on a group of young men who've just passed us. Rae's lips fall open, her cheeks fade to white.

"Rae, what's going—"

But I also don't finish my thought. I've followed her gaze, and suddenly I can't speak either. I see why she stopped breathing. We've all stopped breathing.

Right there, in the middle of a throng of boys, is Danny. His back is to us, but it's him, in the flesh. This is no vision, no flight of imagination, no tortured hallucination. It's obvious that we all see him this time. That sandy mop of hair, the long neck, the bony, slouched shoulders. He's even wearing his favorite black polo. It's him. He's actually here—just twenty feet from us.

Next to me, my mother claps her hand to her mouth; Deenie grabs at Rae's arm. But Rae shakes her off and lets out a piercing shout, her eyes blazing with wild joy.

"Ellie," she whispers. "Oh my God, Ellie—I see him too. *I see him too!*"

"Rae, wait," Deenie begs, "I don't think—" But Rae is already tearing after him.

I'm frozen to the ground, torn between the urge to follow her, yet too terrified to move. They could all see him now. Finally, they could all see him.

But what did that mean for me? Why hadn't he said anything as he passed? He must have seen me. Did he not want to see me? Is this what I've been waiting for all this time? Danny has finally come back, but now he won't look at me.

"Wait!" Rae cries, and launches herself at them. Two startled boys fall back to let her pass. She calls Danny's name and grabs at his shirtsleeve, spins him around so roughly that he totters against her.

An awful moan shudders through Rae, a cry that tears through all of us. The boy is wearing a different face; every part of him is wrong, distorted. To his buddies I know he looks completely ordinary, but to us he's absolutely hideous, because he's not the boy we've longed for. Like a small child reaching for her parent's arm, Rae had accidentally grasped at a stranger. And in that moment, that boy's innocent, confused expression burns us like a monster's sneer.

Rae wilts, her fingers still clutching his sleeve. Mom grabs my hand and quickly draws me close to her. I can barely feel her arms around me as she pulls me into a hug, but I catch a glimpse of her face before I'm buried in her blouse. She looks like she's seen a ghost.

Deenie is the only one who's kept her sanity. "Sorry about that," she calls out to the startled boy. "She thought you were someone else."

"No worries," the boy replies, and gently disengages Rae's hands from his shirt.

I hate his stupid voice. *No worries?* How can he say that? We're obviously worried. Even my mom's calm confidence is blown; she's shaking as hard as I am.

I wriggle out of her arms and start toward Rae; I'm scared she's about to fall to the ground. Deenie is closer, and she reaches her before I do, but she's also too late. Rae's sadness has already evaporated. Fresh outrage sweeps over her; it straightens her back and lights up her eyes. "Where did you get this?" she demands, grabbing the boy's shirt again. "This isn't yours!"

He looks like he's at a total loss. Deenie tries to pull her away, but Rae has caught most of the polo between her fingers; she seems to be trying to yank it off of him.

"This isn't yours!" she repeats desperately. "How did you get this?"

"Look, Rae, there's a monogram," Deenie points out, prying the cloth from her fingers. "It's the wrong shirt."

The wrong shirt, the wrong boy. Rae stares at the fancy orange stitching and throws it back at him with a cry of disgust. The boy makes a face at his buddies, and they all take off down the hall, their laughter lingering behind to mock us.

Rae turns around to us, her jaw set, her eyes blazing. "Stop looking at me like that," she growls. When none of us speak, she clenches her fists. "Stop looking at me!" she repeats, and then takes off.

I head after her, leaving Deenie and my mom behind.

"Go away!" Rae shouts as I catch up to her at the entrance to the restroom. She slams the stall door in my face. "I just need a second, okay?"

"Rae, it wasn't just you. We all saw him. I know how you feel—"

"Yeah, but you see Danny all the time," she snaps. The door lock clicks into place. "Isn't that right? So there's no way you know how I feel."

"Come on, that's not fair—"

"He's always with you. I bet he's standing next to you right now. Is he laughing? I bet he's laughing at me. Go to hell, Danny!"

I take a deep breath. "Fine. I'm going to go."

"Good. See ya."

I linger in case she changes her mind, but there's no sound from behind the closed stall door, so I reluctantly step back into the hallway. On the way back I spot my mom and Deenie near the entrance of Nordstrom. They are facing away from me; my mom is speaking, and I stop to listen, my body hidden behind a purse display.

"You have sharper eyes than I do," Mom is saying to Deenie. "I really thought it was him for a moment."

Deenie looks down at her feet, as if ashamed of herself. "I tried to stop her. I knew it wasn't him."

"How?"

"If it really was him, I know I would have felt—" Deenie hesitates for a moment and shakes her head. "You know that Danny always knew when Ellie was nearby? Even before he saw her. He'd know she was going to call even before his phone rang. He'd never have walked past her like that."

It feels good to hear her say that, to see my mother wipe away a tear. I want to hug them both, to thank them for seeing a part of him I couldn't see. I'm about to step out of my hiding place to join them when Deenie draws closer to my mom. "He isn't coming back, you know," she whispers. "He's never coming back."

"I know," my mother says. "I know, dear."

I step back into the shadow, a surge of anger blotting out my love.

My mother gives her a sad look and gently touches the end of the black braid coiled around her shoulder. "Your hair is so beautiful. Are you really planning to cut it all off?"

Deenie doesn't look up. "Yes, I am," she says softly. There's a ring of regret behind her cool conviction. "I just don't want it anymore."

DANNY MEETS THE RAWR

There was a boy in my basement! It made me giggle when I thought about it. It's not that I'd never been exposed to the opposite sex before—my high school was coed. But religious girls and boys hung out in separate circles for the most part. No girl I knew could truly say that she was close to a boy.

And yet, somehow, I'd managed to convince one to be my friend. Danny's voice had changed sometime after our plane ride and had fallen to a good octave below mine. I didn't know why this excited me as much as it did, but I loved listening to his gravelly rumble. He smelled like a strange cross between talc powder and Old Spice. And he was taller than me now, though not yet close to Deenie's height.

Over that winter break, he only came by during the mornings when my parents were at work. My basement had always been my friends' preferred hangout place; in a clever attempt to supervise my socializing, my parents had equipped the large windowless room like a teenager's dream palace: it housed a collection of massive multicolored beanbags in front of a large-screen TV, a corner Ping-Pong table, and a stocked mini-fridge for late-night snacking.

Danny ate all of Rae's frozen cookie dough and then worked through the kitchen pantry so diligently and enthusiastically that my mother began to wonder if I was finally going through a growth spurt. (I wasn't. He was.)

But the best thing about Danny was the stories he told. Sometimes they were anecdotes from his former life in LA, sometimes tall tales based on real events—and sometimes they were total fantasy.

Deenie objected to the tall tales, especially the ones that overlapped with reality. We couldn't help noticing there were a disproportionate amount of girls in his stories who resembled the two of us; it was hard to believe that most of his past acquaintances were tall, rosy-cheeked brunettes or petite, freckled redheads. "You're basically lying," Deenie pointed out after one of the fictional brunettes did something she didn't like. "How will we know when to believe you?"

He shrugged. "I never lie about anything that's important."

"I bet I can guess which ones are made up," I said.

That's how our favorite game was born.

We were in the middle of playing one morning during winter break, and I was building a pretty strong case for "fiction" (He couldn't possibly have organized a team of ninjas to scale the school fence and steal ungraded math tests, could he?) when the front door slammed and there was a heavy thud on the landing.

"Anyone here?" Rae's voice echoed down the stairs. "I'm home, girls!"

Deenie and I exchanged concerned looks. Neither of us had mentioned our new friend to Rae. She was supposed to be in New York at a Jewish boarding school for "at-risk" religious girls. We didn't expect her back until Passover break, so we figured we had plenty of time to introduce Danny to her.

"Down here!" Deenie called out.

She bounded down the stairs and burst into the basement. "Hey, bitches! What are we smoking?"

Something was definitely wrong. She only called people bitches when she was nervous or scared. Rae looked the same as usual, except maybe her blond curls had lost a little of their bounce. They hung limply around her thin cheeks, and she kept brushing them aside impatiently.

"Who's up for some experimentation?" she demanded, whipping a crushed box out of her jacket. "I've got hair dye and scissors."

"Rae, what are you doing home?" I asked her.

"I wasn't expelled, if that's what you're thinking," she declared, ripping open the box and dumping the contents on the floor. "I left. Turns out, you have to pretty much kill someone to get expelled from that school. And believe me, I tried. To get kicked out, not to kill someone. But they were too busy trying to love me to get that I just wasn't interested in what they were selling. So, I got on a bus."

"You just—left?" Deenie's expression was somewhere between shock and admiration. "Did you call your parents to let them know?"

Rae tensed and turned her back to her. "Come on, Ellie, help me with this dye stuff. I've never done this before. And I'm not going home looking like me." She seemed about to say more when suddenly she paused and sniffed the air.

"Why does it smell like Old Spice in here?" she asked, turning around in a circle until finally spotting Danny, buried deep in a beanbag. He waved and made a show of smelling his armpit.

"That would be me. Too much? Thanks for the tip."

Rae froze, her mouth slightly open.

"Rae, meet Danny," I said awkwardly.

"Hi there." He struggled out of the beanbag and pointed to the bottle in her hand. "By the way, if you really want a change, then that isn't the right dye. It's temporary. Not going to make the statement you want."

It was like waving a flag in front of a bull. My awkward introduction had obviously pissed her off, but she'd been holding back—until Danny's innocent little suggestion sent her straight over the edge.

"You want a statement, shrimpy boy?!" she shouted. "I'll give you a statement. I'm DONE." She walked over to him and grabbed the little kippah off his head. "I'm done pretending to believe this crap. So you can just stick this thing up your skinny butt and run home to your mama. I'm not going to any more 'lost girl' schools and I'm not listening to another rabbi tell me to just follow the rules and be patient. I'm rejecting all of it," she shrieked, brandishing the kippah in his face, then turned back to me and Deenie. "And if you want to replace me with this nice Jewish boy, then go right ahead."

She choked on the last words and made a noise between a sob and a moan. Deenie took a couple of steps toward her and then stopped, one arm outstretched in an aborted hug. I wavered between Rae and Danny, torn between protecting my new friend and comforting my old one.

But Danny didn't need protecting. "It's okay, you can keep that," he said quietly, nodding at the crumpled kippah in her hand. "I wear it mostly to make my father happy. And I would love to run home to my mama, except I can't because she died. That's why I moved to Atlanta."

Rae's eyes widened, and she took a step back. There was an awful, heavy silence; nobody breathed while Rae struggled to find her voice.

"You don't have to apologize to me," he said before she could find the words. "I've eaten about ten batches of your chocolate chip cookie dough, and if you promise to make more, that's better than any apology. But your friends didn't deserve that." Rae's shoulders sagged; she glanced around the room as if looking for an escape. "Hey, I'm with you on the religion thing," he continued, lowering his voice. "But you know it's precious to Deenie and Ellie, and calling it crap would be like me calling your brownies crap. It would hurt you, and anyway, it wouldn't be true. Your brownies are awesome—except that I think they're missing something."

She blinked and cleared her throat. "What are they missing?" she said hoarsely.

He smiled and pulled a white Hershey's Kiss out of his pocket. "So glad you asked."

A little color returned to her cheeks. "That stuff is, like, fifty percent filler. I only use the best ingredients."

He grinned. "Great. I'm looking forward to it."

She took a deep breath, and her lip quivered. Rae never cried. She yelled, she swore, she threw things, but I'd never seen her cry. She came pretty close that morning, though. There was a glassy shine in her blue eyes. "I think I'd better go home now," she whispered. "I need to talk to my parents."

"Do you want me to come with you?" Deenie inquired.

She shook her head and turned away.

"You're coming back, right?" Danny asked. "I'm still pretty hungry, and these two can barely crack an egg."

"Hey!" I protested.

"That omelet tasted like toenails, Ellie."

I chucked a pillow at his face.

Rae's shoulders were shaking with silent laughter. "I've never really talked to my parents about how I feel," she said after a moment. "So it might take a while. But I'll be back. Save your appetites, guys."

Rae was gone for hours. When she returned, her eyes were bloodshot and puffy, but there was something new in her smile, something stronger than faith and kinder than rebellion. I think it was hope. She never told us what she said to her parents, but I believe that was the day that the RAWR was born.

Chapter 6

"But how will you know if he's any good?" Rae asks Deenie as she settles with a sigh into her beanbag and leans back against the cement wall. We've made an unspoken agreement to leave last week's Danny sighting alone. Rae hasn't referred to it at all, and neither Deenie nor I want to bring back the pain of that evening. So we just add it to the list of things that we don't talk about.

Not on that list, apparently, is Deenie's *shomer* conviction.

Rae has become obsessed with the idea that Deenie is going to wake up one day to the horror of a sexless marriage, shackled to a man who's not attracted to her. "Or he could be gay. What if he's gay, and he doesn't realize it until he sees you naked? And then BAM." She makes a deflating motion with her index finger. "Oh, no, there it goes. I'm melting, I'm meeellllting. . . ."

Deenie bats her hand away and laughs. "I guess I'll just take my chances. And, anyway, you can feel chemistry, even without touching."

"She's right," I say. I'd certainly felt it with Danny, way before we touched each other. "If you're in love, the sex will be wonderful."

Rae snorts. "How would *you* know? Weren't you the *shomer* poster child?"

I should have kept out of it. Rae usually tries to hold back when talking to Deenie about religion. But when I get involved, those gloves come right off.

"Are you making fun of me and Danny?" I shoot back.

Deenie looks frightened and immediately tries to change the subject to hair. "I'm glad I cut it myself," she says, running her fingers through the short curls around her neck. "This style suits me."

But I'm not going to be distracted. "So now you're the sex expert, Rae?" I demand. "Even though you've never told us anything about your supposedly hot dates?"

"Really, I don't think that it's any of our business," Deenie says quickly. "We love you, Rae, and we respect you—"

"—even when you decide to date a total douchebag," I finish for her. "And that douchebag tries to destroy us."

Rae deflates a little, but her eyes are still snapping fire. "Greg wasn't a douchebag," she says, her voice shaking. "He made a stupid mistake. And I broke up with him as soon as I found out what he did."

"But it was too late, wasn't it?" I demand. "He'd already wrecked my relationship with Danny."

"He didn't wreck anything. That's all on you, Ellie—"

"On me?"

"You're the one who broke up with Danny!" she points out. "You're the one who wouldn't give him a chance to explain—"

"Since when do you ever give anyone a chance to explain?" I shoot back. She stands up suddenly, and I realize I've hit her in a sore spot. She looks stricken—and scared.

"And now you're lecturing Deenie about sex," I continue, picking up steam. I push myself off my beanbag and step toward her. "So I want to know—where exactly is this coming from?" I hadn't intended to slide off the rails into this territory. I should have just said something spiritual about the bond between two soul mates and then gone back to talking about hair. But suddenly it isn't about defending Deenie's choices, or my own. There's been a poison boiling under the surface, souring every word between me and Rae since the day of the big fight. I'd been trying to ignore it, but old resentments bubbled up anyway, every time we talked. I'm tired of our passive-aggressive sniping. So I've just blown the lid right off the simmering pot. "You never told us. Was Greg really that great?"

Rae shrinks in front of me. "W-we didn't sleep together—" she stammers. "Because I didn't want to."

I'm not ready to let this go yet. "But you're such an expert, Rae!" I shout. "So who was it, then? You never told us. Who was the magic guy? Was it Matt? Or Jeremy? Or that dude who ran off to yeshiva—what was his name?"

"Yonah." Deenie moves between us, like a desperate referee. "Stop it, Ellie. She doesn't want to talk about it."

"Why not?" I persist. "We're supposed to be best friends, aren't we? Then why is it a one-way street? Why are there things that I can't ask?"

"You can ask me anything," Rae replies coolly, but there's fear behind the wall of defiance. "But the truth would be too hot for you to handle. I don't want to hurt your virgin ears."

Her entire body is tense, prepared; she's gripping the edge of the Ping-Pong table to steady herself, as if bracing for an attack. *What is she afraid of?* I wonder. "Rae, there's nothing you can say that would shock me," I insist. But the words come out sounding like a challenge instead of a reassurance. "Friends shouldn't have secrets from each other," I try again, in a softer tone. "But ever since New Year's I feel like we've all been tiptoeing around a minefield." Next to me, I sense Deenie flinch, and I turn to her, in appeal. "You agree with me, right? I'm not imagining it?"

I have no idea why I'm saying these things. It's not like I'm ever going to tell them what I did on New Year's. And yet, somehow I'm convinced that if they're honest with me, if they let down their shields, this awful tension will magically disappear.

"We all miss him, Ellie," Deenie says. "We're all just—dealing with it differently. We're not hiding anything."

It's not an answer—and as I watch her, I realize, it isn't even the truth. Rae has always been both combative and defensive, but Deenie's openness is the one thing I could always rely on. And yet, for some reason, she won't meet my eyes now.

I have no idea what to say; we are glowering at each other, like rivals at a standoff. I need to offer something, a small guilt, as a sacrifice, to break this silence. "Look," I begin, slowly, "I know you both blame me for the fight I had with Danny. And I blame myself, too."

Deenie shakes her head, but she still won't look at me. Her eyes are fixed tearfully on Rae, who is standing with crossed arms and a stony face. "We don't blame you, Ellie. Nobody blames you."

But you should, I think. *You have no idea.*

There's a soft noise from the landing, and I look over Rae's shoulder to see Danny padding down the basement stairs. He isn't supposed to be here; it's well after eight o'clock, and visiting hours are over. Still, I'm not going to tell him to leave. Just the sight of him relaxes, me and I feel my heart rate slow. It's good to know that Danny is on my side, when I truly need him, rules or not.

"You have a tell, you know that?" Deenie says suddenly.

I've heard those words before. Danny used to say that about my easy blush whenever I was hiding something. I put my hands over my cheeks. "Yeah, I know." *She can see that I am lying*, I think. They can all see. My face must be giving me away. "What are my freckles doing now?" I say, straining for a joking tone.

She shakes her head. "I always know when Danny's here," she tells me. "Even though I can't see him."

That was not what I was expecting. "What do you mean?"

"Your eyes go soft," Deenie says. "Every time."

I lower my hands and watch them warily. Where is their judgment? I know it's coming; it always does. I'm waiting for Deenie's pity and Rae's frustration.

But instead Deenie turns away from me. "Nobody blames you," she repeats, softly, as if speaking to herself.

Rae moves to take her hand, but Deenie shakes her off and quietly leaves the room.

MY FRECKLES BETRAY ME

While Danny's revelation that he'd recently lost his mom was not an earth-shattering shock to me, it did make me a little uneasy at first. Several of my friends and classmates lived in single-parent homes, but so far, I didn't know anyone who'd sat shiva for a parent. Though Danny was already past the seven-day grieving period when we met him, I was surprised to learn that he was still in the middle of *shloshim*, which meant that his mother had died less than a month before he moved to Atlanta. I remembered my father's *shloshim* for his dad; he'd barely left the house, ate only when reminded, and slept most of the day, so it was hard to reconcile the image of Danny yelling "penis" in the street with that of a kid in mourning. I didn't know what grief was supposed to look like; maybe it was mostly hidden and would only surface suddenly and dramatically if I said the wrong thing. So for the rest of winter break I tiptoed around him, avoiding any topic that I thought might trigger a painful memory.

I probably took the sensitivity thing too far. Some instinct told me that even the sight of a mother might send Danny into a spiral, so I found clever ways to make sure he was out of our house when my parents returned in the evening. They both worked at Emory and carpooled (Mom was a dermatologist, Dad an ENT), so they generally walked in together, like clockwork, at six p.m. It was easy enough to avoid a meeting during break, but it got more complicated when we all went back to school. Danny had decided to enroll at our local yeshiva high school. It was more religious than he was, but I suspect he chose it because Deenie and I went there, and starting over in a class where he knew no one was terrifying. Plus, he said it made his dad happy.

Rae enrolled in our school too, much to our surprise. For her family it was a compromise: Her parents preferred the more religious girls' seminary, or some institution that concentrated on "at-risk" teens. Rae wanted to attend public school. "I'm just starved for some diversity!" she complained. We couldn't really argue with that. For a community in the middle of a very diverse city, our school (and our suburb) were pretty homogeneous. And for anyone looking for a Jewish education, the only choice in our area was the girls' seminary or our coed yeshiva, neither of which boasted very much diversity.

After school the four of us usually congregated in my basement. That only left an hour until I had to get our new friend out of the house. Danny caught on pretty quick.

"Do I embarrass you?" he said abruptly one afternoon, after I'd trotted out another fake excuse about a doctor's appointment. "Or are you just some kind of after-school hypochondriac?"

I looked over at Deenie and Rae for help, but they were pretending to be engrossed in their math homework. Rae had told me flat out that I was being stupid. *(He just wants us to treat him like normal, Ellie!)* But Deenie had backed me up, so I'd hoped for a little more support from her. All I got was the top of her head.

"What do you mean?" I asked innocently. "I really do have an appointment with the allergist."

He raised his eyebrows. "You have a tell, you know that?"

"A what?"

"When you lie, your freckles glow."

I clapped my hands to my cheeks; behind me Rae snorted with laughter, and Deenie smacked her knee. "Oh my God, they totally do!"

I'd always been sensitive about my skin. I was as pale as a ghost even in summer, with freckles covering every inch of me. I could never hide what I was feeling; my face was like a mood ring, changing color with every emotion.

"Whoa." Danny backed up a step. "And apparently they disappear when you're upset. Where'd they all go? Come back, little freckles!"

"I was just trying to do the right thing!" I could feel my cheeks burning. "And you're making fun of me!"

"Hey, I'm only trying to figure out what's going on. Are your parents so religious that they don't want you to associate with boys? Is that why you don't want me to meet them?" He winked at me and lowered his voice to a seductive whisper. "Am I your naughty little secret, Ellie?"

Rae and Deenie had dropped all pretense of studying and were watching us with unconcealed delight. Rae had *I told you so* written all over her face.

"I was protecting your feelings, okay?" I blurted out. "My parents are perfectly nice. And I'm sure you'd all get along. But I didn't think that you would want all that happy family energy around you—" Even as I said it, I realized how ridiculous it sounded.

"You thought I'd prefer to hang out with a bunch of angry assholes?"

"No! I just thought because you'd recently lost your mom—"

His smile faded as understanding hit. "Wait. You thought because I didn't have a mother, I didn't want anyone else to have one either? You know that's not how feelings work, right?"

"I know," I admitted, hanging my head. There was no way to explain the stupid away. "I was just thinking—"

It was Rae who saved me from further embarrassing myself. "Hey, it's not like we've met *your* dad either," she interrupted. "Every time we bring him up, you change the subject. So why don't we make a deal? You can stay for dinner tonight and meet Ellie's parents if you introduce us to your mysterious father."

Danny smiled broadly and rubbed his hands together. "Awesome. But you're baking, right?"

Rae answered his unspoken question with a grin. "I'll make the lava cakes you like. Extra white chocolate."

My parents were used to my friends showing up for dinner; in fact, they welcomed the platters of treats that Rae brought with her. And as I predicted, that evening went perfectly. Danny got along great with my family, and with Deenie's and Rae's as well, over the next few weeks. And yet, whenever we mentioned a possible visit to Danny's home, he always found an excuse to delay it.

As much as my parents loved Danny, though, his presence in my life brought a new "concern" to their lives. I was aware of whispered conversations behind closed doors for a few days until one morning I found myself staring at my dad over a giant mug of steaming hot chocolate.

"What's up?" I asked, taking a tentative sip of the slop he'd made me. I get my cooking skills from my father. There were lumps of undissolved cocoa floating around a lonely marshmallow.

"Your mother and I are concerned about your new friendship," he began, placing his hands flat on the table, as if trying to steady it.

"Oh, no," I said, and placed my hands beside his in mock gravity. "Not concerned. Anything but concerned!"

"This is a serious matter, Eliana," he replied, ignoring my tone. "There are a lot of issues to consider before entering into a new relationship—especially with a member of the opposite sex."

I sighed. "You know there's nothing between Danny and me, right? He's just a friend." I wasn't lying, either. He was, officially, just a friend. "And you can tell Mom that."

"I understand that," he replied. "But we wanted to remind you that our policy on dating has not changed. Not until you are sixteen."

"That's FINE."

"And then, only a religious boy."

"Danny is religious."

"Who shares our values."

I stifled a groan. I didn't want to hear my father talk about "intimacy," as he called it: how he and my mother had been completely *shomer* while they were dating, and how happy they were that they had. I'd heard it all before. It was their favorite topic, after the excruciating details about their battle with infertility and my miraculous conception on their final round of IVF.

I would have argued with him, but I knew that the best chance for continuing my friendship with Danny was to convince my parents that he was absolutely no threat to their precious only daughter.

So my practical side shut up the rest of me. And I rolled my eyes as if Dad had just reminded me that eating pork was forbidden. "Well, obviously!" I said. "I'd only want to date someone who was *shomer*. Don't you trust me at all?"

At which point Dad insisted (loudly) that he did, and Mom materialized from nowhere and assured me that she was very proud of me, and when we were finished hugging and smiling, my friendship with Danny was safe. I'd been fully parented—and duly warned.

My parents just had THE TALK with me, I texted Danny later that evening.

The sex talk? he replied. **Aren't you a bit old for that?**

No. The DANNY talk.

. . . never had one of those. What's that?

Come on. Do I have to spell it out?

Yep

They just wanted to make sure that you and I are not . . .

Yes?

We're not allowed to . . . you know . . .

What? Allowed to what???

I suddenly realized that my first attempt at flirting over text had wildly misfired. There was no way to continue this convo.

Never mind. Forget it.

No. I need to know. What can't we do?

Seriously, forget it

TELL ME

bye

That was it from me, I decided. It was getting too embarrassing. But I didn't turn off my phone. I couldn't go that far.

We can't play Cards Against Humanity anymore? he asked after a few minutes. **Because it's too sexy, right?**

Exactly. No more sexy card games.

OMG Ellie, what are we going to do???

....

Ellie!!! 😭😭😭😭😭

You are so weird

(Long pause)

We can still play in secret, right?

Chapter 7

I rarely take Rae seriously when she rants against religion. So I can't help dismissing her concerns about Deenie's deepening devotion. Like many kids at my school, I've become more relaxed since I began high school. I still keep the basics, like kosher and Shabbat, but other areas have become a bit hazier. But I admire the few friends that have stuck to their convictions, despite pressures to conform.

Deenie has done more than just stick to her convictions, though. She's by far the most religious student at our high school. The local girls' seminary would have been a much better fit for her. The girls at that school share her views more than any of us do. But she seems happy enough by my side; she doesn't seem bothered by the puzzled looks she gets when she shows up to gym wearing multiple layers beneath her jersey.

In my opinion, there isn't any reason to be alarmed, despite Rae's doomsday predictions. For some kids *frumming* out is a developmental milestone, something they try for a while to see how much of it actually sticks. Deenie's dad was one of the wisest men I knew; so if he wasn't concerned, there was no reason I should be. Deenie told her parents everything, and they trusted her completely.

So when Deenie bursts into my house in tears, begging me to reason with her parents, I'm totally speechless.

"They're acting like it's the end of the world!" she sobs. "And it isn't. There's an understudy for my part. She'll be happy to fill in for me."

I'm a little lost. I know that Deenie has been rehearsing with the Atlanta women's theater group for months. They're performing *Les Misérables* at the end of the fall. But why would she need to call in an understudy?

She answers my question before I ask. "I just can't take the risk," she explains gravely. "Something awful happened today."

I'm still completely lost.

She takes a deep breath before she breaks the news. "A tech guy wandered in during rehearsal this afternoon," she says in a low voice. "And I didn't see him until the end. But by then it was too late. He *heard* me."

"He heard you sing."

She nods, and fresh tears well up in her eyes. "I can't take that back. I can never take that back."

I understand why she's upset, but I know Deenie's distress would be a complete mystery to most people. Deenie had accidentally violated a modesty rule that prohibits women from singing in front of men (excepting close relatives). The scripture compares the voice of a girl to nakedness, so in Deenie's eyes, it's as if the tech guy stumbled in on her while she was in the shower. Among the very religious, solo singing in front of men is discouraged because it's considered provocative behavior. Still, no one I know takes that prohibition so much to heart, and I've certainly never seen anyone in tears over a simple mistake. Despite the wording in the Talmud, a melody from a musical is not the same thing as a nip slip. I want to be sympathetic, but

Deenie's freak-out seems a bit melodramatic to me.

"It's okay," I say, putting my arm around her. "You didn't do it on purpose. It's like accidentally turning on a light on Shabbat. You just say 'oops' and then try to do better next time."

She stares at me intently, her bloodshot eyes narrow with determination. "There isn't going to be a next time," she declares solemnly. "I'm pulling out of the play."

It's my turn to be horrified. "You're quitting? How can you do that? Deenie, you're Éponine!"

She shakes her head. "I can't take the chance. What if it happens again? The audience is supposed to be all women, but I can't control who walks in and out of the theater. And they'll be recording opening night. So anyone can listen to my voice whenever they want. I'll never be safe."

"But recordings are okay," I protest. "It's only live performances—"

"Not according to some opinions," she interrupts.

"What about your dad's opinion?" I demand. "Doesn't that count for something?" I'm trying to keep calm, but my voice rises anyway. For the first time, I'm actually feeling Rae's frustration boiling underneath my words, and I understand why she finds it so hard to deal with Deenie's new convictions.

"I love and respect my father," she replies. "But I have to make my own choices."

"But you'll be letting the whole cast down," I say. "That's way worse. You're breaking your word."

"That's what my father said."

"And you want me to talk to him? Convince him that you're right?"

She looks defeated. Her shoulders sag as she slowly rises from the couch. "Never mind. You can't defend something you don't believe in."

She starts to turn away from me, but I jump up from my seat and grab her by the arms. "I know you don't believe in this either. Are you telling me that you're never going to sing again? Deenie, you've been singing since you were a baby."

Her dark eyes seem strangely hollow when she finally looks at me. "Well, it's time I grew up, then."

I can't let this happen. Deenie's voice is the soundtrack of our lives; she sings without even realizing it sometimes, while doing dishes or working on her homework. I can't imagine a world without her light crystal soprano. "So you won't even sing in front of me?" I plead. "Just once in a while?"

She seems confused. "Well, if it's just you," she says cautiously, "then I guess it's okay. But not if—" She pauses and glances around the room.

"Not if what?"

"Not if Danny is with you."

I'm suddenly glad that Rae isn't here. Because I know exactly what she would say if she were. *Damn it, girls, I don't know which one of you is crazier.*

When Deenie leaves, I send Rae an urgent text telling her that I'm coming over. I need to tell her that she was right and that I finally understand why she was so worried. Today I caught a glimpse of the chopping block in Deenie's mind, the religious guillotine that is slowly slicing away at everything she loved. And it terrified me.

"You're not going to believe what happened," I say as soon as I walk into her kitchen. I don't bother assuring her that I'm alone. "Just guess what Deenie's decided."

She looks up from the cake she's decorating. "Yeah?"

"Deenie is dropping out of the play. She's decided to give up singing."

Rae stops mid-rose, the frosting tip still poised over an ivy leaf. Her expression doesn't change. "Okay."

"Okay?!" I'm nearly shouting. Where is Rae's famous outrage when I need it? "That's all you have to say? Just 'okay'?"

She leans over her rose and carefully finishes the final petal. "What would you like me to do, Ellie? I'm not allowed to talk to her about this stuff, remember?"

"I never said that!" I protest. "Besides, this is totally over the top. How can Deenie give up her voice?"

Rae doesn't look up from her cake; her head is bent over her flowers so that I can't see her expression. "I was expecting it," she says quietly. "I'm just surprised it took her so long."

MY VERY OWN KING SOLOMON

There are many different kinds of rabbis, just like there are many different types of Jews. There are community leaders, pulpit clergy, teen youth directors, the coordinators of the local college Hillel. They are teachers and guidance counselors, experts on the minutiae of practical law, marriage therapists, and dispute mediators. By the time I hit adolescence I'd met dozens of rabbis, both at school and through our synagogue. But no one inspired me to love religion like Deenie's father. Rabbi Garner was a multi-hat kind of guy; he was involved in Jewish events at several local campuses; he lectured on various religious subjects at our high school. He tutored boys on their bar mitzvah portion; he gave talks for women on topics ranging from kashrut observance to marital harmony. But his passion was *Kiruv* work, the time he spent speaking to unaffiliated and unobservant Jewish teens, to draw them closer to our faith. It was said that there was no teenager so jaded he couldn't move them to reflect, no adolescent so lost he couldn't bring them back to the Shabbat table, if only for one afternoon. While we respected the appointed rabbi of our synagogue, we gravitated to Rabbi Garner because he represented the more "modern" track of Orthodoxy. He was clean-shaven and favored jeans over black suits. He'd been a troubled teen and found religion later in life, so we knew he wouldn't judge our choices, even when they conflicted with our parents' conservative ones. And he could relate to our parents, too, because he'd received a law degree before his ordination, so he had a foot in both the religious and the professional worlds.

Rae and I were Rabbi Garner's faithful disciples from an early age. He ran a Torah for Tots group after preschool and gave ice cream to the kids who were on time. Through his stories the characters in the Bible came alive and became human, like us. His lessons were age appropriate and short *(Respect your parents! Don't say mean things about people!)* and were always magically connected to the weekly Torah portion.

His influence continued throughout my childhood; there was no crisis in belief, no discrepancy between science and religion that Rabbi Garner couldn't resolve for me. If something didn't make sense in my mind, it certainly did in Rabbi Garner's. I only had to ask.

A few weeks after Danny entered our lives, I decided to place a dilemma in Rabbi Garner's capable hands. Deenie was sitting in her dad's chair when I walked into his office. Her face glowed when I inquired if the rabbi was free for a consultation. She leaned forward and lowered her voice. "You're here about Rae, aren't you?"

I shook my head. "No, I think we just need to leave her alone. Let her figure things out on her own."

Rae had stopped coming to all nonmandatory religious activities. And as part of her rejection of all things Jewish, she'd cut Rabbi Garner out of her life as well. "What's going on?" I'd demanded. "Are you mad at him or something?"

"Why would I be mad at him?" Rae had replied. "He's always been nice to me."

"Exactly! So why are you rejecting him?"

"I'm not rejecting him. As a rabbi, he's fine. But he's part of the system. I'm rejecting the system."

I found it hard to understand Rae sometimes. Rabbi Garner may have been clergy, but there was nothing stodgy or old-fashioned about him. The man could quote lines from our favorite TV shows better than we could.

The rabbi walked into the office before I had a chance to tell Deenie the reason for my visit.

Rabbi Garner was unusually attractive for a suburban dad. To me, he was just Deenie's father, but even I couldn't help noticing the effect he had when he walked into a room. Most of Rabbi Garner's congregants were used to the fact that their rabbi looked like Ben Barnes with a kippah, but it was funny how flustered some ladies got when they met him for the first time.

He lit up the office with a smile and asked me to be seated. "Well, Ellie, it's been a while," he said. "What can I do for you?"

I glanced at Deenie, who nodded encouragingly and quietly placed a glass of water by my side. "It's no big deal," I told him. "I'm just worried about Danny."

The rabbi nodded at Deenie and folded his hands. "Your new friend.

Deenie's told me about him. Why are you concerned?"

"It's not him exactly," I explained. "But I think something might be wrong at home. He won't let us visit, and he changes the subject whenever we ask. I thought maybe you'd know what's going on. Is Danny's father sick? Is there something we should know?"

Rabbi Garner considered the question quietly for a moment before fixing me with his dark eyes. "Before I answer that, I need to understand your motivation," he replied gravely. "Are you worried for your friend's safety or well-being? Are you thinking about paying a sick call to Mr. Edelstein? Or are you simply curious?"

I opened my mouth to answer and then caught Deenie's eye. "Curious," I admitted in a low voice. "I think Danny's being mysterious just to mess with us. And I wanted to know if I'm right."

"Ah."

"But—but, if he isn't, and something is wrong or if there is some reason I shouldn't go over there—"

The rabbi raised one hand, and I spluttered to a halt. "First of all, I believe you should give your friend a little more credit. But I can speak to Danny's father, if you'd like. If, however, he chooses to keep to himself, you will have to respect that."

It took two days for the ripples of magic to work their way from Rabbi Garner's office to the shuttered Edelstein home. I never found out how he did it. But Danny showed up at my house one afternoon, shaking with excitement.

"I can't cook," he blurted out.

Rae looked up from the bread dough she'd been pounding. "We know. So what?"

"So my dad needs me to make dinner. He wants to have the three of you over for a home-cooked meal tonight. He wants to meet my friends."

There was a moment of shocked silence.

"Well, it's about time," Rae declared, dusting the flour from her hands. "Get out your shopping bags, girls. I'll have a menu ready in fifteen minutes."

Chapter 8

After Danny's disappearance I got asked about my grades a lot. It was the first question on everyone's mind for some reason—psychiatrists, social workers, even my pediatrician at my yearly checkup wanted to know about my report card. I suppose people who are delusional tend to do poorly in school, as they're too distracted by whatever is going on in their mind palace.

I love to tell them the truth, mostly to see the surprise on their faces. "Straight A's," I reply. Their pen always stops over their clipboard for a moment. "They fell a little at first," I admit. "But I'm back on track now."

I'm not lying, either. Ever since Danny returned to me, my grades have climbed back to where they belong. Well, except for a B in physics (but I hated physics before the accident too).

So I'm a little shocked when Ms. Baker returns my latest assignment with a giant red C-minus on it. I'd been expecting some kind of reaction to the crap I'd submitted. Still, a C is pretty harsh.

"See me after class," she says shortly.

"I was debating a failing grade," she tells me as soon as the last student files out of the classroom.

"Come on, it wasn't that bad." I can't help smiling, though. I have a stack of stories piling up at home, but I wasn't going to share them with anyone, least of all my overly enthusiastic English teacher. So instead, I'd handed in a steaming pile of purple prose, complete with a girl "whose tears were diamonds that glistened with the songs of a thousand prayers" and her lover "whose azure eyes shrieked like ocean waves wailing against jagged, splintered rocks." At the end of the excerpt I'd run out of overwrought adjectives, so I'd hit the thesaurus—hard. It was educational, in a way. I'd learned some new words, and then sprinkled them "like confetti over a tortured, putrefied wound."

"You know, when most people self-sabotage, they generally don't advertise it like that," she remarks. There's no humor in her eyes. "It's usually a quiet process ending in failure. Not a 'fanfare whose pomp and grandeur ooze with the poison of a generation's ennui.' What does that even mean, Ellie?"

I smother a grin. "You're the English teacher. Which word didn't you understand?"

She folds her arms and leans back in her chair. "I didn't force you to enter the contest. It was just a suggestion. There was no need to churn out nonsense just to make your point."

I'm trying hard not to feel foolish, but it's not working out too well. I hadn't meant to piss her off so completely. She seems to be taking the garbage assignment personally, as if I've insulted the English language with my paper. "Look, I can rewrite it," I suggest. "I was just having a little fun."

"No, I think you were trying to tell me something. So, I'm going to read between the lines."

I want to tell her that I have no idea what I'd written between the lines. I'd been too busy finding clever ways to say "skin that glowed like a moonlit pond."

"I think you're trying to tell the world that you're tired of being coddled. So, I'm going to treat this assignment like I would treat any subpar work by a student who can do better. I'm not allowing a rewrite. You'll have to work hard if you want to pull up your average by the end of the semester."

She gets out of her chair as she speaks and motions toward the door. The conversation is over. I want to ask her what she meant, want to insist that I never expected to be coddled and that I'm prepared to accept the C if that will prove that I'm happy to take responsibility for the joke. But there's no way to say all that without sounding like a manipulative kiss-up angling for a better grade. I have no idea how to even start a decent apology. Apparently, I used up all my words in that ridiculous essay.

So, I stuff my paper into my bag and walk out the door.

DANNY AND HIS ABBA

If not for the mountains of books, the Edelstein house would've been a study in minimalism. There was a futon sofa in the living room facing a TV stand without a TV. A foldout table in the dining room with five folding chairs. No carpets on the floors or curtains over the shuttered windows. But every surface in the place was covered in books. They were stacked everywhere, crammed into corners and piled in leaning towers and ambitious pyramids throughout the home. There was no theme to the books, as far as I could see. It looked like Mr. Edelstein had simply walked into a used bookshop one day and bought them out. They had everything from science fiction novels to essays on comparative religion, volumes on economics to collections of poetry. Only the math books were grouped together in impressive columns by the TV stand. All the others were scattered randomly wherever they fit.

I'd always believed you could learn a lot about a person by just walking over to their bookcase. But I had no idea what to think of this monstrous collection. Or the fact that the Edelsteins didn't appear to actually own a bookcase.

Danny came up behind me as I was inspecting a copy of *Euclid's Elements of Geometry*.

"Your dad's a mathematician?" I asked.

"Yeah. He used to work as an investment analyst for a local firm, but he left them a couple of months ago. Now he does financial consulting. Mostly at home."

I was about to comment on the comfort of working in pajamas when a door at the far end of the hall opened, and the man himself appeared.

He tottered toward us slowly, then stopped in the middle of the corridor and raised his hand to his eyes to block the light from the window. Danny hurried past me and quickly closed the shutters, and the living room immediately went dark. "I'm sorry, I was going to close them," he apologized. "I'll go get the candles."

"Ooh, I love a candlelit dinner," Rae declared as he set the flickering lights by our plates. "What's the occasion?"

"The occasion is my son is overly concerned about my health, so he likes to baby me," Mr. Edelstein replied fondly. "I keep telling him it isn't necessary, but sometimes it's just easier to let him have his way."

"Do you need some water, Abba?" Danny inquired, ignoring his father's remark. "Here, why don't you sit down and I'll get the pitcher for you."

"Don't you want to introduce me to your friends first?" his father suggested.

Danny glanced around, startled, as if he'd forgotten that we were there. His dad slowly eased himself onto a chair with a soft grunting sound and winced as he stretched out his legs. Mr. Edelstein hadn't been to synagogue since Danny's arrival to Atlanta, and I was surprised to note how much he'd aged since I'd last seen him. He was in his mid-fifties, but he looked ten years older. He was very thin like Danny, but Mr. Edelstein's thinness seemed starved and unnatural to me. A wrinkled knitted kippah was perched awkwardly atop a few strands of sparse black hair that fell over thick black brows. His dark eyes seemed even darker in the sunken shadows over his hollow cheeks. Even as he turned his head to study us, the movement seemed to cause him pain.

I couldn't blame Danny for being worried about his father's health. He didn't look like a well man.

As we settled around the table, Danny introduced us, using our full names, which made Rae chuckle. He came to me last, and his dad turned to me with a twinkle in his tired eyes. "Ah, yes. The redhead from the plane."

"That was a long time ago, Abba," Danny said. "Almost a year."

"And you're the brilliant chef who's been feeding my son," he said, turning to Rae. I could see her blush, even in the darkened room. He gave Deenie an approving nod. "And you must be the singer. I understand you're very talented."

"You didn't hear that from me," Danny protested with a grin. "I'm not allowed to hear her sing, remember?"

I glanced over at Danny and saw that he was watching his father with a relieved expression on his face. He'd barely touched his own food; he was sitting poised and ready on the edge of his seat, waiting for an opportunity to assist his dad. "Do you want more lasagna?" he inquired anxiously. "Let me cut you another piece." I realized suddenly that Danny hadn't been nervous about our meeting his father because he thought he would embarrass him; he was actually protecting his dad and trying to guard his health as best he could. I wasn't sure what Mr. Edelstein suffered from, but Danny seemed to believe that bright lights and noisy friends could make him worse.

"So what do you guys think he has?" Deenie wondered out loud as we walked home.

"Migraines?" Rae guessed.

I remembered a story Danny had told me about a superhero whose heart was failing after years of sadness. I'd thought then that it was fiction, but the man I'd just met reminded me of Danny's description of the sickly hero. I wondered now if there was something very real behind the fiction.

I thought back to my own father's battle after his dad had died, and how he had described his experience during that difficult time.

"I'm not sure," I told them. "But I think it's depression."

Chapter 9

"We're smelling mangoes today?" Danny remarks as I lean over the fruit display and sniff. "Fascinating."

"Rae told me to pick up a couple of ripe ones for the salad she's making. She says it's supposed to smell sweet." I hold one out to him. "What does that smell like to you?"

"Honestly? Like a wasted Sunday afternoon."

"Come on. You like Rae's cooking. I thought you'd want to help."

He pushes the mango away. "You forget that I can't eat her cooking anymore."

I toss the fruit into my basket and head down the aisle toward the vegetables. "Cucumbers," I say, ignoring his comment. "And a leek. What on earth is a leek?"

He bounces on ahead of me and climbs up onto a tower of watermelons.

"What are you doing?" I hiss. "Get down. That's dangerous."

"Really?" he says, and lifts one foot in the air. "Come on, Ellie. What's going to happen?"

I hate it when he does this. When he came back to me after the accident, it was as if nothing was missing. Our relationship was perfect again, complete. But then therapy started, and slowly Danny began to change. Sometimes he's the Danny I know and love, the one I can count on to make me smile, to relax me when

I'm stressed. But recently he's been having these diabolical spells; he tests my sanity and calls himself a ghost. It's like he's trying to hurt me. "You're breaking one of the rules," I remind him.

"There's a watermelon rule?" He wobbles on top of the pile and waves his arms. "Wow, that Nina sure thinks of everything!"

"You know what I mean," I say. "Please get down. I want to talk to you."

He scrambles off the mound, as un-magically as possible. Not one watermelon moves. I hate that, too.

"You want to talk here?" he asks. "Isn't *that* breaking a rule?"

I point to the cellphone earpiece in my ear. "It doesn't count if I talk into this."

He raises his eyebrows and slow-claps his approval. "Wow. Sweet loophole."

"Right?" I am a little proud of myself. Now I don't have to wait until we're alone in my room to talk to him.

"What did you want to talk about?"

I roll my eyes. "Take a guess. Our friend who is slowly losing it."

"Ah. The one who sings ever so gently?" His tone is still mocking, but his expression is sober. "So gently that no one can hear her anymore?"

"We have to do something."

"Like what?"

"I don't know! All I know is that Deenie is making a terrible mistake." My voice rises in frustration. "I'm sure she's going to regret this."

Danny opens his mouth to reply, but there's a noise behind me, and we both turn around to look. Rabbi Garner is standing right next to me, holding a carton of eggs in his hands. "Hi, Ellie," he says. He looks puzzled and a bit concerned. "Who are you talking to?"

I'm momentarily speechless. I can feel the blood rushing to my face; a cold sweat breaks over my neck. This is the reason Danny and I are not supposed to talk in public. Not just to avoid the obvious social weirdness of getting caught, but also because Rabbi Garner's worried expression is yet another reminder that I'm alone. Like the stationary pile of watermelons and the standing Monday therapy appointments and the rules I have to keep breaking. Recently, I can't seem to get away from the reminders. It's like falling into a pit, over and over.

"Ellie, are you okay?" The rabbi carefully lays the carton down and takes a hesitant step toward me. "You look like you're going to be sick."

"I'm fine," I say hoarsely.

I'm really not, though. I know that my parents have consulted the rabbi multiple times over the last few months. And he's actually been the only one on my side. *The rabbi says that talking to the departed can be a normal part of the grieving process,* my father assured my mother in one of their late-night bedroom discussions. *He says we should give her time.* But now the rabbi has just seen me bickering with some watermelons. And I'm pretty sure his opinion is about to change.

Danny sidles up to me and points to the Bluetooth I'd forgotten. "You were speaking to Rae, remember?" he says.

"I was talking to Rae," I blurt out, tapping my ear.

The rabbi's concerned expression doesn't change. There's a distracted, pained look in his eyes, and he seems to be struggling to find words. I've never seen the rabbi at a loss before. "You were talking about Deenie just now," he says, finally. It's more of a statement than a question.

"Well—yeah," I stammer, and glance at Danny for help. "It's no big deal, really, but—"

"It's okay, Ellie," the rabbi says quietly. "You don't have to share your private conversation with me."

"I want to, though," I reply quickly. "I could use some advice."

"I think we all could." He shakes his head and turns slightly away from me. His gaze falls on the spot right beside me where Danny is standing. Danny starts a little and grows very still, like a deer caught in headlights; they stand opposite one another, staring into each other's eyes.

I stop breathing, terrified to break the silence. Is it finally happening? Can the rabbi actually see him? He's looking right at him, with the intentness of a man trying to focus on a blurry picture. I'm dying to say something, but if I'm wrong, I'll look insane. I will Danny to move, to see if the rabbi follows him with his eyes, but he's completely immobile, as if mesmerized. Finally, after what feels like hours, Danny takes a deep breath. "I think it's my fault," he whispers to the rabbi. "I made her stop singing. I'm sorry."

"It's my fault," the rabbi replies. "I encouraged her."

They're talking to one another. It's really happening. Someone else can see my Danny. And yet, I don't understand how that's possible. I've always admired the rabbi's spirituality; if someone had told me that he could communicate with the beyond, I might have actually believed it. But Danny isn't a spirit. He hasn't passed.

"Who are you looking at?" I ask, my voice edged with suspicion. "There's no one there."

His eyes snap back to mine. "I'm so sorry, Ellie. I must have spaced out. I haven't slept much in the last few days."

I take a deep breath; my anxiety eases a little. Next to me Danny jolts back to life; he raises his arms and waves them around in front of the rabbi's face. "Hey, Rabbi, I'm still here! Look at me! Come on, I know you can see me!"

The rabbi ignores him, and after a moment Danny quiets down; he slumps, disappointed, against the vegetable bin.

"You're worried about Deenie too?" I ask the rabbi.

He nods. "I know many people who have embraced religion because it made them happy, brought meaning to their lives. I encourage people who are searching for a deeper connection to learn more, to take on extra challenges. I encouraged Deenie, too. Spirituality can be a beautiful thing."

He falls silent, and his eyes focus briefly on Danny. "But I'm not sure now—" he murmurs. "I don't understand what I'm seeing anymore."

THE GENTLE SINGER

"I think it's all a myth," Danny proclaimed one morning after listening to us talk about Deenie's latest audition. She'd just landed the role of Maria in *West Side Story*. The women's theater group had been choosing musicals with Deenie in mind since she debuted as Annie in a performance that brought the audience to their feet. "Honestly, I don't think you can actually sing at all," Danny taunted. "I think it's a giant conspiracy. And I'm being punked."

Deenie rolled her eyes. "You think a group of twenty women has been putting on fake rehearsals and concerts for years just to mess with a fifteen-year-old boy?"

Danny climbed off the kitchen stool and stood in front of her. His growth spurt had kicked into full gear during the fall of tenth grade, so he no longer had to crane his head back to look into her eyes. In fact, he now towered over all of us. "Oh, I think the concerts are real," he declared. "I just think that you suck. That's why you won't let me hear you sing."

Rae and I exchanged amused smiles. We all knew that Danny wasn't being serious and that Deenie's feelings were totally safe. Danny had been angling for a display of Deenie's legendary voice for months. "I swear I won't find you attractive!" he'd insisted. "What if I close my eyes? What if you paint on a mustache while you sing? What if I stab myself with a fork the whole time?"

Deenie refused each time, patiently and firmly. "You're still a boy and I'm still a girl," she insisted. "It doesn't matter how you feel about it. It would make me uncomfortable."

"So I'll make myself uncomfortable too!" he pleaded. "I'll strip naked while you sing. And dance around."

Deenie flushed bright red. "Well, there's an image," she said in a strained voice.

"Yeah, nobody wants to see that," Rae said, gagging. "Except maybe Ellie."

I threw my spoon at her.

"Fine, then I'm leaving," he said, pouting like a spoiled toddler. "Since I'm in the way here."

"Great!" Rae declared. "We can finally talk about girl stuff again."

But Deenie put her hand out to stop him, her fingers just barely grazing his sleeve. "Hold on," she said softly. "Can you do me a favor?"

He turned back to her, hesitated. "Uh . . . okay—"

She walked over to the bin and pulled out a half-empty bag of trash. "Can you take this out for me, please?"

Rae snorted with laughter. "Wow, Deenie, that's cold!"

But Danny didn't appear hurt. A smile played on the edge of his lips. "Where are the cans?"

She pointed to the open kitchen window. "There. Behind the garage."

He was beaming as he took the bag from her hand.

As the door closed behind him, Deenie walked slowly over to the kitchen sink. "Well, I guess I better get started," she murmured. Rae and I were excited because we knew that she always sang as she washed up, and we were hoping for a VIP preview of the upcoming show. But that day she ignored our requests for *West Side Story* and instead chose a sweet song by Avaya, a new artist that she and Danny had recently discovered online.

And if the world was ending (she sang)
I would be the first to call
I'd thank you for the worst parts
I'd thank you for it all

Oh, I'm dreaming about you, my darling
And what my life would be like if we didn't last the day
Oh, please wake me
From this dream, my darling
So I can tell you I love you
And make sure we leave it that way
If it's the last words that we say . . .

Chapter 10

Monday afternoon rolls around again, and as usual, I find my mom waiting for me in the school parking lot after the last bell rings. I got my license during junior year, and I normally carpool with my friends to school, but my mom still takes off early from work on Mondays so she can drive me to Nina's. I think she believes that a breakthrough won't happen unless she's nearby, waiting for it. She's like my mental health spotter, poised to break my fall.

Only it's not happening quickly enough. So today, on my way to Nina's, my mom decides to speed things up, blunt-mama style.

She dives in as soon as I get into the car. "I stopped by the police station today," she tells me. "They said that there's been no progress on the case."

"Really? How shocking."

The sarcasm in my voice throws her for a moment. I normally get emotional and fragile when she brings up the stalled investigation. But today I'm just massively pissed.

"I know how frustrating this must be for you, Ellie—"

"Frustrating?! He's my boyfriend, Mom. Not a lost bike. 'Frustrating' isn't the word you're looking for."

"You know what I mean." She gives me a pained look and abruptly pulls the car over to the curb.

"What are you doing?" I snap. "We're going to be late to therapy.

And then I might never get better. I might die from all the *frustration*."

She stares at me quietly for a moment, and I stare back at her. I can't help noticing how much older she looks; the auburn hair beneath her bandanna is streaked with gray, and the wrinkles around her lips are as deep as the hollows beneath her eyes. She was over forty when she had me, but I've always been proud of her youth and energy. My father claims it's good genetics, my mother credits her diet and the gym, but I've always admired how she can still outshine women half her age. Yet somehow, without my noticing, her shine has faded. I wonder when it happened. And if maybe I'm the cause.

"I've been reading urban legends on the Internet," she says unexpectedly.

"Legends?"

"About the lake."

I suppress an irritated sigh. "Let me guess. The ghostly lady that drags swimmers under?"

She seems relieved that I know of it. "You read about that?"

"I can google too. That's pretty much all I did after Danny disappeared."

A little more relief in her eyes. The wrinkles relax a bit. It's weird that everyone dances around his name until I say it, like they're waiting for me to summon his spirit before they can talk about him.

"So you know that it might take months—even years until they find Danny," she says. I can tell she's trying to be comforting, but she's struggling to keep the desperation out of her voice. "The closure you're waiting for, Ellie—it might never come."

"I'm not waiting for closure."

"In lake water they usually float to the top right away," she continues doggedly, ignoring my response. "So the recovery isn't delayed, like it would be at sea. But there are always exceptions. People get stuck. Under debris, or beneath rocks, places where divers can't find them. They can get trapped."

"I know."

She reaches her hands out and grabs mine in hers, squeezes them until her rings dig into my skin. "Their loved ones get trapped with them," she says sadly. "Waiting for them, hoping against hope. The dead never get to rest, because their families never got to say goodbye."

I pull away from her so suddenly that she falls back against her seat. "Great talk. But I'm late to therapy."

She throws her hands up into the air. "God, Ellie! Who cares if you're late?"

"You're paying for it. You should care."

"Of course I care!" she wails. "But what's the point of all this therapy? You're still talking to a boy who's been dead for nine months." I push her away as she grabs for my hands again. She's violated our unspoken rule, the only one I've insisted on since Danny disappeared. No one uses the word "dead" around me. I can't allow it. As I struggle to unlock my seat belt, she paws frantically at me.

"Ellie, listen to me!"

"Let me go!"

"Somebody has to say it!" she cries. "We've all been tiptoeing around the topic for months. Nobody can even speak about Danny in the past tense around you. Your father won't let me mention his name, your rabbi thinks you need more time to adjust, and your therapist actually talks to Danny in front of you!"

"I've lost my mind, remember?" I shoot back. Damn this sticky seat-belt buckle. I'm a prisoner in the car. "Nina's probably just humoring me so I don't go apeshit on her."

"You haven't lost your mind, Ellie!" she insists.

"Thanks for the pep talk."

She stops grabbing at my hands and instead lifts my chin up so I have to look her in the eye. "You know that the boy you see isn't real," she says sharply. "Any more than Tzili was."

"Tzili?" It takes me a moment to remember. "My imaginary friend from elementary school? Really?" Why would she bring that up now? The two things have nothing to do with one another.

"Do you know how worried I was about that Tzili business?" she persists.

"Really. Is that right?"

She takes her hand off my face. "You have no idea, Ellie. I was freaking out at the end. Oh, I know that it was harmless in the beginning. She was just a little imaginary friend. Your father and I actually thought it was cute. But then things started to get so intense. You began to lose yourself in your fantasy. It got to the point that I wasn't sure if you knew the difference. Between what was real and what wasn't."

"I knew the difference. What's your point?" I spit the words out through gritted teeth. I can't look at her anymore.

"My point is that we're all grieving. In our own way. But you've gotten stuck in this neverland between denial and acceptance."

"There's nothing to accept!" How many psychiatrists, teachers, friends, and cops have said the same thing? Why does she need to repeat what I've heard a thousand times? "They never found him!" It's the only solid ray of hope I've got. "That must mean something."

"Mean what? What could it possibly mean?" She's crying now, and the sight shocks me. Never once throughout the last nine months have I seen my mother cry. It calms me to see her tears. For once, she's the one weeping and I'm the rational one.

"Are you really asking? You want to know what it means?"

She nods and rubs a hand over her red-rimmed eyes. "Yes. I want to know what you believe happened."

I'm not ready to tell her that. I don't think she actually wants to hear the truth. She's just waiting for me to bare my soul, so she can pick it apart. And yet, I know those tears are real. My mother can't act to save her life. Maybe she's as desperate as I am for the truth; maybe she wants answers as much as I do, and she's just been hiding her pain to spare her daughter. Is it fair to walk away from that? Don't I owe her a few words of comfort?

There's a rustling sound behind me, and I turn to see Danny slipping quietly into the back seat of the car. He grins at me and leans forward over the headrest. "Just tell her, Ellie," he says. "Tell her my story."

My boyfriend's confident smile is my security blanket; it warms me and makes my world sane. It even touches my mother. She stops crying and stares at me, then glances over to where Danny is sitting. "Oh," she whispers. Her eyes widen and focus on his face; her lips go pale. I know she sees him, just like Rabbi Garner did. Just for a second. Danny raises his hand and gives her a little wave. And then she shudders and her vision blurs again.

But that moment is enough to convince me. My mother has finally opened her mind and made the connection. She's ready to listen. If Danny wants me to reveal what happened, it doesn't matter if I'm ready. This is his story, and I'm the only one who can tell it.

"Mom, look at me," I say. "I need you to promise me something."

She clasps her hands together and takes a deep breath. "Of course. Whatever you need."

"I want to tell you what happened that night. But I need you to promise to let me finish, all the way to the end. No interruptions. And when I'm done, I want to get out of the car. No arguments. No lectures on logic or probabilities. I just want to tell you the story, and then go."

"But what about Nina—"

"I'll walk. It's just a few blocks. And then I can take the bus home. Okay?"

She nods and reaches out for my hands again. "Okay."

I take a deep breath. I know I can't start at the beginning, of course. I can never start at the beginning. But I can tell her just enough that she will understand—but not so much that she will hate me. "Danny didn't drown that night," I tell her. "He never fell into the lake at all."

A shade of doubt crosses over her eyes, but she remains silent, as promised.

"I know they found his jacket floating in the water. He climbed up on the bridge guardrail after the accident. He called me while he was sitting up there."

I'm not telling her anything new. This is all in the police report.

"We talked for a little while, and then I heard him shout. He didn't explain what happened then, but I know that's when his jacket blew off into the water below. I told him to wait there for help, but he said it was too cold on the bridge. Then he promised me he was coming home and hung up."

She hasn't said a word; even her expression is patient and accepting. I glance back at Danny for a final boost of confidence and then plunge into his story.

"After he hung up, Danny jumped down from the barrier; I think that's when his phone dropped from his pocket, but it was so windy that he didn't notice. He started to walk up the road. I'd urged him to call the police, but he was too afraid to ask for help. He was scared they would arrest him for drinking and driving. So instead of waiting by his wrecked car, he tried to flag down a passing motorist, hoping for a ride to the nearest gas station, somewhere dry and warm to wait for a cab home. It was freezing on that road, pitch dark and completely deserted. The rain was beating at his face and soaking through his shirt. He was miserably cold and desperate, so when a car finally pulled over and opened the passenger door for him, he climbed in without hesitating."

I can see from the fear in her eyes that she knows where this is going. We've all read the same horror stories. Young teen kidnapped by a stranger, kept in a dank basement as a prisoner, starved and molested for years. I can quote those police reports like a seasoned detective. I've spent months combing the Internet for missing person cases that have ended with a miraculous rescue. I know all the victims' names and ages, their time in captivity; I've tortured myself with the details of their pain. But despite the scores of voices that have seeped into my blood, Danny's case has stood apart. His story is more tragic than terrifying, and it makes me sad without tearing out my heart.

"It was a woman," I tell my mother. "An older woman who took him. She really didn't mean him any harm at first. She just wanted to help; she saw how cold he was and suggested he warm up in her house down the road."

It's hard to guess what my mother is thinking now. She seems to be hanging on my words, waiting for me to finish. Still, there's no judgment or doubt, and for now, that's enough for me.

"The lady actually served him hot chocolate and cookies. Can you believe that?" I tell her. "She talked about her son who was serving abroad. The scene was about as innocent as you can imagine. Until Danny woke up a few hours later in a strange room and couldn't remember how he had gotten there. He tried to open the door and found that it was bolted shut. The only window in the place was barred like a jail cell. He shouted for help and banged on the walls, hoping someone would hear him. But there was no way out. She had locked him in."

My mother shakes her head slightly, opens her mouth to speak; but no words come, and I'm grateful that my mother never breaks her promises.

"The lady is sick," I tell her. "About as messed up as you can be. She has this fantasy that Danny is her son who has come back to her. Her real son died in Iraq years ago. But Danny is around the age that her boy was when he was deployed. He's her replacement, and so she's never going to let him go."

Still no sound from my mother—she's mesmerized by the story. Her silence gives me the strength to tell her my ending.

"Danny was scared at first. He tried to escape, over and over. Pried at the bolt, scraped at the bars on the window. Then he became furious. Screamed his rage for days, swore at her through the walls, threatened to burn down the place with both of them inside. She braved it all quietly, waited for him to calm down and accept his fate. And then one day he did. Not completely. But just enough for her to enter the room without fear. Just enough to listen to her story.

"She talked for hours that day, well into the night. And he listened to her, patiently, as if she really was his mother." I glance back at Danny one last time. His head is bowed over his hands, like he's praying. "Since that day, he's stopped fighting," I explain. "He hasn't accepted his fate, not at all. Every waking moment he hopes that someone will find the remote house, will knock down the door and free him. But he's accepted his captor. In a way, he's almost grown to understand why she did it."

I think maybe my mother has lost her voice. I've never known her to be quiet this long, promise or not. But her eyes speak for her. They shine with fresh tears.

"She's good to him, in her own way," I assure her. "She makes him her son's favorite foods. Which unfortunately aren't always his favorite." I remember the story he told me of the chopped liver he kept choking down, just to spare her feelings. "He's actually put on a little weight," I add with a smile. "Not even Rae could manage to pad those skinny bones, even with all the cookie dough."

There's a ghost of a smile on her face, but the rest of her remains completely immobile. She doesn't speak, and, again, I'm grateful.

"That's what happened to Danny," I conclude.

She takes a deep breath, bites her lip. But no words come. Instead, she just clasps my hands in hers and bows her head, like a mourner at a memorial.

I bristle at the gesture, even though I know she's faithfully kept her promise by remaining silent. Still, there's too much pity and resignation in her bowed shoulders. Somehow, I'd been hoping for more—maybe a spark of hope in her red eyes, some flicker of my faith reflected in her expression. I hate that she still looks like a person in mourning.

"I'm going to go now," I say.

She doesn't move to stop me. Instead, she quietly releases my hands and folds her own in her lap.

"By the way, you're the only one I've told," I inform her. "So please don't share this with anyone."

She appears surprised. "Not even Rae and Deenie?"

I shake my head.

"Or Nina?"

"No. Especially not Nina. Promise you won't say anything to her."

She nods her assent and then swallows hard, like she's forcing down a bitter medicine. I push open the car door.

"It's a good story, Ellie," she whispers hoarsely. "Thank you."

MY DEAR DEPARTED IMAGINARY FRIEND

It was a dark-mood kind of day—for Danny. I could tell by the story he told me that morning.

We were hanging out by Bruster's ice cream shop, stuffing heaps of mint chocolate chip into our mouths. Bruster's had become our favorite outdoor hangout because it was just a fifteen-minute stroll from my house. Conveniently situated in the parking lot in front of the local strip mall, it was still far enough from the busy shops for two teens to enjoy the best ice cream in Atlanta in relative privacy. Just the sight of the red-striped awning emblazoned with the company's cherry logo raised my spirits.

Rae and Deenie rarely rolled out of bed before noon on Sundays, so I knew that if I called Danny early, I'd get him to myself, if only for a couple of hours. Neither of us ever mentioned our ice cream dates to either Deenie or Rae. We weren't trying to lie, exactly, and yet I think we sensed that if we spoke of our private get-togethers, it would create tension in the group. So, it never came up. I admit that I enjoyed our little innocent secret. It felt like we were starting down a path, one that might lead to greater and more exciting secrets.

But that day he was in a gloomy mood. So I asked him for a story to get his mind off whatever was bothering him. He gave me a weary look and then gazed off into the distance. "There once was a snake whose home was destroyed by a winter storm," he began in a low voice. I could barely hear him, so I scooted a little closer to him on the bench. "The snake was freezing and all alone. So, he stole a boy's clothes off a laundry line to get warm, but it wasn't enough. The temperature kept dropping, and he knew he wouldn't survive outside. Just then a young woman came along. He called to her and begged her to help him. She was very nearsighted, so to her he looked like a little boy in need of shelter. She took him into her home and gave him warm soup to drink. But she had no idea she was taking care of a snake. Until one day, the snake boy bit her. 'But I saved you,' she cried as she lay dying. 'Why would you poison me?' The snake bared his fangs. 'A snake will always be a snake,' he said."

I crossed my arms. "Wait a minute," I said critically. "That story sounds weirdly familiar."

He appeared startled, even a little frightened.

"What do you mean?"

"I think that's an Aesop's fable. My mom used to read me those when I was little."

"Oh." He sat back, relieved. "Sorry. I didn't realize. I guess I'm just blocked today. Why don't you tell me a story for change?"

The request made me strangely nervous. One of the reasons I enjoyed Danny's company was that I never felt pressured to impress him. He happily acted as the sideshow entertainer for our little group.

I wasn't nearly creative enough to fill his shoes, even for a few minutes. "I don't think so." I scooped the rest of the ice cream into my mouth, to discourage further requests.

"It can be something true," he suggested. "Something from your childhood."

I licked up the last drops of syrup and stared hungrily at his cup. "You don't want to hear that. My childhood was pretty boring."

He pushed his ice cream across the park bench with the smooth assurance of a dealer handing over a bribe.

"Come on," he urged me. "Everyone has something weird. Tell me your weirdest thing. And I'll tell you mine."

I actually blushed. Maybe because I already knew what my weird thing was—and it was quite unusual. Or maybe because his proposal was the equivalent of "show me yours and I'll show you mine."

I stared into his eyes, like a psychic trying to read his soul. "Promise you won't laugh," I said. He put his hand to his heart.

"Okay, here it is." I took a deep breath. "I used to see people who weren't there. Sometimes I even talked to them."

He blinked once. Twice. Wiped his mouth with a napkin. Then blinked again.

I immediately regretted all my life decisions. A cold sweat broke out over my lips.

"What kind of people?" he asked after the longest pause of my life. There was no mockery in his voice, just puzzled curiosity.

"Not, like, dead people covered in blood or anything," I assured him quickly. "Nothing creepy. Just people I made up. In my head."

He nodded, but it was a cautious nod. "Like imaginary friends?"

"Kind of. That's how it started. When I got home from school, they would be waiting for me in a little circle around my bed."

He smiled, and I felt myself relax a little. Maybe it wasn't so weird, after all. Lots of kids played with imaginary friends.

"So what happened to them?"

I shrugged. "I had a fight with one. Two of them moved to Sandy Springs and didn't want to hang out with me anymore. So, I was left with one best friend."

"What was her name?"

"Tzili."

He grinned. "Ah. 'My shadow.'"

It was my turn to be surprised. "How do you know that? I thought you were terrible at Hebrew." He'd been placed in my introductory Hebrew language class, but he appeared to struggle with even the simplest assignments.

Danny seemed confused for a moment. "I think I saw it in a book once," he said with a careless wave of his hand. "So what happened to Tzili?"

"She died. Nodular melanoma."

Danny gaped at me. "Wow. That is really specific for an imaginary friend!"

"My mom's a dermatologist. She talks about her work a lot."

"So why did Tzili die?"

"I just told you."

"No, I mean in your mind. You were in control, right? You decided her fate. Why did she have to die?"

I'd never asked myself that question. It was just something that had happened over the course of a summer vacation. My beautiful best friend began to get paler and paler, like a consumptive heroine from an old movie. And then one day I came home to find her lying perfectly still on my bed, already wrapped in a white shroud.

"I'm not sure. Maybe I was getting too old for her. And I was growing closer to Deenie and Rae, so I didn't need a fake friend anymore. I don't know."

"So why not just stop talking to her? Why did she have to die of cancer?"

Again, I was stumped. Who questions the motives behind their own fantasies? "I guess I enjoyed the drama," I mused. "My life was pretty boring, as I said, and there was something so exciting about nursing a dying friend. I got pretty carried away with it, actually. I started showing up at breakfast with bloodshot eyes. My parents were worried about me. I even sat shiva for her when she died, though I didn't tell anyone what I was doing."

He smiled sadly; but there was still no judgment in his eyes, so I smiled back.

"So—what do you think? Was that weird enough for you?" I asked.

He didn't reply at first. "You know it's nothing like that, right?" he said finally.

"What do you mean?"

"Grief. It's nothing like that."

I poked at my melted lump of ice cream, suddenly ashamed of myself. Here I was talking about fake mourning to someone who had just lost a parent. What had I been thinking? "Oh God, Danny, I'm so sorry—"

He waved off my apology. "Don't be. I'm glad you have no idea what I'm talking about." He looked down at his hands, his expression quiet and sober. "Grief isn't something you can milk. It's not dramatic at all."

"I know it's not. I'm sure it feels just awful—"

"Not at first. At first it feels like nothing. Like this hole that you've thrown some sand over. You can even cover it so well that it looks totally solid. Only it's not and so you keep stumbling in. Over and over. A hundred falls a day. And yet, each time, you can't believe that you forgot it was there."

I couldn't think of anything to say. It was better to be quiet, for once.

"Being here feels like a vacation," he continued after a moment. "I've started at a new school. I've made new friends. But I think I'm still waiting to go home."

"It hasn't sunk in yet?"

He shook his head. "I guess not. Truth is, the waiting isn't really that bad. You can't be truly sad if deep down you're still waiting."

Chapter 11

I've had as much sharing as I can handle for the day. My mother's reaction to Danny's kidnapping story hadn't been too bad. She'd been just nonjudgmental enough to fulfill her promise. But the admission still drained me, and I'm not ready for any more soul-baring for a while. So, my meeting with Nina is a bullshit session, full of cliché dreams that I made up on the spot and breakthrough epiphanies that had happened months ago. I'm not sure how much of it she believes, and I don't know who is more relieved when the hour is up.

I take a detour on my way home and get off at the bus stop before mine. It's been a couple of weeks since I've visited Danny's father. The obligation has been weighing on me since my last visit, and I'm dreading our meeting. Normally I like going to see Mr. Edelstein. For one, he's the only physical connection I have to Danny. Even if he's too ill to talk much, I enjoy sitting next to him and listening to quiet music and flipping through his collection of antique books. I can hang out in Danny's room for hours; there's no curfew, no interruptions, no judgment. Mr. Edelstein feels Danny everywhere, so he never challenges me or gives me a look when he catches us together. He just smiles and recedes back into the shadows until I'm ready to come out.

Mr. Edelstein is the only person who understands us. But more importantly, he's the only one who truly believes that Danny is coming back. So, I feel totally safe with him, as he does with me. We aren't humoring each other; we accept the other's truth without question.

Lately, though, Danny's dad has been taking a turn for the worse. His joint pains and chronic migraines are the same as always, barely tolerable with the cocktail of meds he swallows with every meal. But the depression that's dogged him since his teen years has come back, and it's worse than before.

His father's struggle was a shadow over Danny's life ever since I'd known him. Oddly, after Danny disappeared, while the rest of us were barely keeping our heads above water, Mr. Edelstein managed to stay on stable ground. Maybe it was the hope for a breakthrough in his son's case that kept him positive, but somehow he held the depression monster at bay. Recently, though, his ghosts have come back to haunt him, and it's terrifying me. I've never known him like this. Danny once hinted at a time right after his parents' separation that ended in a prolonged hospitalization. I wasn't part of their lives at that time, so I can't say if he was nearing that level, but I'm constantly on the alert now. I send him daily messages to check in, and stop by as often as I can. Two weeks is the longest I've ever gone without visiting, even when he was well.

He sees the guilt in my eyes as soon as he opens the door.

"Ah," he says with a faint smile. "I see that Danny has passed it on to you."

I love that he doesn't tiptoe around his son's name. He talks about him just like he always has.

"Passed what on to me?" I walk with him into the kitchen and place a foil-wrapped package on the counter, next to another bundle of foil, which has begun to gather dust. "You didn't eat Rae's pound cake?" I ask, pointing to the lump.

"Sweets are more Danny's thing," he responds, and hobbles out to the living room. "Sweets and worrying about his dad." He nods weakly in my direction. "Which he has now passed on to you. Or so it seems." He sinks onto the sofa with a grunt.

I sit down next to him. "I can't help worrying, okay?" I glance at a thick packet of papers on the coffee table. "What's that? Did you get that at your appointment yesterday?"

He sighs. "Yes."

I squint at the close writing on the booklet. "What is ECT? New medication?"

He sighs again and shakes his head. "I've been through their pharmacy. Twice. There are no new medications. Not for me."

I reach out for the packet on the table. "Can I look?"

"If you promise not to get upset."

I don't get a chance to promise because the word "electroconvulsive" jumps out at me as I scan the writing. And then I get upset. Really upset.

"What is this?" I flip through the pages, barely registering what I see. The "possible side effects" dance in front of my eyes, terrifying me. "They want to give you a seizure? *On purpose?!*"

He shrugs and pulls the papers from my hand. "You've never heard of shock therapy?"

I splutter for a minute before I can respond. "Well, yeah. In movies. Like, as a last resort."

"Exactly. That's where I am. The last stop."

"The last stop before what?" Even as I ask it, I know the answer and I rush ahead to block it out. "Come on, Mr. Edelstein. You don't need this. We'll work through it together. Like you used to with Danny. I'll come by more often, okay?"

"Ellie—"

"No, I mean it. I'm sorry it's been two weeks. It won't happen again, I promise."

"You have nothing to apologize for—"

He has no idea, of course. Nobody does. But I can't let him choose this path; I can't let my selfishness destroy him, too. I have to keep him well until Danny comes back. Nine months ago, I took his son away from him. It's the least I can do now. "Every day. After school. Or after Nina's on Mondays. I'll be here like clockwork. Five p.m., the latest. You can count on it."

"Ellie, I don't expect you to—"

"But I want to. Okay?" My voice is high-pitched, hysterical. "I want to!" I'm grasping the edges of the packet and tugging at it; maybe if I pull hard enough, I can yank this awful therapy out of his mind. "You don't know what will happen to you if you do this! It says here that ECT causes memory loss."

"That's usually reversible—"

"Usually? And what if it's not? Are you going to forget him? Is that what you want? That's why you're doing this? You want to forget him, like everyone else!"

"Ellie!"

I know I've finally crossed the line; his watery, weak eyes are blazing, and there's a glow of rage in his pinched cheeks, as if I've smacked him across the face.

I can't bear to see his hurt expression, so I duck my head. When I look up, Danny is standing in the doorway, just a few feet away, watching us. I'm surprised to see him; since the accident he rarely interrupts me when I'm hanging out with his dad; instead he waits quietly in his room for me to join him. I'm not sure why he's kept apart from us until now. Guilt, maybe. Taking care of his father used to be his job.

Next to me, I feel Mr. Edelstein start; his breathing has gone shallow. I steal a glance at him, but he's staring past me—at the doorway. At his son.

Danny walks toward us and squats down opposite me, his thin knees almost brushing the edge of my skirt. For a moment it seems like he's going to take my hand; I reach out to him, but he keeps his arms crossed on his lap.

"We talked about this, remember, Ellie?" he says.

He knows that I can't answer him in front of his father, so he continues as if I've spoken.

"It was one of my stories. You thought that it was fiction."

The memory is beginning to stir, but I can't quite grasp it. Danny's told me so many stories over the years. It's hard to remember which ones were real.

"The man who is slowly going numb," he prompts me. "He touches the exposed wire on the highway. And loses his memory from the spark. But he's reborn. What's important is that he gets to live."

Next to me, Mr. Edelstein shifts, clears his throat. I'd almost forgotten that he was sitting next to me. "It's not what you think," he offers. His voice is barely audible. "I'm not going to change."

I close my eyes, shutting them both out.

I can hear them breathing next to me—Mr. Edelstein's wheezy rattle and across from me, Danny's calm exhale. At that moment,

I can't tell which one is more real. "But memory is everything," I insist. "You can't love someone if you don't remember them."

Mr. Edelstein's hand grips mine, a sudden cold weight around my wrist. My eyes fly open. Danny is gone, and his father is staring at me with a fierce intensity. "Ellie, *nothing* will ever remove my son from my mind," he says. His voice shakes, but the pressure on my arm doesn't waver. "There isn't enough electricity in the world to steal even one moment of him. Do you understand?"

I nod, silently. *How can he be so sure?* I wonder. But my doubts stick in my throat.

"Danny and I discussed this possibility years ago. It was always an option—if I really needed it. I believe that he supports it."

I'm grateful that, as always, he uses the present tense when referring to his son.

"It won't be as bad as you think," he assures me. "Most of the memory issues are short-term. We're not talking about soap-opera amnesia. I'll still know who I am. And I'll still be waiting for my Danny to come home. I promise."

It's the only thing I wanted to hear. Until that moment, I hadn't realized how scared I was to lose the security of his faith. "Good. Because I'll be waiting with you," I say. "And I'll go with you to the sessions. If that's what you choose in the end."

He sinks back against the couch and releases my hand. "Thank you." His eyes wander over the empty room, before focusing back on me. "And thank you for giving me—a glimpse."

My breath catches. "What do you mean? You—you saw him? Really?"

He shakes his head. "No. But I saw the look on your face. And that was enough."

SEXY ASTRONOMY (OR—MY FRECKLES ARE THE BEST THING THAT HAVE EVER HAPPENED TO ME!)

It was a matter of time before Rae butted heads with the school administration, and I wasn't surprised that it was her new boyfriend, Greg, who ended up being the cause for all the trouble. When they started going out, he didn't exactly join our foursome, because Rae was very careful to keep her dating life and her friends separate. "Boyfriends are for high school, but friends are forever," she'd say. Still, despite her convictions, Greg did manage to create some tension in the group. Personally, I didn't mind it when he joined us. I could see why Rae was attracted to him; he was tall and built, with a thick mop of auburn hair. He was a staunch atheist, prone to go on rants about the subject, but as long as no one got him started on politics or religion, he was actually a lot of fun. Danny also seemed to enjoy hanging out with him and often called him when he wanted some guy time. Only Deenie obviously disliked him. Though Greg was always nice to her, his disdain for anything religious got under her skin in a way that Rae's rebellion never had.

"He actually asked Rae why she was so careful to keep the plates kosher when she cooked!" Deenie complained to me. "It's because she's not the only one eating the food! How can he not understand that?"

"She put him in his place, remember?" I assured her. "Don't worry. Rae isn't going to screw over her friends because of a guy."

And she really did put her friends first. But she also sometimes went along with Greg's ideas. Her decision to wear a "Thank God I'm an Atheist" T-shirt to a school charity drive was definitely his influence. (It was also his T-shirt.) The incident should have ended with a teacher quietly asking Rae to change, but nobody noticed until it was too late.

Someone snapped a photo of Rae in front of the school sign, and the shot was included in an article about the event.

Rae received a call summoning her to an honor council meeting the following day. "They want to discuss how I made the school look bad," she told me darkly over the phone.

An honor council meeting was our school's equivalent of a trip to the principal's office. Students were summoned for infractions such as cheating, smoking on school grounds, and similar sins. None of us had ever been called to one, and we were all a bit scared of the prospect.

I sent a message to the friend group calling for an emergency meeting in my basement. Rae arrived a few minutes after us, but there were no traces of worry on her face as she thumped down the stairs. "They want to lecture me about misrepresenting the school," she declared defiantly. "Well, I've got something to show them."

Without warning, she lifted up her shirt and exposed her lower back, which was covered in sloppy black letters. Hebrew letters.

Deenie and Danny moved forward to get a better look. "What does 'ASHDINAT' mean?" Danny asked, slowly sounding out the print.

"That's the initials of my three best friends," she replied. "It can be like our blood pact. What do you guys think? Who's in?"

We were all silent for a moment, digesting this drastic declaration of loyalty to the group. Would she be expecting a similar gesture from all of us? How could she make a decision like that without asking us first? "Rae, I can't get a tattoo," I said finally. "You know that, right? My parents would kill me."

"And it's forbidden to get tattoos," Deenie put in. "I can't do it either."

Rae dropped her shirt and turned around. Her face was unreadable. "I wasn't asking you guys to do anything. This is my personal statement. They want me to issue some kind of apology. For misrepresenting Judaism." She sank heavily to the ground and put her head in her hands. "But I wasn't trying to represent the school or the Jewish people with a T-shirt. So I'm going to tell them that these are the initials of the only people I want to represent. My three best friends, who've always stood by me."

We all stared at her, dumbfounded. Deenie looked like she was going to cry. "I do support you, Rae. But I didn't want this. I don't want my name branded on you. I never asked for that."

Danny sat down on the floor beside Rae and placed his hand on her shoulder. "We don't actually need to get a tattoo," he said with a smile. "Do you guys own a good razor?"

I gaped at him. "What for?"

He lifted his mop of hair. "There's enough room back here. I bet you can etch all your initials into my scalp."

Rae shook her head. "Are you serious?"

"Why not? I know they'll make me get rid of it. It's against the dress code—or hair code or whatever. But I'm going to go with you to that meeting tomorrow. Wearing your name."

Rae's lower lip actually quivered. For a moment I thought we'd see the impossible: the vision of Rae weeping. But then the mask came down and a smirk lit up her face. "God, you guys are so gullible!" she crowed. She smacked her back. "Do you think I could do that after a real tattoo? Those things hurt like hell! And I'm only sixteen. No tattoo parlor would do this without my parents' consent."

"Whatever," Danny said with a shrug. "The offer is still open. I think it would be cool."

"I want to do something too," I said. "Something personal."

"Didn't Deenie teach you to crochet?" Danny suggested. "You can make us matching bracelets or something."

"Uggghhhhhh." Rae snorted her contempt. "So cheesy."

"Rae, you've got my initials floating over your butt crack," Danny retorted. "You don't get to shoot my ideas down."

She smothered a smile.

"And by the way," he added, "I'm really glad those letters aren't permanent. Because you actually got them wrong."

It was my turn to be shocked. Names were my thing. And Danny was my best friend. How could I not know this?

"What are you talking about? Your name isn't Danny?"

"Of course it is." His calm smile was mocking my surprise.

"Short for Daniel, right?"

He didn't answer.

"Right?" I persisted.

"Ellie, maybe we should focus on Rae," Deenie suggested mildly. "And the meeting tomorrow."

I was shamed into swallowing my questions. But it was going to come up again, I warned Danny with my eyes. This wasn't over.

"I don't know what I can do before tomorrow—" I began.

"I have an idea," Danny interrupted. "Do you have a thin marker?"

We didn't have any markers in the basement, so Danny followed me upstairs to the kitchen. After a little digging in the junk drawer, I pulled out a pink pen. "Will this work?"

"Perfect." He picked it up and took a step toward me. His eyes swept over my face, down my neck, and finally rested on the dip over my clavicle. I followed his gaze, and for a moment we both stared at the little button that held my blouse closed.

"Let's see . . . ," he said. He seemed to be analyzing the little clasp.

"What?"

There was something about his look that made me lift my hand to the button, made me pluck resentfully at it. I was suddenly glad that Rae and Deenie had stayed behind in the basement. I had no idea what he was thinking, but I was very happy that we were alone.

"I bet I can find them, if I look hard enough," Danny declared after a heavy, breathless silence.

"Find what?" My voice was an unattractive croak, but he didn't seem to notice.

"Our initials."

He touched the uncapped tip of the pen to a freckle beneath my jaw. "Like the Milky Way." With a quick, soft stroke he traced a line between two freckles on my neck. "And now they're gone," he whispered, like a magician shocked at his own skills. Predictably, as the pen descended, my skin had flushed and cloaked my thousand freckles in a ginger fog. I never realized that connect the dots could be so sexy. Apparently, neither had Danny. By the look in his eyes, Danny was discovering a whole new side to astronomy.

"Hmmmm. There's really not much room to work with," he mused regretfully.

I don't remember doing it, but I must have popped open my collar button because the next moment Danny was staring in stunned silence at my bare shoulder. "Is that better?" I asked, stepping closer to him.

I knew the effect I was having on him, and it was making me giddy; he was breathing so fast that I was worried he would pass out. My modest clothing had always covered me from neckline to elbow, from waist to knee. I didn't even own a V-neck or anything sheer, so this was the first time he had ever seen this much of me. It was just a shoulder, but for Danny, the vision was as shocking as if I'd suddenly stepped out in a string bikini.

It was no big deal, I told myself. Danny was a close friend; he wasn't actually touching me; it was only a tiny patch of bare skin. We all saw naked actors and actresses on TV every single day. What was a flash of collarbone? It was ridiculous to be so conscious of this bit of nothing. But deep down, I knew I'd crossed a line. And Danny knew it too.

"You were going to find our initials?" I suggested hesitantly. I was waiting for the brush of his pen, like a girl waits for her first kiss. I knew that this was the closest we were going to get, but that afternoon, it was enough for me.

Danny's hand shook as he raised the marker to my neck, and I jumped a little as the tip grazed a freckle beneath my ear.

"If you draw it there, I won't be able to see it," I said as he began to trace.

"So?" His breath was warming my cheek, and the marker was tickling my skin. I was loving every second of this sexy art project.

"I want to know what your real initials are," I teased. "How can I reveal your secret identity if I can't read what you wrote?"

He laughed into my hair, and I stopped breathing for a moment. "Look in a mirror, genius," he murmured.

The closest mirror was hanging on the second floor, and, for us, that might as well have been miles away. At that moment, the idea that we would actually have to leave the kitchen and rejoin humanity was unbearable. As far as I was concerned, Danny had a million initials, and I was ready and willing to be a canvas for all of them.

I didn't say what I was thinking, of course, but as the pen continued its naughty dance over my clavicle, I couldn't help sighing. Loudly.

Twice.

"You okay?" he asked after the second time. It was his turn to sound croaky and breathless.

"Fine. Just—you know—exhaling." It was a stupid thing to say, but I didn't care. There was no way he could expect me to be witty when his lips were inches (centimeters?) from mine.

He smiled and continued his drawing. "Yeah? Felt like you quit breathing there for a minute."

"I didn't want to mess up your sketch, Michelangelo."

He stopped writing and studied his work, and for a moment I was worried he'd run out of letters and the experiment was over. I couldn't think of anything to say. There was no way to say what I wanted to—which was basically, *Don't stop now, just touch me, touch me, touch me, please, I don't care if you make it look like an accident, I don't care if it's only for a second, but please touch me touch me touch me. Please—*

I couldn't tell what he was thinking exactly, but he was almost as red as I was, and his mouth was way closer to my ear than it needed to be. I'm pretty sure Michelangelo never got this turned on by his work.

"I think I messed up," he whispered, and before I could ask him what he meant, it happened. His fingers brushed against my neck. I forgot everything. I forgot how to inhale or exhale. I forgot how to pretend. I forgot that all of this was supposed to be totally innocent. I forgot that we were just two friends. I forgot that I was a religious girl who'd promised to lead a religious life. I forgot that I had already decided what was good and what was bad. Because at that moment the only good thing in the world was the feel of Danny's fingertips on my skin.

I forgot everything and just said, "Oh!"

But it came out all sharp and panicked and not at all like the breathy, fluttering "oh" you hear in movie love scenes. It was the "oh" of someone who's been stung.

Danny pulled his hand back as if I'd smacked him. "Sorry," he faltered. "I smudged a letter. So I just thought I'd—sorry."

"It's okay," I said. "It's just—your fingers were cold." (They weren't.)

"Well, I'm done anyway." (He wasn't. I discovered later that he'd left out his own name.)

"I'm hungry." (I wasn't. Didn't think I would ever eat again, actually.)

"Did Rae and Deenie leave?" (They hadn't. In fact, they were standing in the doorway staring at us when we turned around.)

Rae sauntered up to me and examined Danny's handiwork on my shoulder. "Oooh, hottttt," she drawled. "How sweet, you guys. You did this all for me?"

I was too embarrassed to speak. How much had they seen? And did it really matter? Nothing had happened, right?

Then why did it feel like Danny and I would never be the same again? Was I the only one losing my mind? I looked around at my friends. Danny was shifting back and forth on his feet and staring at the ground. Deenie was suddenly occupied with a flake of fingernail polish and wouldn't meet my eyes. Only Rae was staring straight at me, her head thrown back in triumph. She touched the writing on my shoulder.

"Now that, I think, is permanent," she declared, with a sarcastic wink.

Chapter 12

"I'm quite impressed by your progress," Nina says at our next meeting.

I'm not sure what she means, exactly. Recently, I've been breaking the rules more often than I've been keeping them. I've found ways to talk to Danny in public. He keeps showing up after curfew. I wonder suddenly if her statement is just a sneaky therapist's tactic that she uses before introducing more restrictions. We're due to pull the curfew back to six p.m. this session.

"I noticed that you came today without Danny?" She glances around the room. "That's a milestone."

"Danny's busy this afternoon," I lie. He's actually sitting right next to me; I've simply been careful not to look at him since we walked into the room. Even when he leans over to whisper in my ear, I keep my eyes fixed on my psychologist. "Hey, hey, hey, hey," he taunts. "What, am I invisible?" I don't crack a smile. I know he'll understand. Maybe if she thinks I'm making progress, she'll forget about the curfew thing.

"That's great," she says as she scans the room again. "How is the assignment we spoke about?"

"The stories? They're going great."

"Stories?" she asks, raising her eyebrows. "Plural?"

"Yeah. I'm making a collection." I'm so relieved she's brought up my writing. I can use that to distract her with something innocent, a sign that I am actually following her instructions.

"Here they are," I tell her, pulling my notebook from my bag and flipping through the excerpts. I land on a simple one which I don't mind sharing. With a quick tug, I tear out the pages and hand them over. "Do you want to see?"

She chuckles at the title. "'Love, Lies, and Gas.'" She reaches for her glasses. "Do you mind if I read it out loud?"

Yes. I think. *Please do. Read as slowly as you like.*

LOVE, LIES, AND GAS

"You know, I could just ask your dad," I declared one morning as we dug into our mint chocolate chip ice cream. It was a warm autumn morning two weeks after the beginning of eleventh grade. We were sitting on one of the red metal benches opposite Bruster's. "I'm sure he would tell me."

"Go ahead." He waved his spoon in front of my face. "Cheater."

"How is it cheating if I ask your father about your real name? I have a right to know what it is."

"Do you?"

"I'm one of your best friends! We tell each other everything."

"Do we?"

He was in one of his moods, I realized. Somewhere between teasing and irritable. It wasn't likely that I would pry anything out of him today. Still, I could at least try. All my other attempts to learn his secret had failed miserably. He was Danny Noah Edelstein on all his correspondence, both virtual and paper. I had begun to think that he had invented the alter ego just to mess with me.

"I've told you everything about me," I insisted. "So what's the big deal? Is your real name that embarrassing?"

He frowned and drew a little smiley face in the ice cream droplets that had dropped from his spoon onto the bench. "You tell me everything, huh?" he said, ignoring my question. "Come on, now."

"I do! I'm totally honest with you. But you still don't trust me."

I'm not sure why I was so fixated on learning Danny's real first name. It didn't really mean anything, after all, especially if he never used it. But there was so much more beneath my raging curiosity. I'd been friends with Danny for two years now, and he still refused to speak about his pre-Atlanta days. I knew virtually nothing about his mother, for example. He changed the topic whenever she was mentioned, and he did it so persistently that I sometimes wondered if he was hiding a terrible relationship.

There weren't even any pictures of her online, not on his public profiles anyway. Facebook had been scrubbed of all early photos, and there were large gaps on his Instagram page. A few months earlier while playing with his phone, I was surprised to find entire folders that I'd never seen before. I clicked on one (It wasn't snooping if Danny was sitting right next to me!), and the image of an olive-skinned, dark-eyed woman popped onto the screen. "Wow, she's gorgeous!" I exclaimed. "Who is she?"

His expression didn't change as he plucked the phone out of my hand. "My mom," he replied.

"Your mom?" The woman in the picture looked Yemenite or Moroccan to me; she didn't resemble her fair-haired son at all.

Danny answered the question in my eyes. "My father adopted me after his brother and sister-in-law were killed in an accident. My father—the one who raised me—is actually my uncle. " He pointed to the picture. "And Dalia became my stepmom when they got married."

I was stunned silent for a moment. "Oh, wow," I said finally. "I didn't know that. Why didn't you ever tell me?"

He shrugged and slipped his phone into his pocket. "It isn't a secret. It's never come up, I guess."

"It comes up in your stories," I pointed out. "They're full of orphans and adoptive fathers."

"Brilliant observation, Sherlock," he said.

"You don't trust me enough to tell me anything real about your life," I retorted. "So you just tell me stories instead."

He glared at me for a moment.

"We should head back," he said abruptly. "Your stomach hurts."

"Excuse me?"

"Your stomach is starting to hurt," he reiterated, tossing the empty ice cream cups into the trash can behind us. "It's probably going to get worse."

As he said it, I felt the familiar wrenching twist of indigestion. It had been happening every week for months, and by that point I'd gotten pretty good at ignoring it. I pressed a hand to my belly and swallowed. Until he'd mentioned it, I'd been so focused on our conversation that I hadn't even felt the warning squeeze. So how had he known?

"I think I'm okay."

He shook his head. "I don't get it, Ellie. Why don't you just take Lactaid? Or order the sorbet instead?"

I grunted and took a deep breath. There was a clammy sweat breaking over my brow. The double helping had been a really stupid mistake. I'd known I was lactose sensitive for a while now, but I'd been careful to hide my dairy issue from him. "The pills don't work for me. And I don't like sorbet."

"So why didn't you just tell me?"

Did he want me to spell it out? Ice cream at Bruster's was our tradition. It was the best part of my week. How could I risk giving it up?

An embarrassing roar broke from my bloated stomach, and I sprang to my feet. "Oh God. We'd better go."

I spent the better part of the afternoon in the bathroom, miserable and sweaty, moaning with pain. It was the worst stomachache I'd ever had. But worse than the pain was the knowledge that I'd given myself away and that our Sunday mornings were over. Danny never referred to that awkward morning again. But the following Sunday I got a text from him just as I was getting out of bed. "Where are you? Ice cream is melting."

I was down at our bench ten minutes later.

Two heaping mounds of mint chocolate chip were dripping over the edges. He was carefully catching the drops and scooping them back into the cup.

"But I thought—you know that I can't—"

He held up an empty carton of dairy-free ice cream. "I tried three different brands, and this one's the best. Not as good as the real thing, but pretty good."

And that became our new Sunday tradition. He would eat my portion of Bruster's and fill the empty cup with a serving of nondairy before I got there. And, true to his word, he never asked me why I'd hidden my lactose problem from him. Maybe he already knew.

"Very sweet, Ellie," Nina tells me as she lays the page down. "Gives me a window into your relationship."

"Yeah, what a great guy, right?" I say flippantly. "Oh my, look at that; our time is up. My mom is waiting outside."

I don't give her a chance to answer.

"Wow. That was smooth," Danny says as we head out the door.

"Oh yeah." I raise my hand and give him a mock high five. He goes through the motion but stops just short of my palm. "Curfew is still at eight p.m.," I declare triumphantly. "You're welcome."

He gives me a look. "Why do you care?" he asks. "You're not following the rules anyway."

We pass into Nina's living room, and my mother rises quickly from the rocking chair. "How'd it go?"

I nod and force a bright smile. "Really well. Lots of progress."

Mom follows me out to the car; I feel her watching me as I climb into the passenger seat. Danny catapults through the rear window and stretches his long legs over the back seat.

"You could have opened the door for me," he calls out. "Are you pretending you can't see me now?"

My mother starts asking me questions about the session, but I'm too distracted to answer her. Danny is calling my name over and over. When I don't answer him, he starts drumming his hands on the back of my seat.

"Ellie? Are you listening to me?" asks my mother.

"Ellie! Why aren't you listening to me?!" Danny demands.

I close my eyes to block both of them out.

BUT WHAT WOULD GOD THINK?

Middot lectures were a nuisance to which we'd grown accustomed; about once a month a speaker would speak to our grade about morality—covering topics from drugs and alcohol to modest dress and the dangers of gossip. It never felt very relevant to me until the day Rabbi Garner took his place at the front of the room. The subject of the discussion was going to be relationships, he told us. I sat up in attention. A few people in the back groaned.

"I'm glad Rae's out sick," I whispered to Deenie. "She would hate this."

Deenie nodded. "Yeah. And I bet so will her new boyfriend."

Greg resented every minute of Judaic studies and never missed an opportunity to remind the teachers that his parents were forcing him to attend our school. I glanced over at him warily. His thick arms were crossed over his chest, and his deep-set eyes were narrowed, glowering his disapproval.

"Rabbi, if this is a talk about how God wants me to save my body for marriage, can I be excused, please?" he called out. "I find the idea offensive. It's basically God-sanctioned slut-shaming."

Rabbi Garner blinked. "I see," he said slowly. "Is that what you think I'm here for? To tell you that God is disappointed in you?"

There was a ripple of laughter. "That's kind of your job, isn't it?" Greg remarked. "We sin. You make us feel bad. We repent. Then we sin again. Lather, rinse, repeat. It's the Jewish circle of life."

Rabbi Garner held up his hands in surrender. "Okay. Okay. I don't know what they've told you about this lecture. But I'm not here to talk about God. Today we are putting that all aside. Nothing Divine at all. We are only going to talk about you. I want to take God out of it. Completely."

No one was expecting that. Not from the rabbi, anyway. Take God out of the discussion? That was unheard of. A little scandalous. Possibly even heretical.

We were all ears.

"I have a question that I want all of you to answer," the rabbi continued. "But I want you to do it silently. Don't share your answer with anyone, even your closest friend. This is a personal question. And there is no right answer."

Again, revolutionary. That was the purpose of religion, wasn't it? Religion was supposed to give you the answers. I wasn't sure where this was headed, but I wanted to get on this train.

"I want you to think about what intimacy means to you," he continued after a pause. "Not just sex. All intimacy. A kiss. A hug. A touch of the hand. What does each of these things mean to you?"

I didn't really hear the next few minutes of the lecture—my mind went immediately to Danny, who was sitting just a few seats away from me. His brief touch last week still made me giddy when I thought of it; I was pretty sure a kiss would completely destroy me. I allowed myself to linger on the thought for a moment, but then my face began to warm and I had to shake the image from my mind. I couldn't get all hot and bothered during a sermon. Time to focus.

The rabbi spoke for a while about *shomer* relationships, but to my surprise, he presented both sides of the argument. He described the excitement and discovery from months of pent-up desire but also the anxiety about chemistry, and the fear that all those expectations would be disappointed.

I couldn't believe what I was hearing. Being *shomer* could lead to disappointment? That wasn't possible, was it?

I stole a glance at Danny to find that he was watching me from across the room. Our eyes met, and then he quickly looked away.

I had no idea what that meant. What did he think of what the rabbi had just said? What was I supposed to think?

"There is more than one path," the rabbi concluded. "And whether each path leads to happiness depends on the people traveling it. The question you need to ask yourselves is, how do you define intimacy? And how do you want it to define your life?"

We filed out of the classroom more confused than when we came in. There were a few crude jokes among the guys, but the rest of us kept to ourselves.

Some instinct told me to avoid Danny for a while—at least until I could figure out what I thought about the topic. The two of us had been floating in this weird flirty friends-without-benefits neverland for months, and I wasn't ready to discuss physical intimacy with him yet. What if he was on the verge of asking me out and I ruined it by being too religious?

But then, what if he did ask me out—all the while assuming that I wanted a physical relationship? Deep down, I wasn't sure I was ready for that. I liked the idea of waiting, of discovering my soul mate through words alone. Maybe I did really want to try the *shomer* way. Would it be fair to drop a bomb like that on Danny?

I wrestled with the problem all through math, growing more and more anxious as the minutes ticked by and no answer presented itself. I was damned if I talked about it and damned if I didn't. And the tension between us weighed more and more heavily as I stubbornly avoided noticing the weird faces he was making at me from behind his calculator.

I finally looked up at him as the bell rang. I really didn't have much choice as he planted himself at the edge of my desk and leaned over me as I tried to rise. "Hey, you mad at me or something?" he asked.

"No. Why would I be mad?"

"I don't know." He grinned, relieved. "I started to get worried when my drunk otter impression wasn't getting anything from you." I stifled a smile as he twisted his lips into a lopsided grimace.

"We should get going, Danny. We'll be late to history."

"Uh-uh," he grunted, still scrunching up his face. "Drunk otter is too drunk to go to class. You'll have to show him the way." He reached his hand out for mine, pawing the air between us until he caught my fingers.

I wavered for a moment; I let my hand rest in his for a second longer than I should have. I didn't want to pull back. But he'd put me in a corner—on purpose. Did I have to break it to him now? It wasn't fair to put me on the spot like this, I thought resentfully. He was forcing me to make a statement while he clowned around. I wanted him to be serious, to look me in the eye and ask me what I thought, instead of playing games.

I gently disengaged our fingers. "I can't hold your hand, Danny," I told him quietly. "I thought you knew that."

The drunk otter vanished, and the boy I liked reappeared. He was sad; I could see a flash of hurt in his eyes before he dropped his head. "I wasn't sure," he said softly. "I'm sorry. I won't do that again."

Chapter 13

"You're doing what?"

Rae had heard me the first time, but I knew that this was her way of protesting my idea without actually saying it. Even if you don't agree with it, it's not very nice to object to a therapist's advice. That's how I present it anyway. I'm doing a project for my psychologist.

"I'm gathering material," I tell her. "It will be stories based on real events. Nina suggested it."

"You're writing a biography?" she asks, crossing her arms. "About Danny."

I nod and climb onto the kitchen stool across from her. "Some will be stories about us. But I'm also interviewing his friends and family. There's so much that I don't know about him, even though I'm his girlfriend."

"And you're starting with me?"

"Yes." I'm not sure why I picked Rae to be the first. Maybe I just want her approval. She's so prickly about anything to do with Danny, and even more protective of him than I am. I remember Rae's burst of joy when she thought she'd caught a glimpse of him, her shattered eyes when she realized it was just a mirage. If I could get her to believe in my project, her faith in it would push me to finish it.

She paces the kitchen and noisily tosses spoons and bowls onto the counter. "Dairy, dairy, where's the dairy grater?" she mutters.

"We don't have one," I say. "My mom just buys shredded cheese."

"Ugh."

"Yeah, I know. We're savages. Why are you changing the subject, Rae?"

"Do you want decent focaccia for dinner or not?" she snaps, but she's obviously not expecting an answer. Not about focaccia anyway.

"At least tell me what you think about my idea," I persist. "If you don't have any stories or you'd rather not talk about Danny, I understand—"

"What makes you think I don't want to talk about Danny?"

"Oh, I don't know. Maybe the fact that you glare bloody murder every time I bring him up—"

She pounds the sifter so hard, a cloud of flour explodes around her. "Damn."

"It's okay," I say. "Forget I asked. We can talk about something else."

She doesn't answer me at first. There's a flurry of mixing and pounding and emotional kneading. I sit patiently and wait as the dough rises and Rae calms down.

"I have a story for you," she says finally. "But you have to promise to take it as it is. There's one part of it that I can't tell you. You have to be okay with that."

"Of course." I'm dying of curiosity, but I don't say a word as she chops the onions with frustrating care. Do they really need to be perfect little cubes? Rae seems to think so.

I'm not sure if it's the memory of the story she's about to tell me or the effect of the onions, but her eyes have a bright shine to them when she finally looks up at me.

"I met Danny before you did," she says softly.

I start and lean forward. "Really? When?"

"About a year before your flight from hell. He must have been here visiting his dad."

"What happened?"

"I didn't see him at first. I was busy doing something—" She hesitates, and her knife wavers over a sliver of pepper. Then it comes down with a vicious bang. "Something pretty destructive."

I'm scared to ask, so I remain silent and wait for her to continue.

"I was twelve," she says with an apologetic shrug. "And I was really angry. I'd just discovered something that had torn apart everything I'd believed in. Everything I'd been taught. So I was acting out. I thought the world deserved to know the truth."

The truth about what?

But I say nothing.

Her lips curl, and she shakes her head. "I was painting my feelings in giant letters on the trunk of a car. It was going to rock the community. My sloppy print on the back of a minivan was going to start a revolution. Danny walked by just as I was finishing the first letter."

I can't help smiling at the picture: Rae spattering paint in furious strokes and Danny bouncing past, humming to himself. He probably had no idea what he was in for.

"He tried to stop you, didn't he?" I guess. "And you covered him in paint."

She laughs and flicks an onion skin at me. "Nope. He offered to help."

My mouth falls open.

"'I've got a can of red spray paint in my garage,' he said when I turned around to find him staring at me. 'I bet it will show up a lot better than that.'" Rae grins at my confused expression. "The car was white," she explains. "And all I had were a few bottles of Wite-Out. The fumes were already making me dizzy."

I nod, eager for the rest. "So? Did you take him up on it?"

"Yeah. I headed back with him to pick up the spray paint. But I thought it was only fair to let him know what we were fighting for. Convert him to the cause. We were going to spray-paint our way to freedom." As passionate as Rae is, she's not above laughing at herself. It's one of the things I love about her.

"So what happened?"

"He took FOREVER finding the stupid spray paint. We had to move piles of books to find it. And then the can turned out to be empty." She laughs shortly. "I think he took me on that wild-goose chase on purpose. He was just waiting until I cooled down." She looks at the counter and draws a thin line in the flour dust.

"So you didn't spray-paint the van in the end?"

She shakes her head. "I guess I realized that the gesture wasn't worth the fallout. It was only going to hurt a lot of people. And it wasn't going to help anyone."

I open my notebook and scribble down Rae's last statement. "Danny made you realize that?"

She shrugs and slides the pan of focaccia into the oven. "I suppose. He really didn't say much. He didn't even tell me his name that day, come to think of it." Her eyes go soft as she speaks about him. "He was this little, scrawny kid, you know? Just as ridiculous and immature as the rest of us. But he also had this quality, too, right?"

I nod, my pencil poised over the page.

"When we met a year later in your basement, I know that he recognized me," she continues. "But he never gave me away. Never mentioned the spray-paint thing again. Even when we were alone."

She spaces out for a moment, and her expression darkens as she brings back another memory.

"This other time—I guess it was just about a year ago—I told him something—I told him about this—this crush I had. That I've had for a long time." Her voice is so soft that it hints at feelings far deeper than a crush. She shakes her head at the question in my eyes. "It's not important who it was."

Not important? Rae has never talked about anyone like that. And her statement seemed to imply that she's still holding on to those feelings. I'm distracted from her story; the vandalized neighbor's car was one thing; I don't care about that person's identity. But was Rae actually in love with someone? And no one knew except for Danny?

She senses that she's lost me and frowns her frustration. "Ellie! I said it's not important. It will *never* happen. I knew that then, and nothing has changed since. I'm trying to tell you about Danny, not about me."

But I want to know your story too, I want to say. And yet, I'd promised her I would let her keep her secrets. I can't press her for details; I can't even look curious or she'll take it as a challenge.

"What did Danny say when you told him?" I ask.

She relaxes a little and sits back. "He didn't say anything at all. He just held my hand. That's it. I was crying, and he just sat there holding me with one hand." Her lips twitch. "And eating cookies with the other. He plowed through the entire plate like he was on a mission."

I smother a grin. "That sounds like him."

She returns my smile, and her eyes brighten again. "When I stopped crying, he picked up the last cookie and put it on my lap. I told him I wasn't hungry. And he said, 'That's okay. I just want you to know that you can always have my last cookie.'"

LEGENDS OF A SPITTY ONE-EYED DUCK AND THE NAUGHTY *SHIRT*

Anniversaries are an important part of any relationship, and Danny and I enjoyed twice as many as most couples. The problem was that Danny and I couldn't agree on the actual date which marked the beginning of our relationship. So, we celebrated twice—two days apart. The confusion stemmed from the whole *shomer* thing. We didn't kiss (not at first, anyway), so the moment we became official was a bit blurry.

I date our relationship from the day I received Quackers. I'd gotten weird presents from Danny before. (So far I'd accumulated a skull key chain, a book titled *What's Your Poo Telling You?*, and a Minions sweatshirt, which he let me keep after I stole it from him.) But Quackers had all kinds of symbolism behind him.

It wasn't a romantic story, exactly. But Danny's idea about the moment that sparked our relationship was even less romantic—so I prefer to tell mine first.

I was hanging out with him alone after one of our Bruster's dates. Normally we joined Deenie and Rae after we ate, but that afternoon we swung by his house because he'd "forgotten something." I waited for him on the sofa while he rummaged around his room. After a few minutes he appeared in the doorway, holding a battered stuffed duck in his hand.

"This is Quackers," he told me, holding him out. "I got him when I was five."

It was a pretty poor intro, especially for a master storyteller like Danny.

"Quackers?"

"He's pretty beat up," he said apologetically, turning him over in his hand. One button eye was missing, and the beak looked like someone had chewed on it. "I should have taken better care of him."

"He's cute—"

"My mother got him for me at a fair. At one of those shooting ranges, you know?" He rubbed a hand over his eyes. "She hit every single target, so the guy said I could pick the biggest bear they had. But for some reason I only wanted this duck. I don't remember why."

I had no idea what to say. "Well, you were really little," I suggested.

He nodded. "My parents were still together then." He was staring at the toy, avoiding my puzzled look. "I could hear them arguing after I went to bed, but I didn't want them to know that I could hear. Some days I used to shove the duck's head into my mouth like a pacifier. The night my dad moved out, I bit down so hard that I swallowed the button eye."

I was speechless for a moment. It was the saddest story he'd ever told me. "God. I'm so sorry, Danny—"

"I want you to have it." He walked over and placed the duck on my lap. "I've wanted you to have it for a while."

"Really?"

He sat down next to me and looked into my eyes. "It's important to me."

He was obviously trying to tell me something deep and personal, but the crumpled stuffed animal on my knees was so comically pathetic that I was having a hard time keeping a straight face. I scooped it up and hid my smile in its fuzzy collar. It smelled like corn chips and curdled milk.

"I love it. Thank you," I said, and planted a sloppy kiss on the sad duck's musty neck.

He made a grossed-out face. "Yuck, Ellie. Maybe wash him first? He's covered in kiddie spit."

I didn't say anything, just buried my face deeper and inhaled the rancid odor of its fur. Somehow, it didn't seem gross to me.

Maybe Danny didn't get what I was trying to say then. Like I said, there's nothing romantic about kissing a spitty duck with a missing eye.

But in my mind, that was the moment I became Danny's girlfriend.

In his mind, our relationship began two days later—and on a slightly naughtier note.

This is the story of THE SHIRT.

It was a modest shirt, purchased by my mother at Macy's—on sale, half off retail price. Light green, ballet neck, full-length sleeves.

Perfect for my complexion. Totally modest. Covered everything my mother wanted covered.

But. It was only modest while I was standing upright.

THE SHIRT's dirty little secret? That neckline was very VERY floppy.

And my dirty little secret?

I knew it.

I was wearing THE SHIRT when Danny came over to do our English project. He was looking unusually adorable that day. He'd recently showered, and the ends of his sandy hair were still plastered to his cheeks. The longer he sat next to me, smelling like manly shower gel, the more I wanted to distract him from *Julius Caesar*. So, a few pages in, I leaned over the textbook to emphasize a point. In the process, I emphasized something else altogether. I meant no disrespect to the subject matter. I suspect Shakespeare would have approved. Danny certainly did.

He reached out and shut the textbook abruptly. "Okay. I have to ask you something," he said, and swallowed loudly. His face was blazing red. THE SHIRT had done its work. I sat up straight and pretended to be puzzled.

He took a deep breath. "I just need to know. Please. Am I your boyfriend?"

I opened my mouth to answer, but he rushed ahead before I could speak.

"And if I'm not your boyfriend—then, I was wondering—could I be? Because I think we'd be great together. And I really want to know if I can kiss you." He paused and ducked his head. "I mean, I want to kiss you in theory. Just in theory. I know you'd like to do the *shomer* thing, and I promise to respect that. But I want to know if I can kiss you in my mind. And if you'll kiss me back. Only in your mind. Please."

The way I saw it, we'd already been dating for two days, on account of the duck and its symbolism. But it seemed like a strange thing to say at that moment. So instead I gave him a little wink. "Well, if it's just in our minds, let me tell you," I whispered. "We're *way* past kissing."

He startled so violently, he knocked my book off the table. I considered leaning forward to pick it up, but I was worried it would be too much for him. I'd never seen anyone so brilliantly red before. The table shook as he leaned over toward me.

"Really?" he asked. His voice was hoarse with excitement. "Really, Ellie?" His eyes drifted south for a moment and then focused hungrily on my lips. "So—hold on. HOLD ON. What *exactly* have we done?"

Chapter 14

"What was Rae's story?" Deenie asks when I tell her she's my second subject.

I close my notebook. "I'm sorry, but I can't share that. I don't want it to bias you. Each story needs to stand on its own."

She leans back in her chair and gives me a suspicious look. "And why are you interviewing me?"

I stare at her for a moment before answering. "Are you serious? You're one of Danny's best friends. You must have a story about him."

She reaches across the desk and flips open her father's giant ledger. "You asked to see me in my dad's office, Ellie. I figured you were here to consult him. This isn't the place for this."

I glance around the small room and shake my head. "What are you talking about? The rabbi isn't here yet. And you aren't doing anything else right now. It will just take a minute."

"I don't have a minute." Her jaw is so tense, I have a hard time making out what she's saying. "And I don't have a story anyway. We hung out as a group, remember? You were part of every story."

She's glaring at the ledger in front of her as if she's just discovered a catastrophic scheduling error that could destroy the entire synagogue. I've never seen her this agitated, and I can't understand how my simple request could have disturbed her so much.

"Come on, Deenie," I protest. "You've known Danny for years. You must have had a private moment with him. All I want is one little anecdote."

"I never had a private moment with him," she shoots back. "That would have been *yichud,* and it's not allowed. I thought you knew that."

She's referring to the rule Danny and I broke about a thousand times: a boy and a girl can't be alone in a room together. Most of the religious kids I knew got around that by simply leaving the door open. For Danny and me, a millimeter crack was our loophole. For Deenie, however, looking for a loophole was a betrayal of the spirit of the law.

"I'm not accusing you of anything," I assure her. "I just thought you could add to my collection. Please? There must be something you remember about him. Something I don't know."

She looks up at me for the first time, and a spark of fear flickers in her eyes. "Is he here now?" she demands in a low voice.

"What?"

"Danny. *Is he here now?* In this room with us."

I know that he isn't. But I glance over my shoulder anyway, as if to prove that I have nothing to hide. "No. Of course not."

She relaxes a little and fiddles with her pencil. "He's not going to suddenly walk in as I'm talking to you?" she persists.

"*No.* It doesn't work that way."

"It doesn't?"

"Not at all. He's not some ghost that stalks me." I'm trying to be confident, to chase away the paranoia in her eyes. Except I don't exactly believe myself anymore. Danny has been appearing unexpectedly these days. Much more often than before. Past curfew hours sometimes. And he's not always the comfort I'm expecting. Sometimes he has his own agenda.

"So—you're in control?" she asks. Her body is still tense, as if she's waiting for our friend to jump out and yell, *Surprise!*

"Yes." I deliver the lie without hesitating. What else am I supposed to do? The truth is too weird and confusing. "I'm totally in control."

"Okay." She eases back into the chair and takes a deep breath. Her eyes are still darting around the room, but she appears to believe me. "I have a story to tell you."

"Great." I flip open my notebook in anticipation.

"You remember how Danny was afraid of horses?"

"Of course. His friend got kicked in the face when he was little. He saw it happen."

She nods and stares at her ledger again. "Yeah. But I got him to go riding with me once. About a year ago."

"What?"

She swallows hard. "It was really cute. He was so scared. But he got up on the horse. He even trotted a little by the end!"

"Really."

"Yup. You should have seen him." Her voice is hollow and sharp; there's no trace of the soft sincerity that I'm used to. I barely recognize this Deenie. "He helped me feed the horses afterward," she continues. "One of them, Gretel, started chewing on his hair." She makes a panicked face. "This was what he looked like!" She laughs, waving her hands in the air. "He was totally freaking out! Just batting at the poor horse, yelling, 'Let go! Let go!' Stupid Gretel. I guess his hair did look like a pile of hay, didn't it?"

"Pretty much." I lean over my notebook and pretend to jot her story down. But I haven't recorded any of it. Instead, I write what I'm thinking: *What the hell, Deenie, what the hell??*

Because here's the thing: Danny never went horseback riding with her. I'm absolutely sure of this. About a month before he disappeared, I tried to convince him to go with me to Cedar Crest Farm, mostly for the Instagram photo op. After an embarrassing amount of begging, he finally agreed. But then he asked if Deenie could come along. *She's been trying to get me to go forever,"* he explained. *"And I keep saying no. If I go with you and don't include her, she'll feel bad.*

I'd thought it was sweet of him. I still do. But we never actually went through with the plans. Things fell apart pretty quickly after that, and so neither of us mentioned the idea to Deenie.

So, the only true thing that she'd said so far was "I have a story to tell you." Because her entire tale was fiction, start to finish.

FICTIONAL KISSES: AS SEEN ON TV

I didn't want to tell Deenie and Rae that Danny and I were finally official because I was worried that it would change our friend dynamic. But Danny insisted on being honest with them, so I took them aside the next day after school to let them know the news.

Their reactions were both predictable and a bit anticlimactic.

Rae gave me an exaggerated look of shock and exclaimed, "What? You guys are dating?! How on earth will we be able to tell the difference?"

But Deenie didn't react at all. She seemed completely unsurprised. "You guys are going to be *shomer?*" was the only thing she asked.

I assured her that we were because at the time, I didn't doubt we would be.

My *shomer* commitment with Danny was an achievement that made me proud, so I shared our progress on Instagram, a little documentary about our triumph over temptation. We had a whole series of romantic *shomer* pics: at the Georgia Aquarium standing side by side with a dolphin photobombing us from behind; at Lullwater Park, beaming at the camera, our arms wrapped fondly—around the tree between us; Danny presenting me with an enormous bear he'd made out of marshmallows and glue (I discovered the glue after I attempted to eat it). Each of my pics garnered about a hundred likes. The pic where Danny posed suggestively behind the giant bear got over a thousand. Still, despite my commitment, I spent hours fantasizing about our first kiss, and of course I couldn't help sharing those dreams with my friends.

We liked to compare famous TV and movie romances and rate them according to hotness. Rae, Deenie, and I had wildly different ideas about which TV kiss was the best of all time. Deenie's answer was sort of predictable, as she'd been obsessed with Pam and Jim from *The Office* and had watched it so often that she sometimes quoted lines from the show without realizing it. So that first kiss between the two best friends, after Jim confessed his love, was hands down Deenie's favorite. "He loved her for years, and he could never tell her!" she gushed.

Rae rolled her eyes. "Oh, please," she said. "He was just scared she'd reject him."

"Fine," Deenie huffed, turning her back to her. "Ellie, what do you think was the best kiss of all time?"

I had my answer prepared.

"That's easy," I told them. "Christina Ricci and—"

"Oh my God, that was mine, too!" Rae exclaimed, to my surprise. "You've seen *Around the Block*?"

"Around the what?"

Rae looked confused for a moment, and then her face flushed. "Oh. Never mind."

"I was talking about Christina Ricci and James McAvoy in *Penelope*. Who did you have in mind?"

"It doesn't matter." Rae gave an irritated shrug. "It wouldn't have been your thing, anyway. *Penelope* was cute. A bit vanilla. But cute."

"Cute?" I clasped my hands together. "How can you say that? Don't you remember the scene? There's this amazing buildup of tension and romance that ends in this kiss that just—"

"Yeah, yeah." Rae waved her hand, dismissing my passionate description. "So, what you're saying is—you still haven't kissed Danny?"

"What?"

"I said—you and Danny still haven't—"

"I heard you," I snapped. "And no. We haven't."

Next to me, I felt Deenie bristle. "Rae, leave her alone. I don't know why you keep bringing it up."

"Hey, I don't care what they do when they're alone," Rae protested. "It's just that Ellie so obviously wants to."

"Of course I want to," I replied. "And I know that he does. That's not the point."

"So? What is the point?"

Deenie and I exchanged looks. She understood my resolution to stay *shomer*. She was my *shomer* buddy, strengthening me when I needed a boost of self-control, applauding me when I told her about our "touch-free" dates.

I shrugged. "I'll tell you. But only if you promise not to judge."

Rae's eyes flashed. "Judge? Look who's talking. That's the entire basis of your religion, isn't it? To decide who's clean and who's dirty? Isn't that what you're about to tell me? That if I sleep with my boyfriend, I'm ruining myself? While the two of you are staying pure?"

"It's not about purity!" I exclaimed. I needed to say something to break up the cloud brewing over Rae's head. "That's what people don't understand. And it's not about judging anyone. Being *shomer* is about building a relationship based on communication, not physical attraction."

"That's a nice idea," Rae said. "But I think you can have both. Greg and I fool around, and I know more about him than anyone else."

Deenie bit her lip; I could literally hear her swallowing her thoughts.

"I'm serious," Rae insisted, answering her look rather than her words. "Do you know that his name was Gedaliah until he changed it, like I changed mine? Do you know that he can't speak his mind at home, because his parents and older brothers act like they can't hear him? When he started asking challenging questions, they decided it was just easier to ignore him until he grew out of it."

"That's sad, but not every religious person is like his parents—" Deenie protested.

"Well, that's all he knows." Rae shook her head. "The last girl he dated? She actually broke up with him because she said that he wasn't religious enough for her. It broke his heart."

"I remember that," Deenie admitted. "Wasn't she kicked out of seminary last month for selling her brother's ADHD pills?"

"Yep. That little hypocrite. He denies it, but I think he still hasn't gotten over her."

Deenie raised her eyebrows, but Rae waved off her doubtful look.

"And I'm okay with that," she assured us. "We all have someone we'll never really get over. And no one actually ends up with their high school boyfriend anyway." She grinned at me. "Except you, Ellie. You and Danny will ride off into the sunset together one day. On separate horses, of course. So that you don't accidentally touch each other."

I couldn't help smiling at the image. Horseback riding would make a great Instagram post. I wondered if I could book a lesson at sunset. And somehow get Danny to overcome his fear of horses. "You can make fun if you like, Rae," I told her. "But while you're wasting time with the wrong person, the right one might pass you by."

"The right one will never look at me that way!" she retorted. She paused and shook her head, as if regretting what she'd just said. "I mean, Greg is fine with a bit of messing around. He doesn't expect anything deep from our relationship."

"Okay, well, I guess Danny and I are the opposite, then. We want the deep part, without the messing around."

She opened her mouth to reply and then paused and crossed her arms over her chest. "Hold on. So, Danny is on board with this?"

"Of course he's on board!" I hesitated, glanced between Rae's teasing face and Deenie's encouraging eyes. "I mean, it isn't easy. We're both human. But he respects me and wants this to work. So, we find other ways to make each other happy."

Rae grinned and gave me an approving nod. "So—sexting?"

"A little bit." I felt the color rising to my cheeks. I lowered my voice and leaned toward them. "Actually, Danny really likes it when we—"

"Wow, that's great, Ellie!" Deenie interrupted, clapping her hands together. "I don't think we need the details, though, right?"

Rae shrugged her surrender. "Whatever. As long as you're both happy, I guess."

Chapter 15

I hadn't intended to start interviewing adults until I'd covered most of Danny's classmates, but Ms. Baker sidelines me during recess a few weeks after I start my project.

"I have a story for your collection," she says, motioning me back into the classroom.

I hesitate and slowly follow her back to her desk. She indicates a chair opposite her, and I settle into it reluctantly. It's not that I dislike Ms. Baker. She's actually a great teacher, and a genuinely kind person. But she makes me uncomfortable for some reason. I feel like she's waiting for me to fulfill some lofty goal; she's like an overeager mama hen hoping that her baby bird will one day soar into the air. And I'm that miserable chick waddling around muttering, "I'm a chicken! And chickens don't fly."

I just want her to believe in someone else and leave me alone already.

"Who told you I was gathering stories?" I ask her suspiciously.

She shrugs and draws a folder from her desk. "I've been debating showing you this for quite a while. Do you remember that writing assignment I gave your class last December? It was due right before break."

I nod, and my throat gets tight. We were supposed to hand in an original composition using Lois Lowry's *The Giver* as inspiration.

"I wasn't sure what to do with Danny's paper. It seemed, at first, to be a breach of confidence if I showed it to anyone. Then I thought perhaps I should hand it over to Danny's father." She sighs. "I called him a few weeks ago—but he told me to keep it until his son returns and then give it to him." She glances up at me, and her pale eyes grow large with sympathy. "It's been more than nine months. I think it's okay to share this now. And, anyway, it was so obviously written for you, Ellie. I believe he meant for you to have it."

I'm so curious about the contents of that folder that I forget my earlier question. It doesn't matter who told her about my project. She has something from Danny, something he wrote down. Something for me!

It's hard to keep a calm face as I wait for her to hand it over. She doesn't know the value of what she holds. Danny told stories to me every day. And yet, no matter how many times I urged him to, he never wrote a single one down. *I look at* you, *and I tell you a story meant for you*, he explained to me. *I can tell by your eyes, by your reaction, where the story is meant to go. How am I supposed to speak to people I've never met?*

"But I want them on paper so I can read them whenever I want."

"What's the point?" he replied with a shrug. "I'll always be here to tell you a new one."

Except now he wasn't; he hadn't been for a long time. I was dying to hear him tell me a new story. Not the ones I told in his voice, but authentic Danny.

Was it possible that he'd actually pushed through his self-doubt and recorded one of his ideas? I'm holding my hands in my lap, my fingers intertwined in a painful fist; it's all I can do not to grab the folder from her and run.

But she doesn't seem to be done yet. Apparently, "I have a story for your collection" didn't mean just Danny's composition. Ms. Baker has something to tell me too.

"He was one of my best students," she says with a smile. "I was going to use his essay on *Leaves of Grass* as an example for future classes. But when I announced the creative writing assignment, I actually saw his face fall. The first draft he handed in was a silly little poem that I refused to grade." She flips open the folder and draws out the first sheet.

> *"There once was a boy who was blank*
> *Whose writing actually stank.*
> *His girlfriend was lost,*
> *Their stars were all crossed,*
> *So he just watched his GPA tank."*

I feel my stomach tighten as she reads the poem out loud. The words may seem silly to her, but they hit me like a fist to the gut.

"What does he mean when he says, 'his girlfriend was lost'?" she asks when I don't speak.

I hesitate before answering, then realize that there's no reason to hold back. Most of the class knows what happened between us. "We were fighting when Danny wrote that," I explain. It hurts to talk; I'm scraping the words out one by one. "Normally I would have helped him with the story assignment. But we weren't speaking to each other then."

She nods silently and looks down at the folder again.

"I mean, I wasn't speaking to him," I amend miserably. "He was speaking to me. He was trying to, anyway. I wasn't listening."

"I see."

I'm pretty sure she doesn't. From where I sit, I can make out the date scribbled on the corner of the paper. She can't possibly know that the night before he'd written that poem, he'd sat outside my window during the bitterest freeze in Atlanta history, with his phone clasped in his chapped hands.

Please talk to me, Ellie. I'll wait as long as it takes. Please.

I was going to, of course. Eventually. But I was still so angry. I thought I would punish him a little longer.

That was the last text he ever sent me.

Ms. Baker is watching me closely; she turns to the next page and begins reading the passage out loud, but after a moment she pauses and seems to reconsider. With a quick motion, she flips the folder shut and slides it over to me.

"Maybe you'd like to read it for yourself, Ellie?"

I would, but not now, and not in front of her. I need the privacy of my room, the safety of solitude. Her sympathy is choking me.

"Can I take this home with me?"

"Of course."

Time skips. There are three more classes, a car ride home with Deenie and Rae, and a phone call from my grandmother that I have to pass through to get where I need to be. The only thing that matters is closing my bedroom door and being alone with my precious folder.

Danny is sitting on my bed when I finally hurry to my room.

"You have it," he says as I settle down next to him.

"I'm scared," I tell him.

"So don't read it."

I tear my eyes away from the typed page in front of me and look at him. He's only inches away, his thin shoulders jutting forward, his arms on either side of me. I can almost feel the warmth of his cheek near mine. Almost.

"If you're going to read that, I'm leaving," he declares.

I bow my head over the folder, slide away from him. He sighs loudly and then disappears as I start to read.

THE SECRET KEEPER

Emory Island was unlike any other land. Its people had long ago discovered the key to happiness. They had learned from countless conflicts and wars that the source of human suffering was falsehood. So, they decided that the only way to rid themselves of lies and deception was to remove all secrets from their society.

They appointed a Secret Keeper, someone who would draw the poison out of their lives and store it away. Their Secret Keeper had an odd power; the moment someone deposited their story with him, the pain of the memory would vanish, and they could return to their families happy and unencumbered.

The post was obviously a sacred one; the Keeper had to be trustworthy and wise. In many ways he was like the community priest, but unlike a priest he could not forgive their transgressions, because he wasn't God. He simply stored the sin, so it wouldn't hurt the rest of the world. The Keeper loved his job because he saw that he brought peace to his people. But their problems and hidden thoughts lay heavy on him, and before long he was bowed down by the burden. His hair turned white; his back was bent double from the weight of their cares; his breathing became labored and wheezy. And then one day he learned the worst secret of all, the one his wife was keeping from him, and his heart broke from the shock. They buried him in the back of the cemetery, hidden behind a row of rosebushes, so that no one would be reminded of the darkness that he had carried for them.

The Keeper's son was appointed to take his father's place, but the boy was young and not ready for the gravity of his post. He had barely hit his growth spurt and was still trying to speak without cracking his voice.

And yet, the people of the island rushed to bring him their latest pain, unloading decades of insults and betrayals in a single afternoon. The boy groaned under the strain but took it all in; he knelt at his father's grave and swore to him that he would make him proud and bear whatever was laid at his doorstep.

By the time he reached puberty the boy had learned the hidden guilt of everyone on that island. He managed to take all their secrets and store them faithfully, and never once did a disloyal whisper escape him. Even his mother's confession was safe with him, though it tore through him whenever he thought of it.

And then one day the boy fell in love. It happened in a moment, aboard a sinking ship. He spotted her, clinging to the railing, crying into the ocean. It was the worst moment in the world to fall in love, because he had to be brave for her, though he was ready to heave and smelled strongly of sweat. But somehow, the girl never noticed this. When he spoke to her, his voice became calm—almost like an adult's. As he looked into her frightened gray eyes, he opened his mouth to tell her his name—and the world's stories poured from his lips. He never once betrayed anyone's secret, their tales twisted and intertwined until their owners became unrecognizable, but she was nevertheless mesmerized by his words. And he discovered that he could never get enough of her.

For years they talked about the world around them and all of its stories, but he never told her how he felt about her, because that was his secret, and he was, after all, the Keeper of Secrets. Besides, it was a heavy thing to be the Keeper's girlfriend, for he wasn't sure he would be able to open his heart to her, while guarding his people's cares. What if he should slip one day, and tell her everything? It was better not to take the chance.

If he hadn't kissed her, they might have remained happy friends forever. But he did kiss her, and then he kissed her again, and then suddenly his life became a race between kisses. He could never get to her fast enough, and when he was with her, it was a countdown until they were forced apart.

Every love song spoke to him; none of the breakup songs made sense. How could love make you cry, as those lyrics claimed? Love made him jumpy and restless, and sometimes it made him breathe really heavily. After a couple of hours of steady making out, it made him pretty hungry. But there was never a reason to cry. Because after they were together all he wanted to do was tell the whole island that he'd just kissed the most beautiful girl in the world. And she'd actually kissed him back.

But the people kept bringing him their secrets. Some of them were complicated and confusing. Some made him sick to his stomach. Some were whispered in shame, others shouted in anger. One was never even spoken, just given to him with a look. And he couldn't tell his love a single one, because they didn't belong to him.

He was carrying them all, he was holding on to his own, and she was kissing him through all of it. But no matter how close he got to her, he never betrayed his people's secrets.

Instead, he betrayed her.

There were no excuses.

He didn't have a reason.

He just did it. He didn't even realize what he'd done, until he saw the look on her face. And because there was no justice on that island, only peace and blindness, the people never stopped loving the boy, even after he betrayed her.

But they spit at the girl and drowned her in their scorn.

The boy wanted to give up his post immediately, to hide himself away and seal his lips forever. He'd never hear another secret because he should never have been the keeper of anything, much less her happiness.

He promised he would never tell another story.

None of them mattered now.

Because she wasn't listening anymore.

I flip the page and encounter a blank sheet, with our teacher's red scrawl at the bottom. "Nice beginning but incomplete," Ms. Baker had written. "B-minus. Please finish the story."

The irony of her comment was probably only obvious to her after Danny had been gone awhile. I wonder if that's why she'd hung on to the assignment as long as she had. She'd never had a chance to hand it back to him, and he'd never had a chance to finish it.

When he wrote that story, he was still waiting for me to talk to him. And now, almost a year later, he was still waiting. Somewhere out there, Danny was counting the minutes until I found him, just as he'd counted the minutes huddled outside of my bedroom in the freezing cold.

"Danny," I whisper, and suddenly he's there again. "I forgive you. I've forgiven you a thousand times, you know."

He doesn't answer because he can't. Nothing he says will make me feel better, and he knows it. So he just slips into my bed and buries his head deep into my pillow. I snuggle close to him and lay my face as near him as I can, without touching him.

That night I dream that Danny's hand is covering my eyes. For the first time in months, I can actually feel his skin against mine, and it's the best dream in the world. I can't see anything because he's blocking the light, but I don't care. He will tell me what I need to see. Honestly, I'd rather keep my eyes closed forever than wake up and find that he is gone.

IF PILLOWS COULD TALK

I didn't want to get into it with my friends, but my *shomer* relationship wasn't the happy little tea party that I'd been painting. Sure, Danny and I had awesome late-night conversations about everything from celebrity scandals to the meaning of life. He'd even commented once that our talks were what made us a great couple—the best couple in our high school, in his "unbiased" opinion.

But after he hung out with Greg, our conversations sometimes took a different tone.

"I'm crazy about you, Ellie," he said in a voice that sounded more like an accusation than a declaration of love. "I've told you that a thousand times. And I've never kissed you once. How is that normal?"

"But we've talked about this already," I reasoned with him. "You don't have to kiss me. I know you care about me as much as I care about you."

He stared stubbornly at his lap, refusing to meet my eyes. "Yeah, well, that's nice to hear," he muttered after a moment. "It's just hard to believe sometimes."

And suddenly we didn't feel like the best couple—anywhere.

So, I came up with ways to show him how much I cared about him, while not breaking the rules—sort of.

Some were sweet and made him smile. (I'd kiss a piece of white chocolate and then place it on his tongue. "Look at us—we're *shomer* French-kissing!")

And some were freaking crazy.

Once, we were discussing how weird the whole kissing thing was, if you truly thought about it. I figured that if we overanalyzed it, it would lose some of its appeal. (I was wrong.)

"I mean, if aliens were watching us, they'd think we were insane," I pointed out. "Two people basically mushing their lips together, for a few minutes. It's weird, right?"

He stared at me for a moment before answering. "Just a few minutes? That's all you'd want?" His eyes had the bewildered hurt-puppy look he got when I teased him about his skinny legs. "After all this time, it would just be a few minutes?"

I couldn't handle it when he looked at me like that. "Not for us," I assured him quickly. "For us, it would be hours."

He grinned. "Hours? Come on. You're all talk. You wouldn't last thirty minutes."

I crossed my arms. "Wanna bet? Just wait. When we finally do kiss, I'm not going to let you go. You'll probably end up starving to death."

He inched a little closer to me. The puppy look was gone. He was staring at me like a hungry wolf, and the fire in his eyes made him so unexpectedly sexy that I had to look away.

"Is that right?" His voice was hoarse and strained. I was trying to keep it together, but looking away wasn't helping at all. I could literally feel the heat radiating off his body, just inches from mine. "Come on," he teased. "You've never kissed anyone. You wouldn't know what to do."

"I know better than you!" I retorted. "I've practiced. A lot."

"A lot, huh?" He sounded like he was choking back a laugh. I still couldn't bring myself to look at him. "So you're an expert, then?"

"You don't believe me?" I grabbed my pillow and held it between us, pushed him back against the wall. He made an "oh" noise that sounded like a cross between surprise and desire. I was panting with frustration, drunk with excitement. I'd never felt so wanted before, and I was scared that the feeling would break me. I wanted to be strong; I was the sensible, calm one who was supposed to guide us along the impossible path of virtue. But at that moment I dared to look up at him, and the expression on his face undid me. He wasn't mocking me anymore. Danny was all desperation.

I wanted to show him how I felt. I needed to kiss him, once, fiercely, perfectly, to banish all his doubts forever.

But I couldn't because it was forbidden.

So instead I attacked the pillow between us with such fierce energy, it would have made a porn star blush. There were sounds, and tongue, and so much messy, misdirected passion that I think I shocked the breath out of him. When I finally came up for air, he was totally still, and bright red all the way to his hairline. The pillow was lying crushed between us, a battered testament of my love for him.

"Are you going to—hurt me?" he gasped. He was staring at the jagged hole in the lace lining.

I shrugged. "Only if you deserve it," I whispered. I was trying to sound seductive, but it came out more psychopath than siren.

He didn't appear to notice. Maybe weirdness turned him on. Or maybe he was so frustrated that even a damp pillowcase seemed sexy at that moment.

"God, Ellie, that was so—hot," he growled.

I pursed my sore lips at him. "Told you so."

And then he grabbed the pillow from my hand. "Oh, baby, you ain't seen nothing yet."

Like I said, sometimes the *shomer* thing got freaking crazy.

Chapter 16

Danny is with me most of the time now. I rarely wake to my alarm because he whispers in my ears every morning until I throw a pillow at his face. He hides in the closet while I get dressed and pretends not to peek. Sometimes at breakfast he licks one of my pancakes when I turn my back and then dares me to figure out which one. He comes with me to school and hangs around my chair while I try to concentrate. And, of course, he snuggles with me as I fall asleep.

I know we're breaking every single one of Nina's rules, but I don't care. Her eventual goal was to wean me of my need for him, but I don't want to be weaned. I like being with him. And I don't see the harm. Danny's my private joy. I *know* no one else can see him, so I'm not shouting at empty street corners. And it isn't like my grades are falling, or I'm becoming a hermit. I still hang out with Deenie and Rae most afternoons, I play board games with my parents on Shabbat, I visit Mr. Edelstein after school, and I go on my morning runs. Danny helps me do all these things. He's my rock, and I can't imagine my life without him.

Besides, he's coming back soon. I'm not going to pretend I'm over him just to please my psychologist and my parents. And I'm not going to let him disappear like everyone else has.

According to Nina, I'm making "progress." The therapy is just a Band-Aid for my parents, some scheduled reassurance that I won't scare them again, the way I did after Danny's accident. Now my mother can say, *Ellie's seeing someone,* to anyone who asked how I was coping. *She's doing so much better.*

And she's right. I am. But it has nothing to do with Nina. I'm doing better in spite of her. And it's a good thing I am, because the Jewish High Holidays are just around the corner, and I know I can't get through them without Danny.

The Jewish New Year, or Rosh Hashanah, falls in October this year. It's a pretty long affair, a two-day holiday with a five-hour morning synagogue service. Rosh Hashanah is followed by Yom Kippur, Sukkot, and then Simchat Torah, all within a four-week period. Each holiday is celebrated with multiple feasts. My dad complains that he always gains ten pounds between September and October. I don't mind the eating, but the hours in synagogue do get pretty boring. We repeat prayers. A lot.

The previous year I hadn't minded the interminable mornings. I could see Danny sitting in the men's section next to his father. He was just on the other side of the crack in the curtain that separated the women from the men. That curtain was meant to prevent us from becoming distracted during prayer. I know I'm supposed to focus on God, repentance, and my soul. But God also put that crack in the curtain. So, the service had been a game of "What faces can I make at Danny without my mom noticing?" By the time our parents caught on, we were nearing the end, and the two of us had had the best five hours in synagogue ever.

This Rosh Hashanah is different. It's eerie how nothing else has changed since the previous year—every face is familiar, every prayer sung exactly the same. I sit in the same seat, my mother on my right, Deenie and her mom on the left. Someone has sealed the crack in the curtain, and anyway, there's nothing to see on the other side. I spend a few moments studying the Memorial Wall beside me; it contains hundreds of names illuminated by little light bulbs; each name represents a departed soul looking down at us from heaven. I follow the names up toward the ceiling and gaze at the ornate arched windows. At that moment the sunlight breaks through and lights up the *bima* where the rabbi is standing. It's breathtaking; as the *Shema* is chanted the hall is bathed in a Divine glow.

I bow my head over my *siddur* and mouth the prayers with the congregation; I close my eyes and rock to the rhythm of the songs. I float, buoyed by the Hebrew melodies; I bow before the ark, pulled by the weight of worship. I believe God is here with me; I can hear Him in the murmured voices around me. So, I speak to Him with my own words, the ones I've said a thousand times. "Please, God, bring him back. I know it's my fault that he's gone. But I'm begging you. Please, forgive me and bring him back."

"Ellie! Come outside!" Danny's whisper is so sudden and unexpected that I jump in my seat. I glance over my shoulder, and there he is, bouncing quietly on his toes behind me. He's wearing jeans and his favorite black polo, and his hair is way too wild for synagogue. I know I can't speak to him here, but I shoot him a guarded smile. *What are you doing in the women's section? And where is your kippah?* I ask him with my eyes. He whips his kippah out of his pocket and mashes it down on his head.

"There. Now will you come outside?"

I steal a glance at my mother and then back at Danny. Why shouldn't I take a break? No one will notice if I'm gone for a few minutes.

As I sneak out into the foyer, a gust of wind whips around me and slams the heavy door shut behind me. It's blessedly quiet out here, the drone of the prayers just pleasant background noise in the empty corridor. "Where are you?" I whisper, and he's there before I finish the question, teetering cross-legged on top of the radiator. "I've only got a few minutes," I warn. "Then I have to get back."

"Or what?" He grins and cocks his head to the side. His kippah slides off his head onto the floor. "God won't forgive you?"

"I was trying to concentrate on the *davening*, for once." I'm forcing myself to be serious because some part of me feels guilty for talking to him here in this holy place. It's one thing to break Nina's rules or my parents', but how can I expect God to be on my side when I'm flirting with my boyfriend right in the middle of Rosh Hashanah services?

Danny takes the cue, and the smile on his face fades. "What were you *davening* for?" he asks.

"What do you think?"

"Me?"

I nod. "Of course. Always you."

He climbs off the radiator and walks up to me. "You were pretty intense back there," he says quietly. "Like you really believed."

"I do." I look up into his eyes. They're darker than I remember, like the color of the ocean before a storm. "You know I've never lost faith."

"And you never will?"

I shake my head. "I say the same prayer every Shabbat. And every holiday. I pray that they'll find you and bring you home. It's the only thing that keeps me going."

He doesn't seem pleased. I step closer to him, but he begins to edge away; he ducks his head and his hair falls forward, blocking his eyes. "What if God never answers you?" he asks.

"He will. God always answers our prayers."

"Does He?"

I take another step toward him, but he scoots back, like he's trying to escape me.

"Rabbi Garner says that our prayers are always answered," I explain. "We just can't see the big picture, so we think God's ignoring us. But He isn't."

Danny leans forward. "What if *this* is the big picture? What if this is the closest I ever get to you?"

"Don't say that."

"I'm serious. Haven't you asked yourself how long this can go on? How long am I going to be Schrödinger's cat?"

"What?"

"Remember that thought experiment we learned in physics? The cat in the poisoned box—the one whose fate no one knows. So, he's both dead and alive at the same time."

"Stop it. We both know that you're alive—"

"*You* know," he says. "You're the only one who still believes."

I start to retreat, but he advances suddenly and backs me into a corner. His eyes flash, and his lips curl into a smile. I barely recognize him now; it's like a demon has possessed the boy I love.

"Maybe I'm just a tiny bit dead," he muses. "In your mind. And this is what doubt looks like."

"I don't know what you're talking about—"

He cuts my protest off with a cruel laugh. "Perfect faith, my ass." His voice is biting, shrill and bitter. He's never spoken to me like this before. "You don't really believe I'm coming back."

"I do. I *do*—"

"Then why aren't you honest with your friends? If you really believe that I'm okay, why won't you tell them what really happened that night?"

"What do you mean?" I duck my head to avoid his eyes. "Everyone knows what happened. You left the party. It was sleeting, and your car skidded into the bridge railing."

"Not that part. Before. Why don't you tell them what happened before? Why don't you tell them why I left the party?"

I'm struggling to catch my breath; his voice is like a hand to my throat. "I can't. Danny, you know I can't. I can't tell them that."

His eyes narrow, and he shakes his head. "Yeah? Well, I don't want to keep your secret anymore."

"What do you mean?"

He smirks at me. "Aren't these the days of repentance? That's what this holiday is about, right? So why aren't you repenting? Why are you out here with me?"

"You told me to come out—"

"If it weren't for you, I'd be sitting inside next to my father right now."

I flinch and shut my eyes. But no matter how hard I squeeze, I can't block him out.

"Have you ever thought about that, Ellie? Have you?"

"Yes! I think about it every day—" Tears stream down my cheeks.

"Tell my father what you did," he whispers in my ear. "Tell Rae and Deenie what really happened."

"I can't," I sob. "Please, Danny."

"You have to believe, don't you, Ellie?"

"What do you mean?"

"If I do come back, no one has to know, right? You'll never need to tell anyone that story."

"Is that what you want from me? You think that if I just tell Rae and Deenie what happened—"

There's a clicking sound behind me, and my eyes fly open. Deenie is standing there, staring at me, with a shocked expression. I look around for Danny, but he's disappeared; all I can hear is the moaning wind whining through the open windows.

"Don't say anything," I warn her as I wipe my wet cheeks with my sleeve. "Please don't."

She hesitates and takes a tentative step toward me. "I heard my name. What were you saying about me?"

Oh God, how loud had I been? I wonder. "How much did you hear?"

Deenie studies my face for a moment before answering. "Were you talking to Danny just now?"

I nod, and she reaches out to take my hand. "Oh. It really didn't sound like him."

I stare at her openmouthed. "You heard him? *How?* How could you hear—"

"Ellie, I haven't heard his voice since New Year's. What I meant was you didn't sound like you were talking to Danny. He always used to make you happy."

I realize that she's right, but I can't admit that—not out loud. I'm still shaking from his awful words, and it's hard to keep my voice steady when I speak. "He does make me happy. I was just missing him, that's all."

She doesn't appear to believe me, but at least she doesn't

argue. "If you want, I can stay with you out here until you're ready to go back inside."

I take a deep breath. "I'm ready now."

"Really?" She pulls a tissue from her pocket. "You sure?"

I nod and turn toward the sanctuary. "Yeah. I'm okay."

I'm really not. But I don't want to stay back in the empty foyer alone. I'm terrified that Danny's going to come back.

THE BOY BEHIND THE BLANKET (OR, MY FIRST KISS)

There were a few ground rules that Danny and I established at the beginning of our relationship. Besides the *shomer* thing, I was determined to follow Rae's example and not do anything to mess up the dynamic of our happy quartet. "We're not going to be that couple that drops their friends the moment they start dating," I told him. "I don't want Deenie and Rae to feel that anything has changed."

At first it was the easiest thing in the world. Danny and I didn't touch, so there was no annoying PDA to irritate our friends. In front of them, we were pretty much the same as always.

Except . . . there were only so many hours in the day. And since most of them were split between school, friends, and sleep, something had to give.

School was not negotiable, and as far as we were concerned, neither were our friends. So sleep became optional.

Danny would leave my house with Deenie and Rae when it was time for bed. And after they parted ways, he'd double back and scale the tree outside my window. And our late-night dates would begin.

Nobody suspected at first. We kept our voices low and turned out the lights so my parents would think I'd gone to bed. And we never told anyone that Danny was sneaking home at two a.m. every night. We managed to fool even Deenie, who complimented me on our healthy relationship.

"It's so easy to get carried away," she told me. "I'm so glad you guys are keeping things casual."

I smiled at the compliment, but I couldn't help the pang of guilt that followed. Because I knew that half an hour later Danny and I were going to be alone together. And there would be nothing casual about my dark bedroom, the flashlight under my blanket, and the whispered promises of the boy I was falling in love with.

"I'm not even tired," Danny declared one night. We'd been surviving on four hours of sleep for days. "What about you?"

"I'm a little tired," I admitted. "But it's worth it."

He smiled. "Do your parents suspect?"

I laughed, and the blanket over our heads shivered like a tent in a storm. "They don't even know that we're dating," I said. "So they have no reason to be suspicious."

He wrinkled his brow and leaned closer to me. "But I want them to know. I want everyone to know."

I punched him playfully. It was our only loophole—one that we'd made up for ourselves, based loosely on actual rules. I was allowed to touch him if it wasn't a romantic gesture. There weren't many ways to touch someone non-romantically, so I ended up punching him a lot. He seemed to like it, but then, it was the only action he was getting.

"Come on. You haven't told your dad."

"Sure I did," he protested. "And he's known for weeks that I wanted to ask you out."

I was about to ask him what his dad thought when I was distracted by a gentle weight on my knee.

We both looked down at the same time. His hand had come to rest on top of the blanket, which was covering my leg. I jumped, and he pulled back, an apology on his lips.

"It's okay," I assured him. "It doesn't really count, right? Your hand was on the blanket."

He paused, and a mischievous little smile dawned. "Wait. It doesn't count?"

I hesitated. I could still feel the warmth of his hand on my knee. It was making me giddy, plucking at my convictions, begging me to bend the rules and embrace the desire coursing through me.

"I—I don't think so. We weren't actually touching, right?"

His eyes sparkled as he lifted my blanket and held it up between us. "Interesting," he said, examining the threadbare edges. "So many possibilities. I wonder what I can do with this." He shook it out and placed it carefully around my shoulders. "There," he said, pulling me close. "So I can actually hug you now?" he asked. "That's okay, right? As long as I only touch the blanket?" I didn't know what to say. I hadn't intended to open Pandora's box. But there was no going back now.

"I guess so," I told him. "If it's through a blanket—you can hug me."

I was already wrapped in his arms. It was the thinnest of covers, and I could feel everything through it, the rise and fall of his chest, the sinews of his thin arms, the tickle of his hair on my neck.

Wait—I wasn't supposed to be feeling that, I realized with a start. I glanced down and saw that the cover had slipped off my shoulders and his cheek was resting on its edge. I wriggled one arm out and lifted the blanket to my lips. His eyes widened, and he took a deep breath. "Really? That's okay too?" he whispered.

My smile answered him. And then his lips were pressed against mine, with only a thin piece of cloth between.

My first kiss was through fabric. It was just a tease. My second was just on the edge, as I tugged at the barrier between us. It was close to perfect.

The third one was the real thing. His lips met mine.

It was like an answered prayer.

Danny murmured, "Just one more, okay? Just one." And kissed me again. And again. "One more?" he repeated. "Last one. And then we'll pick up the blanket. I promise." But the blanket had vanished along with my inhibitions. I smoothed his tousled hair away from his face and wrapped my arms around his neck.

"Just one more," I echoed. "Just one." And then we stopped counting.

Chapter 17

We go back to school a couple of days after Rosh Hashanah, and I'm worried that Danny will suddenly appear in the middle of class and freak me out again. But I don't see him until my appointment at Nina's, and he's perfectly respectful and pleasant as he accompanies me into her garage office. He doesn't even speak as she greets me, just perches cross-legged on the ottoman and quietly studies the weird bric-a-brac on her desk.

"It's okay if you want to cut our hours," I tell her evenly. "I think I'm ready."

You can do whatever you want with Danny's curfew, I think, as she beams at me proudly. *He's not going to listen to you anyway. And neither am I.*

To my surprise, she doesn't take me up on it, doesn't even mention the rules. Instead, she asks me about the project I'm doing.

"I feel like I'm connecting to other people through their stories about Danny," I tell her. That, at least, is true. Word has gotten around, and now people are seeking me out to add to my collection. One girl even stopped me on the street to submit her entry. Many of the tales are whimsical and silly, and some are clearly exaggerated for effect, but each gives me a shade more information about the boy I love.

She nods thoughtfully. "And who have you interviewed so far?"

"Rae and Deenie. Ms. Baker. A few classmates. That's it. The holidays got in the way."

"I see. And what about Mr. Edelstein?"

I steal a glance at Danny to see his reaction. He doesn't even appear to be listening. He's pulled out his phone and is scrolling through my Instagram page. "I'm not in any of these pictures," he mutters under his breath.

How did he get his phone back? I wonder. Last thing I heard, the police still had it in an evidence locker.

I'm so distracted that I forget that Nina has just asked me a question. "Ellie? You with me?"

"Sorry." I shake my head and focus on her worried face. "No, I haven't asked Danny's father yet. I don't think that's a good idea."

"Why not?"

I haven't asked him because awakening those thoughts seems like a selfish thing to do, especially when I know how vulnerable he is. Anxious as I am to hear them, I'm scared that retelling those stories will only make his depression worse. He hasn't mentioned the ECT treatment since we first talked about it, and I'm hoping that he's put that idea behind him. But I'm afraid to say anything that will send him back to that clinic.

"Because—" I hesitate again and look at Danny. He holds up the phone and points to a pic of me in my scarlet Shabbat dress. "Nice," he murmurs. "Who says redheads can't wear red?"

I smother a smile. *Cut it out*, I tell him with my mind. *Not here.* He doesn't seem to hear me. "Can you put that on later?" he asks with a flirty smile. "I've never seen you in it."

"Ellie?" Nina's voice distracts me again. "You were saying?"

I don't remember. I have no idea what I'd been talking about before Danny interrupted. She seems to realize that I'm totally lost and prompts me with a hint. "You don't want to ask Mr. Edelstein because—"

"It's not healthy for him," Danny says.

"It's not healthy for him," I echo.

She doesn't answer for a moment, and when she finally does, her voice is cold. "Ellie, is that your answer, or Danny's?"

I just smile innocently at her. What is she going to do about it? Her rules only have power over me if I let them.

When we get home, I instruct Danny to wait in the basement for me and then run upstairs to change into the red dress.

Before heading out the door, I check my reflection in the mirror. He was right; the dress looks like it was made for me, despite the color. It's tight at the waist with a flowing, floor-length skirt, a daring dip at the collar, and scalloped lace sleeves. I'd loved it when I'd tried it on at the store, but it was a bit too fancy for a regular Shabbat. So, I'd posted a pic and then put it away, and it had stayed tucked in the back of my closet until—

Well, until Danny could see it. Deep down, I guess that's what I'd been saving it for.

My mother calls out to me as I'm heading down the stairs. "Deenie and Rae are here," she says, and then stops short as I come into view. "Why are you all dressed up?"

I realize how weird I must look, dancing around the house in evening wear on a Monday afternoon. "Deenie and Rae want to see my new dress," I tell her, and rush down to the basement before she can ask me anything else.

My friends' expressions mirror my mother's when they see me. "Wow," Rae says. "Where's the party?"

I glance around the room, and my face falls. Danny isn't there, and I feel like an idiot. I look like a girl who's been stood up by her prom date. "I was just trying it on."

Deenie clears her throat and nudges Rae in the ribs. "What?" Rae snaps. "You're the one with the stupid sign."

Deenie chucks a piece of white cloth behind her and shakes her head. "I don't want to use the sign. You're right. It's stupid."

"What are you guys talking about?" I walk over and poke the crumpled sheet with my foot. "What is that?"

"We have to talk to you," Rae declares. "Alone."

Her voice has an edge to it, and I'm immediately on my guard. "Okay." This feels like the beginning of an attack, not a conversation. "What's going on?"

She glances around the room. "Are we alone?"

"He isn't here," Deenie says softly. "Go ahead."

Rae appears confused. "How do you know that?"

"I thought it was obvious."

"It isn't obvious to me!" Rae retorts. "Am I the only one who hasn't joined the Danny Dream Club?"

"Rae, you promised you wouldn't make jokes like that!"

I pick up the crumpled ball of cloth on the ground and unroll it. The word "Intervention" is scrawled across it in red ink. "Are you serious, guys? Like from *How I Met Your Mother*?"

"I told you it was stupid," Rae mutters.

"I already agreed with you!" Deenie snaps back. "I just thought it was better to start off funny—"

"Well, there's nothing funny about this." Rae turns back to me.

"This is the first time we've been alone with you in weeks, Ellie! Do you realize that?"

I want to argue, but my mind is blank. *She must be exaggerating,* I think. *I just can't prove it at the moment. . . .*

"Listen, it's okay if you talk to him occasionally," Deenie puts in. "Lots of people do that when they're mourning—"

"I'm not mourning," I mumble.

"But it's become an obsession," she continues without acknowledging my interruption. "He goes everywhere with you now."

"Not everywhere," I protest. "We have a curfew."

"Real boyfriends should have curfews," Rae says. "Daydreams—or hallucinations—or whatever he is—"

"You have no idea what you're talking about," I tell her. "I'm fine. I'm still going to school, aren't I? Getting decent grades? Hanging out with you guys?"

"What about college applications?" Rae points out. "You haven't even started looking."

I don't want to think about college; how can I make plans like that without Danny? We'd talked about applying together before he left, but that was all on hold now. "You haven't filled any out either," I say.

"I'm going to take a year off and then go to culinary school. That's always been the plan," Rae counters. "You know that."

"And I'm going to seminary in Israel for a year," Deenie adds. "I'm still trying to decide which one, but at least I'm looking."

So you'll be halfway across the globe when Danny comes back, I think. *How can you accept that? How are either of you still making plans?*

"You've changed, Ellie," Deenie says. "It's like you're hiding behind Danny."

I feel his presence behind me before I turn to find him coming down the basement stairs. It's such a relief to see him, to have someone here on my side.

"Rae gave up on me the minute the cops told them I was missing," he says, walking up to me. His voice is distant and cold. "And Deenie just buried herself in God. They never tried to find out what really happened."

He's right, I realize. They never fought for him. They just accepted that he was gone and tried to move on. And now he needs me to call them out.

I cross my arms and take a step toward them. "Deenie, you really aren't one to talk about hiding, you know that?"

"What do you mean?" Deenie's voice is guarded suddenly; her eyes drop down to her dress. She knows exactly what I mean.

"Look what you're wearing," I say, pointing to the flowing ash-colored outfit she has on. "Where in the Torah does it say you need to wear a garbage sack?" Deenie flinches; her lips fall open, but she doesn't respond. I wonder if I've gone too far, but Danny gives me a curt nod of encouragement.

We aren't done yet.

I focus on Rae. "When Danny comes back, he's going to ask you why you gave up on him." I barely register the hurt in her eyes before I swing back to Deenie. "And why *you* look like a cult member."

They both stare at me, and Deenie starts to cry silently. Rae puts her arm around her.

"Danny would never say that, and you know it," Rae tells me.

Deenie wipes her cheeks. She takes a deep breath, and her eyes shift upward to focus on Danny's face. They stare at each other for a moment. "I don't know who's standing behind you,

Ellie," she tells me in a hushed voice. "But that isn't Danny."

#KISSAGINGER
OR
#MYGODWOULDAPPROVE

I expected to wake up the morning after our first kiss feeling guilty and sinful. After all, we'd just gone from borderline *shomer* to full-on making out in my bedroom until two in the morning. My parents would have been scandalized. Deenie would pretend to understand, but I'd know she was disappointed. Even Rae would have been shocked.

But the only thing I felt was impatient. I wanted to break the rules again. I wanted to discover new boundaries, just so we could tear through them. We were better than the rules, I decided. We'd crossed the line, and nothing terrible had happened. Danny loved me and I loved him. We hadn't said so exactly—we'd been too busy discovering each other's lips and neck (and very briefly the top of my chest). But it was understood.

Something else that was understood: our adventure the previous night was our little secret. I'd made sure of that before he'd left.

"You won't tell anyone, right?" I'd pressed him as he scrambled over my windowsill and grasped the overhanging tree branch.

He grinned. "I was live-tweeting the whole thing," he teased. "Check out #kissaginger."

"I'm serious!" I insisted. "It's just between us. Okay?"

He shrugged and swung himself onto the branch. "I don't care who knows. I'm not ashamed. But I won't tell anyone if you don't want me to."

"Promise?"

"I promise. The best night of my life is a secret. Don't worry. I got it.

I'll see you at Bruster's at ten." He winked at me and then vanished into the shadows.

I crawled back into bed, but I didn't even bother trying to fall asleep. My head was exploding with plans for the coming days.

Our first few kisses had excited him and even made him moan once—toward the end. It was hard to tell what was more intoxicating—my own excitement or the sound of his. But it was no longer enough for me. I didn't just want to be Danny's first kiss. I wanted to be his one and only everything. I wasn't repentant or guilty; I was impatient. We'd already broken the biggest rule, and it had been glorious. So why couldn't I have a little fun?

Chapter 18

"I have a story for you."

I jump when I hear her voice. Deenie is standing in my bedroom doorway clutching a math book to her chest.

I shove away my homework. "I thought you were coming over to study trig. And besides, you already told me a Danny anecdote. That thing about the horses." I don't add that I know that her tale was actually a pile of horse crap.

"Yeah—about that," she says uncomfortably. "It wasn't true." She sits down next to me and lays her textbook on my desk. "I'm sorry."

"Oh." I'm not sure how to respond. I wasn't expecting a confession from her, not after our last meeting. We were still walking on eggshells around each other after that botched intervention. "So why did you lie?"

"You took me by surprise when you asked," she explains. "And I panicked. So, I just made something up."

It's a strange explanation, but I don't call her on it. I can't imagine why a request for a story would make anyone panic, but I decide it's best not to challenge her right now, not if I want her to open up. I pick up my pencil and flip open my story notes to a blank page. "Okay, then. Go ahead."

She reaches out her hand and shuts the notebook. "Please just listen. It's kind of an embarrassing story, and it'll distract me if you're writing."

I'm dying to hear it now, even though I'm not completely convinced that I'll agree with Deenie's definition of "embarrassing." She gets embarrassed pretty easily.

"I'm ready when you are."

She drops her eyes and pulls nervously at her sleeve. "It happened right before you guys started dating. At the end of tenth grade." She pauses again and glances around the room.

"Don't worry, Deenie. He's not—"

"I know he's not here," she interrupts. "It's just that I've never told anyone this before. And I'm kind of nervous."

"Well, I really appreciate it," I tell her sincerely. "I know how much Danny means to you. And how hard it is for you to talk about him."

She meets my gaze for the first time since walking into the room, and I'm struck again by the emotion in those large, innocent brown eyes. I've known Deenie since elementary school, and I've gotten used to her looks, but she still makes me lose my breath every so often. She doesn't even realize her own power; there isn't a touch of makeup on her skin, and she's dressed in the most unflattering clothes, but nothing she can do can hide her natural beauty. I want to tell her how sweet she looks right now, but I know it isn't the time—and anyway, I don't think she wants to hear it. Compliments seem to hurt her more than criticism lately.

"It's hard. But I don't like secrets," she says. "Not between friends."

"Me neither."

She takes a deep breath. "So here goes. Secret number one."

I can't help laughing. "Jeez, Deenie, how many do you have?"

She ignores my interruption and barrels ahead, as if worried that a pause will break her nerve. "Okay. So, this one time I caught Danny doing something really embarrassing. And I totally freaked out at him."

I'm suddenly glad that she made me close my notebook. No way this is going in my collection. Not if the embarrassing thing is what I think it is—

"Ugh, Deenie." I put my fingers in my ears. "Maybe this should stay a secret. I'm not sure I want to hear this."

She flushes to the roots of her hair and waves her hands. "Oh, no! Not that! He was just watching something on the computer. But I caught a glimpse of it before he shut his laptop. And it wasn't—nice."

I'm trying really hard to keep a straight face, but she's making it impossible. Deenie looks like she's about to melt into a puddle of shame at my feet. Her misery is more interesting than the story, because, really, we live in the twenty-first century. And we all have access to the Internet. So sometimes videos get sent and things get watched. Sometimes they get watched a lot. That's why we have an "erase history" button. Still, I'm guessing Deenie has never had to use hers.

I allow myself a little smile at her expense. "Are you saying that you caught him watching porn?"

She exhales and clasps her hands together. "Are you upset? I don't have to continue if you don't want."

I'm giggling now; I can't help it. "I'm fine. Keep going."

She seems offended by my laughter. "It isn't funny, Ellie. It totally freaked me out."

"Why?"

"Because he's my friend. And it was wrong."

I'm about to protest; I want to assure her that most of the young men we know had probably dipped into that side of the Internet at some point in their lives and it's no big deal. But I can't help noting that she'd just used the present tense when referring to her friendship with Danny. And that detail feels more important to me at this moment than anything else. So, I let it go.

"What did you do?" I ask her.

"I screamed." She smiles faintly at the memory, but her cheeks are still glowing. "I grabbed the computer from his hands and threw it against the wall."

"Oh my God."

Her smile broadens. "Yeah. That's what he said."

"And then?"

"I just kept screaming. 'How can you watch that stuff?' I yelled at him. 'Don't you know that it's demeaning to women?' He didn't try to defend himself. He just kept repeating, 'Okay, okay. I'm sorry.' Over and over. 'I'm sorry, Deenie, I'm sorry.' But I kept screaming. Like, right up in his face. So, he climbed onto his bed to get away from me. I'm pretty sure I scared him to death."

"I bet you did."

Her cheeks have faded to a normal color, and her expression relaxes a little. She seems to be enjoying this part of the story; she gives me a little smile before continuing.

"'How could you watch that?' I asked him. 'Many of those girls have been abused as children. Did you know that? You're basically supporting the exploitation of women when you look at that stuff.' He put his hands up in surrender. 'I'm sorry,' he said again. 'Someone sent it to me. It was my first time.' I waved my finger in his face, and he shrunk back against the wall. 'Okay, almost my first . . .'

"But it wasn't good enough for me. I pointed at the computer bits on the ground. 'I'm glad I smashed that idol,' I told him. 'But you still have your phone. And the TV. So, I need you to promise me.'

"'What?' he said. 'What do you want?'

"'Never again,' I said. 'You will never watch anything X-rated again.'

"'Are you serious?'

"I crossed my arms. 'Yes. If you want to stay friends with me. I can't stand it. I can't stand knowing this about you.'

"'Deenie—relax. It has nothing to do with you.'

"'It has everything to do with me! Would you try to peek at *me* while I'm naked?'

"'No! Of course not! That's totally different.'

"'It isn't! The woman in that video deserves as much respect as I do. And she can't demand it for herself. So, I will for her. Now I want you to promise. Can you do that?'

"He sank down onto the bed and leaned against the wall. We both stayed silent for a few moments while he considered it. Watching him think about it actually calmed me down a little. If he'd promised quickly, I would have wondered if he was just lying to make me go away. But I could tell that he was planning to take this vow seriously. That meant a lot to me.

"'What if I mess up?' he asked finally. 'What happens then? Do I have to confess to you?'

"This was getting way too creepy and personal for me. I didn't want to be his confessor, especially not for this. I just wanted him to promise so I didn't have to think about it anymore. But Danny needed to iron out every detail before he committed.

"'How hard is it to just—not?' I pointed out. 'Don't click on it, okay? That's it.'

"'I know, I know. But what if I screw up? People screw up, right? We have a whole prayer on Yom Kippur about the million human screwups that we repent for. I want to know how I repent for this.'

"I hadn't thought past smashing his computer. What was the penalty if he broke the rule? I couldn't keep destroying his electronics. 'How about this?' I suggested. 'If you watch that stuff—you have to exile yourself.'

"He laughed for the first time. 'Exile? Like a leper in the Bible?'

"'Yes. From the group. You can't hang out with the three of us. For a whole week.'

"He considered again. 'Okay. Do I have to tell you all why I'm staying away?'

"'No, that would be weird. It'll be our secret.'

"'All right. I promise.'"

Deenie pauses, and I shake my head in awe. "Wow, Deenie. Remind me to never make you mad."

"Well, I did buy him a new computer," she says defensively. "I used most of my bat mitzvah savings."

"So have you ever wondered if he kept his promise?"

She hesitates. "Well—"

I slap my hand on the table. "Oh my God. At the end of summer vacation, when Danny disappeared for a week. Remember? He said he had really contagious pneumonia? And that we weren't allowed to visit him because we could catch it. Was that really—"

She grins and gets up from her chair. "He sent me a text too. It just said, 'Soul pneumonia. See ya in a week.'"

MY KNIGHT WITH AN ICE CREAM CONE

Naughty girl or not, I wasn't quite ready to venture outside of PG-rated territory. I wouldn't be throwing all boundaries out the window—not for a long, long time. Whatever Danny and I did would need to be within the bounds of regularly scheduled TV programs, not HBO or Cinemax. So, I had to come up with something shocking while still conforming to acceptable daytime TV fare.

Translation: all clothing would stay on.

And the twist? My outfit would simply be missing a crucial item.

Danny was waiting for me on our usual park bench with my dairy-free sundae. He half rose to greet me, and his face lit up in a smile as I slid in next to him. I was playing it cool, though. I wanted to see how long it would take until he noticed that I was considerably freer beneath my shirt. So, I watched him over my spoon as I took dainty licks of my ice cream. He quickly finished off his double helping with a puzzled *Oh, so we're just pretending everything is normal?* expression on his face.

When he was done, he just sat there next to me, fiddling with his cup and smiling at me. But there was no shock, no curiosity, nothing out of the ordinary at all. He was actually looking at my eyes! A total gentleman!

And I couldn't exactly undo centuries of women's struggles by declaring, "Hey, buddy! My chest is down there!"

"So," I said, after he dropped the cartons in the trash and wiped his hands. "What now?"

He glanced around the empty hill. We were shielded from the ice cream stand by some trees and scrubby bushes. It wasn't exactly private, but there was no one around at that moment.

"What did you have in mind?" he asked.

I had something very dirty in mind, but I couldn't actually say it. So,

I grabbed him by the shoulders and pushed him backward until he was pressed up against a tree. "Oh," he said. "But—"

I don't know what he'd been planning to tell me, but he didn't manage to say anything for the next few minutes. I stole all his words. It was amazing—so much better than our first kisses.

And yet—he still hadn't discovered my surprise.

The problem was that his hands were too tame. They rested respectfully at my waist, and though his lips explored the angle of my jaw and the dip over my clavicle, his hands stayed put, as if glued to the small of my back. I finally gathered up the courage to push them upward, and he responded by running his fingers up my spine and through my hair.

There, I thought. Surely he got it now. I leaned back a little and gave him a sexy smile.

"You're so beautiful," he whispered. He was looking into my eyes again.

This penny was never going to drop, I realized. Silly jokes aside, Danny was actually more innocent than I was. I couldn't believe it. Was I really the naughty one in this relationship?

"How am I so lucky?" he said, pulling me back toward him.

The only kiss I regret was the one that followed those sweet words. Because only a second later, the moment was shattered by a high-pitched shout. Then I heard my name, and Danny gasped as I spun around.

There, standing just a few feet in front of us, were my parents. Dad was holding a melting ice cream cone in his hand. Mom's was on the ground by her feet.

There was a horrible, shocked silence. My dad was glaring at Danny, but Mom's eyes were fixed on me; they traveled from my burning face to my flimsy top and stopped there. My arms flew up to cover my chest, but my reaction was too slow. My father was obviously clueless, but Mom had immediately spotted my missing bra. She inhaled sharply; her eyes narrowed and flashed a warning. She was going to keep my secret, she told me silently, but she was never going to let me forget it.

Before I could speak, Danny jumped between me and my parents. "Don't be mad at her!" he blurted out. "I know it doesn't look like it—but what you saw was my fault." He was breathing so fast, I thought he was going to pass out. "Ellie is totally *shomer*," he insisted. "We've never touched before, I swear." He swallowed and looked at the ground. "Well, only once before, but that was also all me. You should be mad at me." Was that a flicker of a smile on my dad's face? It vanished as quickly as it came, but I relaxed a little, though my mom's eyes were still burning a hole through me. There was no hint of a smile there; she was as serious as death.

"You can be mad at me," Danny repeated desperately when nobody spoke. "I made a mistake. Two mistakes." He swallowed again. "Okay, a lot of mistakes. But I won't make any more. I promise."

I needed to say something, to try to rescue Danny from the babbling mess he was becoming. It wasn't fair that he was taking all the blame and I was cowering behind him.

Danny glanced back at me, and the fear on his face faded a little. "I'm so sorry," I mouthed. He took a deep breath and squared his shoulders, turned back to my parents.

"Except it wasn't a mistake," he declared, his voice a little steadier. "It wasn't a mistake because I love her."

There was no response to his declaration. My father's eyebrows rose a centimeter, and my mother sighed loudly, but nobody spoke. Except Danny, who seemed unable to stop talking.

"And I will keep loving her. Even if you banish me from your house. Even if I am never allowed to see her again. I'm never going to give up. You should know that now. I can't give her up."

Danny was carrying the noble knight thing a bit too far; my father was definitely smiling now, though he was obviously trying to keep a straight face. Even my mother had downgraded her death ray to "stun."

I needed to say something to save him, but still no words would come.

Danny had actually said he loved me for the first time. I couldn't believe it.

It didn't matter that he'd said it to my father. It was everything to me. I had to think of a way to help him.

But Danny never gave me a chance to speak. He seemed to have discovered fountains of hidden courage, because he was suddenly standing with his legs spread apart and his arms extended, like a proud warrior about to sound a battle cry. "I am not ashamed that I love Ellie," he declared. "And if kissing her is a sin, I'll gladly spend the rest of my life in hell if I can just do it one more time."

Holy. Crap. Well, we were officially screwed. Danny had totally crossed the line. That was all my parents needed to hear.

I was marched back to the house, and my phone and laptop were confiscated. Then they left me to stew in my bedroom while they had a heated discussion for two hours about my "behavior." I caught bits of it when my mom's voice rose and pierced the walls. Halfway through their war conference, Deenie showed up with a basket of muffins.

My mom beat me to the door. (I guess she was trying to intercept Danny, just in case he was ballsy enough to come over after they had ordered him to go home.) "Rae made too many," Deenie explained sweetly as my mother stared at the offering. "She asked me to drop these off."

Deenie winked at me as my mother placed the basket on the dining room table. When I looked blank, she gestured quickly at the basket before closing the door behind her.

I waited until my mother had returned to her room and then overturned the basket. At the bottom there was a crumpled note wedged into the wicker lining.

It read: "These muffins which I'm sending may contain: nuts, chocolate, and beef. For questions and complaints you, should definitely call your brilliant friend Rae's sad and extremely handsome boyfriend."

I recognized Danny's handwriting immediately, but it took me longer than it should have to decipher the meaning of the note. It was the misplaced comma after the word "you" that finally clued me in to the hidden message. I tried reading every other word, every third, and then finally every fourth until I got it. It said:

"I'm nuts for you,

your sad boyfriend."

He'd called himself my boyfriend in a love note. Granted, the declaration was wedged in between an allergy warning about beef muffins. But still. It was my first love note. It read like poetry to me.

I was ready to brave whatever lectures my parents had in store for me.

Turns out they decided to start at the beginning. Literally. Like, at the moment of my conception. Because Jewish guilt is not truly effective if it doesn't invoke years and years of suffering, which may or may not have anything to do with the topic at hand.

My mother began by reminding me of the miracle of my existence.

"Ten rounds of IVF," she told me in a grave voice. "Ten. Do you know what that does to a woman's body?"

I'd heard this story before. They'd told it at every one of my birthdays since I was three. But my successful conception was usually toasted with a glass of wine and happy tears. Now the years of injections and tests were being invoked to maximize the guilt. As if that petri dish with my sorry little embryo would have been better off on the floor than growing up into a girl who made out with her boyfriend.

"In public!" my father put in. "Where anyone could have seen you."

"I'm sorry." I wasn't, but I didn't know what else to say. I think if they'd simply been concerned, I would have been more remorseful. After all, I had gone against my religious upbringing, an upbringing I actually believed in. But they were relating to me as if I were simply acting out, breaking rules for the hell of it. I wasn't trying to rebel; there were simply two very powerful forces pulling at me: the religious and the romantic. And they should have realized that faced with a new love, even sixteen years of teaching never stood a chance.

"I don't believe you're sorry," my mother said. She could be surprisingly perceptive sometimes. "And don't tell me it was a spur-of-the-moment mistake, either. I know that's not true."

I glanced down at my loose shirt and then quickly averted my eyes. It was just my luck, I thought. I'd tried to be sexy for my boyfriend, and the only one who had noticed was my mother. At least my dad was still clueless.

I needed to distract them, or they would end the conversation by saying I wasn't allowed to see Danny again. I could have given them the standard "but I love him" speech. But they were expecting that, and I knew it wouldn't change anything. So I decided to take the less-traveled route; I turned the cop's interrogation lamp on them.

"You and mom dated for ten months," I began. "Are you telling me that in that whole time you never once wanted to kiss her? Not once?"

Dad cleared his throat. "Well, of course I wanted to but—"

"I know that you two were *shomer*. But you're telling me that you never slipped up once?" I challenged him. "Even though Mom was prettier than most models?"

Dad's face was growing hotter. Next to him, Mom's iciness was melting. She looked uncertain—almost fearful. I was obviously on the right track.

"Well, I'm *shomer* too," I concluded, in what I hoped was a confident voice. "But I'm also human like you. I know you guys are disappointed—and ashamed of me. But I don't want to be ashamed of myself. Not for this."

I'd never seen my parents so confused, and I hadn't even planned that speech. It was just process of elimination: I'd only said things that I knew they couldn't dispute. Now I just had to head off the worst punishment in the world.

"Please don't say that I can't see Danny anymore," I begged. "I know that would be the easiest thing to do. But he's my best friend." I raised tearful, repentant eyes. "Please, Mom. Please, Dad, just don't say that."

Chapter 19

Two days before Yom Kippur, I make a private appointment to talk with Rabbi Garner. To my surprise, the rabbi agrees to see me, even though his schedule must be full to bursting.

"I notice you called me directly, instead of going through Deenie," he remarks as I sit down in the comfy chair across from his desk. "Is something wrong?"

"With Deenie? No, I'm here for another reason." I pull my notebook out and flip to a blank page.

He nods and leans back against his seat. "Aha. I wondered when you'd ask me for my contribution. This is for your collection?"

"Yes! You heard about it?"

He shrugs. "Word travels."

"And you think what I'm doing is okay?"

"How do you mean?"

"This—project. Is it a good thing?"

He considers the question carefully. "Why are you worried about that? You're keeping Danny's memory alive, aren't you?" The rabbi leans over his desk and gives me a reassuring smile. "Whatever the outcome, honoring someone's memory is never wrong."

"I'm so glad you approve," I say, relieved. "I wasn't sure you would."

"Of course I approve."

"But I mean—" I study his face for a moment and consider my next question. I hadn't really planned to ask him, but now I can't help wondering. He's usually so right about everything. The rabbi's words were as close to prophecy as I could get in this world.

"What is it, Ellie?"

"You think I'm right, though? You think that Danny is coming back? That it isn't just about his memory. I have a reason to hope, right?"

The seconds before he answers feel like hours. I wanted an immediate affirmation of faith, not a careful consideration of the evidence. Even the flicker of doubt in his eyes feels like a smack to the face.

"I think that while there's life, there's hope," he says finally.

I slump down in my chair. "That's just something people say. It doesn't mean anything."

"Ellie, I just said that there is hope—"

"But you don't want me to believe," I interrupt. "You want me to give up."

"No, of course not." He pauses again and looks down at his hands. "You were hoping I'd tell you that it will all turn out all right."

"Yes." I sigh and close my eyes. "You don't have to, though. If you don't believe it."

"But I do believe it."

My eyes fly open, and I lean forward again. "You do? Really?"

He shakes his head, his brow furrowed with regret. "Ellie, things don't always turn out the way we imagine they will." He holds his hands out in a calming gesture. "Please. I'm not a prophet. Don't look at me like that. I'm just as fallible as the next man."

"But you do believe that Danny's coming back? You think that they will find him?"

He swallows and takes a deep breath. "I do. I think that they will find him." His face crinkles in sympathy. "I do."

I exhale my relief and sit back in my chair. For a moment I consider telling him my theory about Danny's disappearance; it would mean the world to me if he supported it. But then I remember my mother's reaction and decide against it. Some things are better left unspoken.

"So, do you want to hear my story?" he asks me abruptly. "It's quite an old one. I've never told anyone this."

His expression reminds me a little of Danny's, the first time he ever told me a story. There's that desperate hope in his eyes that pleads, *Hey, if I make you laugh, will you forget that our ship is sinking?*

"Okay." He smiles as I scribble his name on the top of the blank page. "Go ahead."

"It must have been about five years ago," he tells me. "Right around this time of year, if I recall. I was heading out to give a lecture when I stumbled on this little kid, hunched over the fender of my car. He was carefully scraping at the paint with his fingernail, and then flicking the dried flecks onto the grass.

"'Hello, there!' I shouted, and he jumped so hard he fell right over onto his back.

"I reached out and pulled him up, but he was hyperventilating like I'd just brought on a heart attack. I gave him a moment to get himself together and leaned over to inspect my car. There was a white slash of paint over the fender that had been partially peeled off.

"'So—what are you doing here?' I asked him.

"'It wasn't me. I didn't do that,' he said, when he could speak.

"'Okay. Who did it, then?'

"He shook his head. 'I can't tell you. But I'm sort of responsible. So, I was trying to get my part off.'

"'Your part? What are you talking about? Who are you?'

"He seemed to have calmed down a little, but he took a deep breath before answering. 'Danny Edelstein.'

"'Ah, of course. I know your father. How old are you, Danny?'

"'Twelve.'

"I would have guessed that he was closer to nine, he was so small. He was basically a shivering little stick with a mop of crazy hair. I picked up his kippah off the ground and handed it to him. 'And what would your father say if he saw what you were doing here, Danny?'

"He stuck out his chin. 'He told me to do it,' he squeaked. 'I'm supposed to take responsibility. And I'm responsible for this part.' He placed his hands over the top of the streak. 'So I'm peeling it off.'

"'I see. And why just that part?'

"'Because that's when I came along. But I didn't stop the person doing it. Not right away. When I told my father what happened, he said that I'm kind of guilty; it's almost like I painted that part—because I could have stopped it. And I can't go to *shul* on Yom Kippur and repent for it if I haven't even tried to make it right.'

"'So he told you to peel it off?'

"He dropped his head and kicked at the flecks on the grass. 'No. He told me to apologize to you. But I didn't want to do that.'

"'I see.'

"'Even though I really am sorry.' He looked up at me, and his eyes got very large. 'I really am. But it wasn't my secret. And I knew you'd want me to give it up.'

"'It's okay,' I said with a smile. 'I'm not going to ask who did it. You can relax.'

"He didn't seem convinced. He just kept staring at me, like he was trying to work something out.

"'Look, I forgive you,' I assured him. 'You can *daven* on Yom Kippur with a clear conscience.'

"He hesitated and slowly turned away. 'I really hate secrets,' he said. 'There should be something in the service about getting rid of secrets.'"

The rabbi pauses and looks down at his desk. He seems suddenly older to me; the lines around his eyes look like deepening scars. "I should have told him that we do, that our secret sins are right there in the Al Chet prayer, close to the beginning. But I was kind of preoccupied with my own concerns at the time, and I just didn't think of it. I really didn't see Danny much after that, even after he moved to Atlanta to live with his dad. So, I'm sorry that's the only story I have for you. But I thought you might enjoy it anyway."

His expression is open and untroubled; he's recounted the memory without hesitation or doubt. On the face of it, he's the same honest man I'd trusted since I was little. But there's something wrong with this story. "Did you ever find out who did it?" I ask him faintly. "Do you know who painted that stripe?"

He waves his hand dismissively. "No, I didn't bother. Some bored kid, probably. I don't think it matters, does it?"

He looks completely innocent to me; it obviously hasn't

occurred to him that the mark could have had a deeper meaning. But I know something he doesn't. I actually know who did it, and I know that Rae wasn't just some bored kid. She'd told me that she'd found something out that had shattered everything she'd believed in, that she was splattering her disappointment on that car for the whole world to see. But what had she found out?

Was that just her first rant against organized religion and the rabbi simply a symbolic target? Maybe that was why she'd dropped the idea halfway through. Perhaps she realized that it was immature to focus on one member of our religion, even if he represented an institution she was rejecting.

When Rae had told me her story, I'd wondered at the coincidence of Rae and Danny's first meeting. But now it made sense; the rabbi's house was just around the corner from the Edelsteins'.

"I guess it doesn't matter who did it," I say finally. "But I agree with Danny. I hate secrets."

The rabbi had spaced out a little after finishing his story, but my comment catches his attention. He rouses himself and focuses on me. "Well, this is the time to rid yourself of them. We are in the final days of repentance, remember?"

"I know." I look up quickly; his understanding smile is making me nervous. "I didn't mean myself, personally," I assure him. "I don't have anything to confess."

He laughs and rises from his chair. "I'm not a priest, Ellie. I don't demand confessions, because I can't give absolution. Only God can do that."

I drop my head and focus on my notebook. I can't look him in the eye; I know he'll see right through me, right down to the guilt rotting inside me. "But what if—what if the sin wasn't against God?" I ask.

"You mean, if you've hurt another human being?"

"Yes."

"I believe you know what you have to do. Have you asked this person for forgiveness?"

Yes. A thousand times.

"No. I can't."

"Well, I'm afraid God can't forgive a sin *ben adom l'chavero*," he explains, using the Hebrew phrase meaning "between man and his friend." "It's up to the injured party to forgive."

But what if he can't? I want to ask the rabbi. *What if you've pleaded and cried, and he just can't hear you? What if you've been waiting for him to come back so that you can beg for his forgiveness?*

What if you're responsible for everything that happened?

What if you're the reason he's gone?

THE FIGHT

The verdict that came down from my parents was far more generous than I'd expected. It was barely a punishment. In short, Danny and I were never to be alone together. We could hang out with Deenie and Rae, or in any public setting, but my mother would be monitoring his comings and goings more carefully now that she knew we were a couple. I accepted their judgment meekly and without argument. They were only enforcing *yichud* rules, which had been in place in religious communities for generations: unmarried boys and girls were not allowed to be alone together. Mom and Dad had been very lax about that, but my little transgression by the ice cream stand had opened their eyes.

I updated Danny as soon as I got my phone back. He was tapping on my window fifteen minutes later.

"Do they know about the tree?" he whispered as I pushed up the glass.

I shook my head. "They'll cut the branches if they realize you've been climbing into my room. Or they'll just seal my window."

He scrambled over the sill and dropped quietly onto the rug. "So what do you want to do?"

I shrugged and walked over to my door. "I'll say I'm going to bed before you come. And then I'll turn the lock." I clicked it softly into place. "There." I smiled as I turned back to him. "Now, where were we?"

I did feel a little sorry for my parents. They were really just trying to protect me. But by enforcing the "no alone time" rule, they inadvertently made the whole adventure even hotter.

And it was so so hot. That extra layer of forbidden made every kiss into a victory, the thrill of each touch more wild and electric, as we crossed boundary after boundary.

We still stopped just short of PG-13 territory. Panting, sweaty, and shaking, we generally managed to pull apart before things went too far. We were, after all, religious kids, and I wasn't ready to throw away all my convictions. But it was pretty impressive how very flexible those convictions were, and how quickly they were tested.

We managed to keep the *shomer* couple charade going for two whole weeks before Deenie and Rae found out. They'd both suspected ever since the coded note in the muffin basket, but one afternoon we got a bit sloppy and sneaked a kiss in the basement while our friends were upstairs gathering snacks. Rae came down sooner than expected, and her reaction was predictable.

"Well! It's about time."

Deenie's reaction was stunned silence.

We swore them both to secrecy even though Rae protested that nobody at our school cared whether we were *shomer* or not.

Turns out, they did.

Just three weeks after I promised my parents that Danny and I had gone back to being *shomer*, a video of the two of us making out appeared on the class WhatsApp group—sent from Danny's phone.

The effect was immediate. People who didn't even know us shared the video; in one morning it spread to neighboring schools. Elderly members of our congregation saw it. Rabbi Garner saw it.

My parents saw it.

Two teens kissing wouldn't normally have caused such a stir, but Danny and I were known as the "*shomer* couple of the year." Parents had used us as an example when talking to their kids about relationships in high school. So our classmates couldn't wait to knock us off the pedestal.

Everyone enjoys a good rumor—and everybody hates a hypocrite. We never stood a chance.

The day that video went viral Danny and I were hanging out on the bench behind the parking lot. It was our secret spot, the perfect place to make out during free period. After about an hour, I finally checked my phone; we'd heard it buzzing in my purse, but Danny and I had been otherwise occupied for a while and I'd ignored it. There were two messages from Rae, one from Deenie. And about ten from my parents.

Rae's texts basically spelled out what had happened. "Check your WhatsApp! Everyone's seen it. There's a rumor going around that you're pregnant."

I stared, speechless, at the screen for a moment. Next to me, Danny was glaring at his cell. His face had gone white.

"It came from your phone," I said. "Did you tape us—"

"God, no!" he cried. "How could you think that?"

"Then how did this happen?" I asked him. "I thought no one knew about our hideaway."

He wouldn't meet my eyes.

"Danny. Who could have filmed us? Who knows about this spot?"

He swallowed hard. "I told Greg about us," he admitted in a low voice. "But he said he wouldn't tell anyone—"

"You told Greg?" I exclaimed. "After you promised you wouldn't?"

"I'm sorry. I can't believe he did this—"

"Danny, he was playing with your phone after history this morning. I saw him. Of course he did it!"

"Let me just talk to him—"

"Talk to him?!" I shouted, springing to my feet. "I don't care what he has to say! That doesn't matter—don't you get it? What matters is that you promised me you wouldn't tell anyone. And then you went ahead and bragged about it—"

"I didn't brag—"

But I wasn't listening anymore. My phone lit up with another text from my mom, and I tossed it at him with a cry. "It's over, do you understand?" I yelled at him. "My parents know everything. They're not going to let me see you again—" I shuddered as Rae's words flew through my mind. "People are saying that we're liars, Danny! Have you read the comments on the group? Everyone is laughing at us. Why would you do that to me?"

Danny had risen to face me; he tried to grab my hands, but I pulled away from him.

"Don't you touch me!" I screamed. "You're not supposed to touch me!"

"Ellie, calm down," he begged. "It's only stupid gossip. Nobody really cares about this—"

I cut him off with a sharp laugh. "You don't have to go home to my parents! You aren't going to be grounded forever."

"I'll talk to your parents—"

"And tell them what? That we—" I picked the phone off the ground. "That I make cow noises when you touch me?" I scrolled through the texts. "That we like to make out in my parents' bed? Ugh! God!"

A brief smile flashed across his face. "They're just jokes."

"To you! This is a joke to you!" My voice was rising to a hysterical pitch. It cracked as I waved my buzzing phone in his face. "How can, you be smiling? This is just a funny story to you, isn't it?"

"Look, I know I shouldn't have told Greg," he pleaded. "And I am sorry. But I don't understand why you care so much about the gossip. Why are you so worried about what everybody thinks?"

He reached out to take my hand again, but I batted him away.

"You don't get to touch me!"

"Ellie, I messed up. I get it. Let me try to make it right. Can I at least give you a hug?"

I pushed him back. "No! That's not allowed, remember?" I snapped. I turned away, ignoring the pained look in his eyes. "I have to go face the music at home. Don't follow me, okay? Don't come tapping at my window tonight. Just leave me alone."

Chapter 20

I'm at Publix, picking up last-minute ingredients for Shabbat, when I run into Greg in the cereal aisle. It's too late to back away; he calls out my name as he approaches, and I steel myself for a conversation I've been trying to avoid for months.

In the end, I never actually called out Greg for what he did. At the time, my fight was with Danny, and I was so angry about his betrayal, I had no space for smaller battles. Only a week after our fight, Danny disappeared, and all my energy went to desperate prayers for his return. In the urgency of my despair, my anger at Greg evaporated and I welcomed his support, the hours and late nights he volunteered with the search party, the updates he posted on the Bring Danny Home page. And then the efforts dried up, hope dwindled, and I faded from the world. The video that had started it all no longer mattered. And so, neither did the person who'd filmed it.

Rae broke up with Greg when his role in our fight was revealed, and shortly afterward he managed to convince his parents to let him finish up the year in the local public high school. So he vanished from my radar, and I was grateful not to have him as a constant reminder of the worst days of my life.

And now, here he is in front of me, holding a crumpled box of Froot Loops in his arms. He's even taller than I remember, but the thick muscles he'd trained so hard to build have shrunk; he seems gaunt, bowed by the weight of his own broad shoulders.

"I hear you're collecting stories about Danny," he says with no introduction. "I'm a little hurt you never asked me for one."

"Yeah, well, I'm a little hurt you never apologized."

He doesn't say anything for a moment. "I did apologize," he says in a low voice. "He didn't forgive me."

"Of course he didn't. You were the reason we broke up."

His dark eyes flash and he straightens suddenly. "No, Ellie, *you* were the reason you two broke up."

"You sent the video!"

"Yeah, I sent it because I wanted to knock that self-righteous chip off your shoulder. I didn't know you would blowtorch your relationship over it. But you went ahead and broke up with your boyfriend because he ruined your good-girl image."

"What are you talking about? I don't care about my image!"

He rolls his eyes. "Well, you sure did then. Seems like it was all you cared about."

I bristle at the insult, but he doesn't let me speak.

"And it wasn't enough that you were a total hypocrite. You made Danny a hypocrite too. That's what I couldn't handle."

I don't know what to say. On the one hand, I know he's right. I was a hypocrite. But wasn't everyone a little bit of a hypocrite online? No one posts their true self on social media. That's not what it is for.

I glance around the aisle desperately, searching for a hint of Danny's shadow behind the shelves. He always shows up when I need him; if he were here, he'd say something that would soften the sting of his friend's words.

When I don't speak, Greg shakes his head, and the light in his eyes fades. "Just—forget it. That's not what I came over here to say." He sighs. "And, look, I'll say I'm sorry, if you want. I'll say it a hundred times, if you'll just listen to my story."

I study his earnest expression for a moment and shake my head. "I—I don't understand. Why do you care so much about my collection?"

"I don't care about it. But I want you to have this story," he explains. "Because I know he'd want you to hear it."

I nod and feel my anger fade with his. It really doesn't matter now, I realize; it never really mattered.

He takes my silence as agreement and draws a deep breath. "A couple of weeks before the New Year's party, the two of us were walking behind the school," he tells me. "Danny was trying to get me to apologize to Rae for—something. Some stupid disagreement. I didn't understand why he cared.

"'It's all temporary anyway,' I told him. 'We're not going to last. High school relationships spoil quicker than milk.'

"He shook his head. 'Speak for yourself,' he said. 'Ellie and I are going to last.'

"I laughed at him. 'What—like through graduation?'

"'No. Like forever.'

"'Are you serious?!' I shouted. 'She's your first girlfriend. Nobody marries their first girlfriend. Nobody even *thinks* of marrying their first girlfriend!'

"He shrugged. 'That's because they start off dating the wrong people. It's different for us. I can't picture my life without Ellie.'

"'Yeah, well, I can't picture my life without Rae right now,' I said. 'But you know she's going to dump me eventually. Then we'll both move on. And one day I'll have trouble remembering her last name. That's high school. You can't get too attached.'

"'What if I like being attached?'

"'Of course you like it. You two have been joined at the hip since you hit puberty. You don't know any better.'

"He just grinned at me. 'Whatever. We should get back. Lunch is almost over.' I could tell that he was sorry he'd spoken to me. But I wasn't going to let it go.

"'Dude, you haven't even kissed her yet,' I pointed out. 'Do you understand how weird that is?'

"He'd started to walk away from me, but he turned around then. Cleared his throat. 'We're late to class,' he said, but I could see that he was hiding something—and not very well, either. It wasn't going to be hard to get him to spill; I knew exactly where to push.

"I grabbed him by the shoulder. 'You're talking about marrying this girl? And you haven't even touched her. Look, if she cared about you at all, she'd have shown you by now.'

"We'd had this conversation a hundred times, and he'd always defended you, defended religion, defended whatever. But now he didn't fight, didn't react at all—and I knew I had him.

"'Hey, what's going on?' I challenged him. 'Are you holding out on me?'

"He didn't answer me at first. Glanced at his watch and at the school entrance.

"'You *have* kissed her!'

"He smiled at me. Hesitated for a second. And then he caved. 'What can I say? It was worth the wait.'

"'Holy shit, Danny! It's about time!'

"It took a couple more pokes, and the details came spilling out.

He told me about climbing into your room at midnight. Told me about the bench behind the school."

Greg pauses and glances at me for the first time since beginning the story. He scans my face, as if trying to read my thoughts. And in that moment, I don't care if he sees the tears in my eyes. I'm too upset to care that I'm transparent. I want him to see how much his words have hurt me.

I knew that Danny had told Greg our secret. I thought he'd bragged about it, the way some guys brag about their "conquests." But that's not what had happened at all. He shouldn't have done it, of course, but then, I hadn't let him explain his side of things. I'd imagined how the scene had gone, and then convicted him based on the story I invented.

"Danny made me promise not to tell anyone," Greg concludes when I don't speak. "He said he didn't want anyone to know.

"'Know what?' I teased him. 'That you finally made out with your girlfriend? And so now you think you have to marry her?'

"He stopped, his hand on the door, and turned around. Looked back at me. 'What are you talking about?' he asked. 'That has nothing to do with it. I've known she was the one since I told her my first story.'"

Chapter 21

I don't want to hear any more stories. When I'd started the project, it had felt like the beginning of an adventure; every new entry into my journal had given me a little glimpse of the boy I loved. Classmates stopped me in the halls to tell me an anecdote they thought I'd want, and I welcomed all of them. But Greg's story has wrecked me, and now my guilt turns each new memory bitter.

It seems I no longer have control over Danny's stories, though. They continue to find me even when I'm too spent to enjoy them. During my visit with Mr. Edelstein that evening, I try to talk about mundane things. For once, I want to discuss anything but Danny. But he isn't having it. He's heard that I'm writing about his son, he tells me. Would I like to hear about Danny's biological parents?

Of course I don't say no, no matter how tired I am. I've wanted to learn that story for years.

He draws an album from the corner bookcase and flips to the middle. "My brother," he says, pulling out a wrinkled photograph of a teenager on a skateboard, poised at the top of a cement ramp. "Adam was almost fifteen years younger than me, and as different from me as you can imagine. I don't think there was a single daredevil stunt he didn't try before he was twenty. Mountain climbing, skydiving, swimming with sharks. Adrenaline junkies I think that's what they call people like my brother. Always looking for the next thrill. He loved traveling, so he obtained a pilot's license. For a while he worked for a transport company that flew racehorses across the country."

I can't help smiling at this. So Danny's father really was a pilot, after all. I love that the first story Danny told me was actually true.

I gaze at the brash, lopsided grin of the boy on the skateboard. Danny's father. His face is rounder than his son's, but Danny had inherited his dad's hazel-green eyes and wild sandy hair.

"This is Tamar," Mr. Edelstein says, pulling out a photo from the bottom of the page. The girl in the picture looks barely older than me. She's petite and athletic, sporting thick blond curls framing a sunburned face. "I couldn't believe it when Adam wrote that he'd married her. They'd known each other three months. Met during an expedition in the Andes and eloped without telling anyone. He was impulsive in everything he did, though, so I suppose I shouldn't have been shocked. Nine months later Danny was born—while they were camping on a mountain. Tamar barely survived the birth, and they were forced to move to Tel Aviv to live with her mother while she recovered. They stayed in Israel for a couple of years after that, but my brother's wanderlust couldn't be tamed. So when his wife was well, they took off again, leaving Danny with Tamar's mother. A few months later his grandmother had had enough; she was sick and couldn't take care of Danny anymore. So they promised to head back. Two days before their flight, their train derailed outside of Nepal. Everyone in their car was killed."

I stare at the carefree faces of Danny's parents. He probably had no memory of them, and they'd never really gotten to know him. But I can see the imprint of his mother's smile on her son's face; the teasing spark in his father's eyes is so familiar. I wonder how differently Danny would have turned out if they had lived to raise him.

"How did you end up being his guardian?" I ask.

Mr. Edelstein turns the album to the next page. "Would you believe I was the one Adam had named in his will? I didn't, or that he even had a will to begin with. My brother and I had never really gotten along. I was religious; he was an atheist. I lived a frugal life; he'd spent most of our parents' inheritance by the time he died. And I hadn't even met my nephew until I flew in for his parents' funeral. Maybe it was just process of elimination. Tamar's mother wasn't well enough to raise a toddler. And I was the only close relative left. So Danny came back with me to LA."

He draws out a picture of a chubby, pink-cheeked little boy with long blond hair hanging to his shoulders.

"It must have been hard taking care of him on your own," I remark, turning the pages of the album. The rest of the book appears to be a montage of Danny-made disasters. One shows him grinning amid a pile of shredded newspapers. In the next he's sitting in a puddle of red paint, streaks running down the wall behind him.

Mr. Edelstein laughs quietly. "I was losing my mind. He was just like his father, and I had no idea how to handle him. After he was thrown out of daycare, I was forced to bring him to work with me. Lucky for me, that's when things began to turn around."

"What happened?"

"Danny met his mother," he tells me, turning the page again. "She saved me—saved us both."

He points to the last photo in the book, and I recognize the dark-haired woman from Danny's album. "Your ex-wife."

Mr. Edelstein nods. "She was the office beauty. I'd been crazy about her forever. But every one of my colleagues wanted to date her. I was almost twenty years older than her—and"—he waves a deprecating hand over his balding head—"even then, not much of a looker. I never had a chance with her. Or so I thought."

"But she fell in love with you?"

He shakes his head sadly. "She fell in love with my little boy. I was—I came later."

"What do you mean?"

He runs his hand over the photo, rests it just over her hair. "Dalia had her own history. She was recently divorced, and, I learned later, unable to have children. And she wanted a child—desperately." He shrugs and looks sadly at her picture. "We did have a few interests in common. I believe she meant well—that she did care about me, in her own way. Even after things started to go sour, she really did try to make our marriage work, if only for Danny's sake."

I remember the story of the suitor cursed with sadness who brought home an orphan and won the heart of his beloved. Danny had told me that story several times in different forms over the years. It was his parents' story, and I'd never realized it.

"But—but Danny ended up with your ex," I say. "After the divorce." I can't help judging her, though I've never met her. "He was *your* nephew. How could she do that to you?"

He smiles and closes the album. "There was no court case. We settled things amicably. I didn't fight for custody even though I could have. My lawyer kept insisting that I had a strong case. But children don't care about blood relations or legal rights, Ellie. I had to think of what was best for Danny."

"But it must have broken your heart to let him go," I protest. "Why didn't you fight?"

He goes silent for a moment. "Parents always say that their kids come first," he tells me after a long pause. "But when they split, they tear their babies in two. I wasn't going to do that to Danny. He loved his mother. He deserved to be with her. So I moved out. I lived down the street from them for six years, and I saw him almost every day. When my job transferred me to Atlanta, I hoped Dalia might agree to follow. I thought I could convince her that it was best for Danny."

"But she refused."

He studies my critical expression for a moment and shakes his head. "Maybe she wasn't being fair. Still, I could hardly expect her to uproot her life and move across the country for her ex-husband."

"But you sacrificed everything for her!" I exclaim. "You gave up custody of your nephew. Didn't Danny ever ask you why his stepmother got custody of him?"

There's an uncomfortable pause. "See, this is why I don't like speaking about Dalia," he tells me finally. "Everyone gets very harsh when they hear the details. Truth is, Ellie, I loved her. Even when she wasn't exactly reasonable." He chuckles softly. "Maybe especially when she wasn't being reasonable. Who knows? But I shouldn't have gone along with it for as long as I did. That's for sure."

"Gone along with what?"

He grips the armrest of his chair as if bracing himself for a hit. "Dalia was a good woman—" he begins defensively. "But she was stubborn—with some very definite opinions about child-rearing.

She believed it was best—that Danny not be told that he was adopted." His face flushes with shame as his eyes meet mine. "He was too young to remember his biological parents, she argued. Tamar's mother passed away soon after we married. There was no one to tell him otherwise. So Dalia decided that he didn't need to know. She made me promise not to tell."

My shocked silence speaks for me.

"Oh, she planned to tell him eventually," he adds hastily. "But then she got sick. And so she put it off—and put it off. I don't know what she was afraid of, really. When Danny finally found out, it wasn't the truth that upset him. It was the fact that she'd lied to him."

"No wonder Danny hated secrets," I say, understanding suddenly. Until I'd met him, his entire history had been a secret.

"It was my fault too," Mr. Edelstein insists. "I lied to him when he asked me why we had so few baby pictures of him. Told him I was a lazy photographer."

"But you were married three years after he was born. That's sort of unusual for a religious couple. He never asked about that?"

"Divorced couples don't celebrate their wedding anniversaries or display their wedding photos. It never came up somehow—until he found out. He overheard a conversation between his mother and a friend. When he understood what she'd been hiding, he lashed out at her—I'm not sure what he said; he never told me the details. But he called me that night with a hundred questions about his parents. At the end of our conversation, he begged me to fly him out to Atlanta so he could get away for a while. So I bought him a ticket." He pauses and nods at me. "As it turns out, that was the flight—"

"The one where we met!" I remember the boy with the goofy smile, the Kit Kat bar, and the wild stories. I'd assumed he was just taking a regular trip to see his dad. "I didn't realize he was going through all that. He actually helped *me* get through that flight."

Mr. Edelstein closes the album and runs his hand over the leather binding. "When I picked Danny up at the airport, he seemed really distracted. I asked if he was okay, and he told me that it was a very rocky trip. And then he just spaced out—the whole way home, he didn't say a single word. That was *not* like Danny at all." He grins. "You thought he was distracting you on that plane? I'm guessing that it went both ways—"

I'm smiling now. For once, there's nothing awful to sully this perfect memory. I'd made a painful time in Danny's life better. That's all I needed to hear.

But Mr. Edelstein isn't finished. "I truly wish I hadn't bought him that ticket," he admits. "I should have insisted he patch things up with his mother first." He sighs and picks nervously at the album binding. "Dalia took an unexpected turn for the worse while Danny was visiting me. She was undergoing a minor procedure when she suffered a massive stroke that left her comatose."

I stare at him in silence for a moment, trying to absorb the unexpected twist in the story. It shouldn't shock me as much it does; I knew that his mother died later that year. But I'd imagined a more gradual goodbye.

"Are you saying that Danny never got a chance—" I begin. But I can't bring myself to ask the question.

His father finishes my thought. "No, he never got a chance to say goodbye. When we got the call that she was in the hospital, I flew back with him to LA. Danny was desperate to speak to her, to tell her that he was sorry for what he'd said before he left. But he never got the chance. His mother never woke up. She passed a few months later."

This isn't the story of how we met, I realize. It's the story of Danny's guilt. The weight of it takes a moment to sink in before I remember the fable he told me once over ice cream. I'd thought that it was fiction. But to him the story of the poisonous snake was more true than any he had told me. The poisoned lady had to be Dalia, the woman who had raised him. And in his mind, Danny was the snake in his own story.

Chapter 22

Yom Kippur is the final day of repentance, the culmination of a ten-day period of self-reflection and atonement for a year's worth of sins. Before the sun sets we have our last meal, and then settle in for a twenty-four-hour fast, about half of which is spent in synagogue chanting prayer after prayer. For me, this day had always been a chore to get through, and I was usually one of the loudest complainers as the hours dragged by. My head hurt from fasting and dehydration, and my back ached from hours of sitting in a hard chair; the endless droning and repetition frustrated and bored me. (Why did we say everything so many times? Why?) By the end I was usually sneaking out for breaths of fresh air; twelve hours wedged into a small sanctuary with two hundred fasting congregants made for a pretty dense atmosphere.

I'd never understood the point of the whole thing, honestly. How could I concentrate on bettering myself when all I could think about was pizza—and breath mints?

I'd never really carried a burden before, so I'd never needed the nishment that is Yom Kippur. Sure, I'd sinned like everyone else, t they were little-girl sins: talking back to my mom, fighting with , gossiping. I'd never really hurt anyone intentionally, and I'd en a quick nod of forgiveness from anyone I had harmed by dent. While the rest of the congregation pounded away at their sts and wailed their regret, I was usually daydreaming.

I'd often wondered if Rae had the right idea. She spent the day in quiet meditation at home. I was afraid to ask her if she fasted because I didn't want to know the answer, but she put my doubts to rest one day.

"Of course I fast," she said scornfully. "I may not believe in God. But I fast on Yom Kippur."

That didn't exactly make sense to me. But the swaying and chanting made even less sense. Half of the prayers were about things I'd never even done.

This year is different.

This year, a day of fasting isn't going to be enough. Ten repetitions of the prayer are far too few. Yom Kippur is all I have, my last resort. God hasn't listened to my prayers yet. But today has to be different. Today I'll find the right words.

As we settle into our seats, my mother shoots a concerned glance at me. I can't really blame her for wondering what's going on. It's the first time I've made it to the morning service on time, and I haven't even complained about wanting coffee. The only other people in our row are Deenie and her mom; even the most devout women straggle in a few minutes late. Deenie looks over at me and smiles, then glances anxiously around the room. It's obvious she's remembering Rosh Hashanah services and that awful scene wit[illegible] Danny in the foyer. But I don't bother reassuring her that I've com[illegible] alone today. She'll realize soon enough. Today it's just me and Go[illegible]

I open my *siddur* and place my finger on the first line.

I sink deep into the text, mouth the words, and sway. As [illegible] *Shema* is recited, I close my eyes and call out the incantation:

"And you will not follow after your heart and after your eyes by w[illegible] you go astray."

Had I strayed, even as I tried to keep faith? I ask myself. There was a boy that followed me everywhere, who lived in my dreams, both day and night. Was he a kind of idol? Everywhere I looked, my Danny was there. He was my comfort and my rock.

But what kind of rock? Was he simply my friend? Or was he a stone god that I'd created?

Everyone seemed to think I needed to let him go. Was that what God wanted too?

He didn't really expect me to give up, did He? I couldn't.

I wouldn't. It was too much to ask.

"Then the Lord's wrath will flare up against you, and He will close the heavens so that there will be no rain."

My eyes fly open as a clap of thunder rocks the *shul*. The people around me exchange startled looks. What a strange coincidence, their eyes say. Thunder—right at that moment!

But I know that it's no coincidence. Outside another crack of lightning cuts across the sky, and I listen to God's majesty as the skies open up and the rains come.

In His own way, He's speaking to me, and I'm finally ready to hear Him.

Do You need me to give him up? Is that what You want from me?

My mother's voice cuts into my prayer. "Ellie, are you okay?" he whispers.

I nod and close my eyes again, lean down over my *siddur*.

I can't give him up, I plead. *Please don't make me. Ask for anything Anything.*

The rain beats down, but God is silent. I don't know what He ts me to do.

I've sinned, but others have paid for my sin. Deenie, sitting so quietly next to me, has no idea that I've robbed her of her best friend. But she stopped singing weeks ago, and I'm not sure if she ever will again. Rae, waiting for us at home, is as strong and brash as ever. But she breaks down when she catches a glimpse of Danny, and she's stopped baking with white chocolate because she says it tastes too sweet. Mr. Edelstein is sitting next to an empty seat, which he reserved for Danny, just in case.

And none of them know the truth, because I'm too much of a coward.

What if I tell them what I did? Will that make it right?

I have no idea what God wants from me. I don't know how He wants me to atone.

He's trying to speak to me, but I can't hear what He's saying.

So, I look back to the prayers. What am I repenting for? It's all written out for me in rhythmic verse. I chant out my sins and beat on my chest. The words burn with new meaning; I've committed each and every one of these sins. I've finally tasted guilt, and I'm not sure I'll ever be able to taste anything else.

I've lied, I've judged, I've erred both in thought and in deed. And this last one: the sins committed with a confused heart. That's it right there. It is in the text; it's always been there staring at me. God knows that I was confused that night; He knows I hadn't meant to give Danny the worst advice in the world. But He punished me anyway, and worse, He punished Danny.

I'm waiting for Danny to come back. But how will I face him after what I've done? How will I admit that I kept this guilty secret all these months? That's why Danny scorned me ten days ago in this synagogue. He mocked my hypocrisy. *If I do come back, no one has to know, right?* he'd taunted me. "You'll never need to tell anyone that story."

He was right. I'm collecting people's stories because I love learning about him. But they're also an escape, to keep from remembering the story I can't bear to tell. I want Danny to come back because I love him. But I need him to come back because I can't live with myself.

Danny hates secrets. And he'll hate the person I've become.

I have to tell the world what I did. God won't bring Danny back until I truly repent. And I can't do that without admitting what I've done.

I'm going to do it tonight, I vow. *As soon as the fast ends, I will make this right.*

My resolution weighs on me like a stone on my chest. People say that repentance brings peace to the soul. But I can barely breathe when I think about what I'm going to do.

"Are you okay?" Deenie whispers.

I open my eyes and wipe the tears from my cheeks. Deenie is staring at me; she's dropped her *siddur* onto the lectern in front of her. "Do you need to lie down? You look really pale."

She looks pinched and weak too, but she reaches out to steady me. "I'm all right," I tell her. "Just a little dizzy."

"I'll walk you home," she suggests. "You should rest for a while."

I pull away from her. "I want to stay for the whole thing. I'm not leaving early."

Deenie exchanges worried looks with my mother. "We just finished *musaf*," my mother tells me gently. "Everyone is going home for a break." Around us the congregation is rising from their seats and moving toward the exit, but the normal roar of chatter sounds muted and strange to me. Their voices ring hollow, as if I'm hearing them through a fishbowl.

They lead me home, and I do my best to look calm and in control. Our mothers settle on the living room sofa while Deenie accompanies me back to my room. She fluffs up my pillow and covers me with a blanket.

"You were so intent," she says as she sits down on the edge of my bed. "I've never seen you have *kavana* like that."

"I had a lot to think about this year."

She nods and looks away. "Yeah. So did I."

I reach out and take her hand. "I bet we were thinking the same thing."

She glances back at me, and her eyes widen; I can feel her fingers tightening on mine. "I don't think we were," she says, and quickly pulls her hand away.

It suddenly occurs to me that Deenie will know my secret before the end of the day; maybe this is the last time we will sit like this together. I'm not sure she'll even want to speak to me again, much less comfort me the way she's done since Danny went away.

But what if, at the end of the service, I don't go through with it? There's nothing preventing me from going back on my vow. I'm not sure that I trust myself to keep my resolution. So far, the only one who knows about my plan is God. I need someone to push me back onto the path if I start to wander off. Someone I see every day. Someone who never forgets God.

"Deenie, I need you to swear something," I tell my friend.

She gives me a surprised look. "Now? On Yom Kippur? This is the day we annul our vows."

"I know. But it's important. And it isn't such a big thing to promise. Not for you, anyway."

"Okay. What do you need?"

I take a deep breath. "Tonight, after Neilah, before I break my fast, I'm going to talk to Mr. Edelstein."

"Talk to him? About what?"

"I can't tell you yet. He needs to be the first to hear it. But I want you to promise that you'll make me go. If I try to back out of it."

"Ellie, I don't even know what this is about."

I sit up and reach out for her hand, but she pulls away from me and scoots back on the bed.

"I promise you'll understand everything soon. You can stay with me when I speak to him. I don't want to have any more secrets from you. But Danny's father has to be the first to hear. He deserves to know the truth about what happened that night."

"The truth?" Her voice vibrates with a new fear; her pale face turns a shade whiter. "What kind of truth?"

"It's okay," I tell her softly. "I've been holding something in for months, and I can't stand it anymore. I want everyone to know." She doesn't reply, but the bed shakes with her trembling. I reach out to her again, but she recoils from my touch. "Deenie, what's going on?" I ask her. "Why are you so upset?"

"I'm not upset," she whispers. "I just think it's a bad time to talk about this. It's Yom Kippur."

"I know. But I can't say I'm repenting while I'm sitting on this lie. I can't wait anymore."

She nods and turns away so I can't see her face. "Okay," she says finally. Her voice is barely audible.

"Okay? Is that a promise?"

A long pause this time. She squares her shoulders and takes a deep breath. "I swear. I'll come with you to make sure you go through with it."

"Thank you," I whisper, and lie back on my bed. "You're a good friend."

She doesn't reply, and it occurs to me that this might be the last time I will tell her that. I'm not sure she's going to want to speak to me again after my confession tonight, and the thought that I might lose her hurts so much that I can't bear to look at her. Deenie and Rae are my closest friends, but I'm more afraid of what Deenie will think when she hears about what I did. Deenie had no role in the events that took place on New Year's. She wasn't even at the party and only heard about Danny's disappearance hours after we did. Rae was there; it was her grandparents' cabin. She'd helped set out the snacks and appointed herself key-keeper for the kids who'd had too much to drink. Sometimes I wonder if Rae will be surprised by my confession. She's no stranger to spur-of-the-moment decisions, both good and bad, so I think on some level she'll be able to relate to me.

But Deenie? Her moral compass has always guided her every action, so I don't think she'll ever understand what I did. I believe Rae will eventually make her peace with me. But I don't think Deenie will ever forgive me. She'll say she has, because it's the right thing to do. But there will be a wall between us forever.

"Deenie, you're a good friend," I repeat softly, because I want to say it now, as many times as I can, while I still have the chance.

She doesn't answer me, and when I open my eyes, the room is empty. She slipped away when I wasn't looking, and I have a sick sense that this is it. Deenie has always been there for me before, no matter what. But that was for the old Ellie, who never would have hurt the boy she loved. Everything is about to change, and I get the feeling that I'm staring into our new future. And it's so, so quiet.

THE ACCIDENT

I was enjoying my own anger. I doubt I would have admitted it, but it felt kind of good to be righteously mad, to be absolutely certain that I was right a thousand times over. I knew that Danny was probably sitting somewhere, miserably alone—and thinking about me. Maybe he was even crying a little. I'd never seen him cry, and the idea that I was the cause of it, that his love for me was wringing his heart, felt a little romantic.

I let myself enjoy the picture of a forlorn Danny for a moment, before shaking the image from my mind. What kind of a person enjoys the pain of the one they love? "Psychopath," I said to my reflection in the mirror. "You're a real sicko, you know that?"

My puffy, tear-streaked face stared back at me. It was kind of a pathetic face, all droopy and blotchy. My swollen eyes were a testament to the sleepless nights I'd spent, agonizing over our fight and what I'd said to him. I wasn't a psychopath, I assured myself. Not really. I had every right to be furious, and Danny deserved to be sorry.

And I really had been through hell over the last week. I'd suffered through two days of school after our fight until winter break began. So now I didn't have to see Danny, but I also couldn't see anyone else. I was so grounded that even Deenie and Rae weren't allowed to come by. My parents were very clear with me. They may have understood the violation of the *shomer* rules. But the lying and sneaking around were inexcusable. I pointed out that they hadn't really left me a choice. That didn't make things better. All communication with my friends was cut off. Deenie managed to slip me her phone when she ran into us at the supermarket. After three days of isolation I was finally able to send messages to my friends. I sent them pics of my puffy face.

Danny used the opportunity to send me the most pathetic apology ever written. He was sitting at the base of our tree when he wrote it. I refused to come to the window.

An hour later I relented and leaned out to look for him. He'd given up and gone home, and I climbed back into bed, disappointed.

I was sorry he had gone. Without realizing it, I'd gotten over my anger. The boiling part of my rage had passed sometime with my last cry, and now I just felt righteous and wounded.

But I wasn't ready to pick up the phone yet. I was getting to the point where I could imagine our make-up kiss, but I wanted him to take the first step.

Or rather, the next step. He'd already taken a bunch of first steps (which I'd rejected). So, I was waiting for his last try.

At the end of the week my grounding was lifted and I was allowed to rejoin humanity. But I had nowhere to go.

Still, it was pretty lonely being righteous in my room. Rae begged me to come to the New Year's party. "It'll take your mind off things. You'll have fun. Cut loose a little."

"I may not be grounded anymore, but my parents won't let me go to a party," I pointed out. "Why don't you ask Deenie if she—"

She laughed before I finished the question.

"A party with alcohol? You know she'll never come," she said. "Come on. Tell them you're sleeping over at my house. They won't mind that. Please?"

"But Danny will be at the party," I protested.

"So what? School is starting again next week. You can't avoid him forever."

"I'm not ready yet."

So I sat at home while my friends drove off to the lake cabin. I waited, hoping for someone to call, but by midnight I still hadn't heard from anyone. The party was already in full swing, I told myself. It was too late to change my mind.

I studied the raw peeling skin around my nose and the limp red curls clinging to my forehead. My mother was taking me to get this awful haircut fixed on Monday. "The Ginger Bermuda Triangle," Rae had called it.

I couldn't believe how upset I'd been about something so temporary. Just two weeks ago, my biggest worry had been my puffy hair. Danny and I hadn't had our big fight yet; we were still the happy couple. Only two weeks ago!

My silent phone stared at me from between my pillows. No one had posted anything about New Year's yet—not a single pic or tag. I'd checked. Twelve times. The party had probably flopped and they'd all gone home. Maybe Danny was already in bed, staring at his phone, like I was. He hadn't logged in to Messenger in over an hour, though. I wasn't sure what that meant.

My cell buzzed, and I shot forward to grab it as it slid off my pillow.

"Hello?"

"Ellie?" Rae's voice had an urgent ring to it. I could hear the roar of music and laughter in the background. Party was still on, then. "Did I wake you?"

"No. What's going on?"

There was a short pause, and I could hear her breathing heavily.

"Rae, is everything okay?"

"Yeah, I'm stepping outside. I don't want anyone to hear."

"Hear what?"

"Ellie, can you get down here? Like, right now."

It was such a strange request, and her voice was so shaky, it scared me a little. This wasn't a normal party invitation. "Why? What's going on?"

"Nothing." She swallowed hard and took a deep breath. "I just think you really need to be here."

"Why?" I said. "Tell me what's wrong!"

"I just—" She paused again and swore under her breath. "Wait, you're home, right? So you're, like, an hour away."

"Where else would I be?" I glanced outside. The rain was beating at my window; just a few minutes earlier a spray of hail had crackled against the sill. "Rae, if you really want me to come, I'll have to sneak out. And I'll probably get grounded for a month if my parents find out."

"Yeah, never mind. I don't want you driving an hour in this weather. I didn't really think it through."

"You still haven't told me why."

Another pause. A long one. Behind her an entire verse of "Counting Stars" played out until she finally answered me. "I need you to do something for me," she said.

"Of course. Whatever you need."

"Call Danny. Please."

"Rae. I told you I wasn't ready—"

"Do it now. This minute. As soon as I hang up."

I considered the urgency in her voice. I'd never heard her so upset. "Okay, I'll call," I promised her. "But can you at least tell me why? What's the emergency?"

She sniffed and cleared her throat. "Danny's here at the party."

"I know he is. So?"

"He's had a lot to drink, all right? And I don't think he's thinking clearly."

It was my turn to be scared; Rae was trying to warn me, to protect me from something. I was stuck in my bedroom while something terrible was happening to Danny, and I was powerless to stop it. Why hadn't I listened to her and gone to the party when she'd asked? "What's going on?" I demanded. "What is he doing?"

"Nothing," she replied quickly. Her voice sounded congested and muffled. "Nothing."

"What happened?" I persisted. "Are you okay? You sound like you've been crying."

"I'm fine. I'm not crying. Just—" She cleared her throat again. "It's just that—there's this girl here—"

There was a crash behind her, and she swore again; a door slammed, followed by a brief episode of yelling about a broken vase.

"I have to go," she said. "Just call him, okay?"

"Hold on! What girl? You were telling me about a girl."

"Yeah, she's just—she won't leave Danny alone." Her voice shook. "She's kind of attached herself to him."

I felt my pulse quicken.

"Rae, what are they doing?"

"Nothing. It's nothing." She sniffed and muttered something I couldn't hear. "Look, Ellie, I gotta go."

She hung up before I could thank her, and I sat there staring at the phone, confused and miserable. What would I say to him? I wondered. Should I ask him about the girl? I couldn't do that. I didn't want him to think I was some jealous overprotective girlfriend, just calling to check up on him, to make sure that no one else got their hands on him while I stewed at home. That's not who I was. He was free to do as he pleased. And yet—that's exactly why I was calling, I thought, as I pulled up his number. I was calling because the image of that nameless girl and Danny was freaking me out.

He picked up on the second ring.

"Ellie?" He sounded out of breath. "Is that you? I'm just stepping outside." There was a door slam, and the noise of the party vanished. "Where are you? Are you here?"

"No. I'm home."

"Oh." There was a brief pause. "I thought maybe you'd changed your mind."

"I did." I was suddenly desperate to see him. Right then. I couldn't wait until morning. "I miss you."

"I miss you too." He said it so quickly that the words blended together. "I wish you were here."

There had never been a nameless girl, not for him. I knew it the moment he spoke. The party could have been filled with random flirty girls but Danny wouldn't have noticed them.

"I really want to see you," I said. "Can you come back?"

"I want to see you too. But—I don't know if I can get back tonight. Rae took my keys." He had to repeat it twice before I could understand the slurring.

"So get them from her."

He hesitated. "I can't—I can't talk to her right now. And anyway she's not going to let me drive like this."

I considered for a second.

In my fantasy world, the one where I got to kiss Danny as the sun rose, I smiled and told him to go lie down. To sleep it off. And he listened to me, because he loved me. Just hours later, when dawn broke, he woke me up with a tap at my window.

In the real world, I barely paused a moment. "Remember the Purim party? She put the keys in her purse and stuck it under the kitchen sink."

He hesitated again. "Okay. I'll try to sneak into the house. I have to make sure Rae doesn't see me."

"Great. I'll be waiting."

I wish I could say that I regretted my advice the moment he hung up. That I dialed again before he even got inside and made him promise to wait until he'd sobered up. But the thought never even crossed my mind. He loved me and I loved him, and our love was invincible. Danny was coming back in less than an hour; I could actually count the minutes until I saw him. That was the only thing that mattered.

The second hand on my alarm clock ticked off twenty minutes until my phone buzzed again.

"Ellie?" He was shouting into the phone. "Can you hear me?"

"Yeah. Where are you?"

I could hear his teeth chattering. "I'm not sure. Sitting on a bridge somewhere." He sighed and his voice shook. "God, I don't know what to do. I really screwed up."

"What happened?"

There was a shout and some muffled swearing. "Great. Just what I needed."

"Are you okay?"

A minute of silence passed before he spoke again. "I totaled the car," he told me. "Plowed right into the guardrail. My dad's going to be furious."

"Are you all right?"

"I'm fine. But I need to get off this bridge. It's so windy up here, I can barely hear you."

"Can you wait in the car until somebody comes? It's freezing outside."

"The windshield's shattered. There's glass all over the seat. I cut my hand trying to get out."

"Are you bleeding?"

"No. I don't know. Only a little."

"I can sneak out," I suggested. "I'll come get you. Just send me your location—"

He cut me off before I could finish. "No. I don't want you to drive in this weather. Don't worry, I'll figure something out."

"Can you call a cab or a Lyft?"

"I have to find someplace warm to wait." He sighed and went quiet. I could hear the wail of the wind and the patter of freezing rain beating against him.

"Don't wait up for me, Ellie," he said finally.

"It's fine. I don't mind—"

"No, I need a few hours before I call anyone. Or I'll lose my license. I shouldn't have been driving tonight." He wasn't slurring anymore, but I realized he was probably right. If the cops picked him up in his current state, he would be in serious trouble.

"What are you going to do?"

He sighed again. "I'll see you in a few hours, okay?"

"Okay. I'll wait for you."

"No, get some sleep," he said. "I'll tap on your window in the morning."

In my fantasy world, that was when I told him that I loved him. That I forgave him and that I wished I'd forgiven him sooner. That I'd dream of kissing him until I saw him again. That I would wait forever, if that's what it took. That I would never give up.

But I wanted to say those things in person. So all I said was, "All right. Be careful."

Considering what happened next, maybe "be careful" were the only words that mattered that night.

Chapter 23

The final hours of the Yom Kippur service are a test, and I'm determined to make them count. I stand through the entire thing, even though the cantor urges those who are weak to sit down to preserve their strength. I say every single word, I bow, I pound my chest with renewed energy. This hunger is nothing, my thirst doesn't matter; I'm running on pure terror and conviction. The verses of neilah are no longer just a prelude to the breaking of a fast. This is my last prayer before my true act of repentance. These are the words that will bring Danny home.

Deenie sags in her chair by the end, but as the shofar is blown to signify the end of service, she climbs to her feet and grips the edge of the pew. Her head droops against her chest, and she sways slightly before I reach out to steady her.

Her mother tries to take her hand, but Deenie shakes her head. "Ellie and I have to talk to Mr. Edelstein tonight. I'll meet you at home."

She's so pale that I want to take it back; it seems selfish to prolong her fast. "Deenie, it can wait—" I begin, but she cuts me off.

"No, it can't. I promised."

Our mothers exchange looks, and my mom gives me a brief hug before heading out with Mrs. Garner. "Rae is eating with us tonight," she calls over her shoulder. "Don't be too long; we'll be waiting for you."

Deenie and I take our time walking toward the foyer. There's a brief night service after the close of the holiday; most of the men stay for that while the women rush home to heat the food for the breaking of the fast. When it's finally over and they all file out, Deenie and I stand patiently by the exit, waiting for Danny's father. But Mr. Edelstein doesn't appear. I peek into the empty sanctuary and shake my head.

"He's not here. Maybe we missed him?"

Deenie sighs. "I suppose he went home early. I guess we can just meet him at his house."

As we cross the parking lot, I hear someone calling my name. Rae is rushing toward us and waving for us to stop.

"Your mom said you were going to the Edelsteins'?" she gasps when she catches up with us. She has the pale, pinched look of someone who hasn't broken their fast. "Hold on a second. I want to come with you." She leans over and grips her side. "Just give me a minute. I ran all the way."

"Thank you for coming," I tell her.

Rae acknowledges my thanks with a grunt. "Well, I know how you feel about fasting. So if you're putting off dinner to talk to Mr. Edelstein, I figured it had to be important."

Deenie sways again and puts a hand to her forehead. "We should get going. We don't want to interrupt Mr. Edelstein's meal."

I have a feeling he won't be in an eating mood after I speak to him, but I nod and reach out for Rae's hand. We walk mostly in silence. Deenie comments once about the weather. Rae makes a moaning noise and clutches her growling stomach. "Out of all the Jewish stuff, this is the one I chose to keep. Unbelievable. God better appreciate it."

"I thought you didn't believe in God," I point out.

She shrugs. "Old habits die hard." She smiles and sticks her tongue out at the sky. "Hear that? I don't believe in You!"

"Who are you talking to, then?" I tease. "The man in the moon?"

"Come on, guys. Could we maybe not mock God on the night after Yom Kippur?" Deenie suggests weakly.

But I want to keep joking. It's distracting me from thinking about our destination and the conversation I'm about to have.

And I'm desperate for one last laugh with my two best friends. I'm light-headed and sick to my stomach, but I don't want this moment to end. As we round the corner onto Deenie's street, I stop in the middle of the road and point at the ground.

"Do you remember that spot, Deenie?" I ask. "It was right here."

She stares at me.

"The day you met Danny," I explain. "He was yelling those dirty words? And you refused to hit him, remember?"

Rae grins and nudges her with her elbow. "What did he say?"

Deenie blushes and shakes her head. "I can't tell you."

"Poodle sex," I declare gleefully.

Rae crows with laughter. "Seriously? What else?"

"Butt plugs!" I shout.

Deenie hushes me and glances toward her house. "Come on, Ellie. People will hear you," she whispers. But then her eyes twinkle and she leans forward toward us. "Dildo face," she whispers.

I almost collapse on the pavement. Rae is doubled over, hiccuping and giggling as she clutches her belly. "Good old shrimpy boy," she gasps. "He can still make us laugh."

We stand in the road for a few minutes, smiling. Behind me, a lone pair of headlights brightens up the street, and we scoot onto the sidewalk to let the car pass.

"A cop car," Rae points out as we start off again. "That's weird. On this dead-end road?"

"It's not an emergency." Deenie shrugs. "The siren isn't on."

"They seem to be looking for someone," I point out. The car passes Deenie's house and then slows down, as if checking the numbers on the homes.

"The Bergers are probably fighting again," Deenie remarks. "One of them always ends up calling 911."

The police car passes the Bergers' and rounds the corner.

"Oh." Deenie's eyes widen. "There are only three houses in that cul-de-sac."

The Edelstein home is one of them. It's not a premonition, exactly, but we speed up a little, and Rae grabs at my hand as we turn the corner.

The cop car is sitting in Danny's driveway when we reach the top of the hill. Deenie stops dead in the middle of the street and pulls us back toward her. Two policemen exit the car; the short one quietly checks the number on the porch and nods at his partner. They walk up the stairs, side by side. The tall one rings the doorbell.

"We should go," Deenie says, but none of us move. We're rooted to our spots, our eyes glued to the thick shoulders of the large cop.

The porch light flares and the door swings open; Mr. Edelstein totters into view. The flickering lamp over his face makes him blink. He seems confused by what the cop is saying. He nods slowly and clasps his hands together.

"Can you hear anything?" Rae whispers.

We can't, but we can read faces and body language. The cops' shoulders are heavy; their arms hang limply at their sides. The short one points at the door, as if asking to come in. Mr. Edelstein shakes his head and gestures wildly with his hands.

The cops exchange looks. The tall one indicates a porch chair and tries to lead Mr. Edelstein to it, but he shakes him off and shouts at him.

The cops look at each other again.

And then one of them leans forward and speaks.

Says a few words.

Mr. Edelstein takes a step back. There's a beat of silence. The cop bows his head.

Danny's father sways in the doorway. We can see his face under the glare of the porch light. His lips are hanging open, but he doesn't make a sound. The cop steps forward with one arm extended. But he's too late. Mr. Edelstein crumples over like he's been stabbed and topples to the ground.

THE LAST TIME I HUGGED DANNY

As the sun rose on New Year's Day, Danny woke me with a tap on my window, just as he promised he would. I jumped out of bed and stumbled across the room to let him in.

But somehow he was already inside, rubbing the cold from his blue hands and stamping his feet on my carpet. Clumps of muddy slush dropped from his boots onto the rug. Little shards of ice clung to his eyelashes.

The snow on his lips tasted sweet when I kissed him.

"You're warm," I said as he wrapped his arms around me. "How are you so warm?"

"I think that's you," he murmured. "I'm freezing."

"Here, get under the blanket," I whispered, pulling him toward my bed. "I'll cover you up."

He kicked off his boots and climbed in, and I pulled the comforter over our heads. He sighed and buried his face in my hair. "One last hug, okay?"

"What do you mean?"

"I mean I'm about to be grounded for the rest of my life."

"So? I can sneak out and see you for a change."

He laughed. "I just climbed into your room at dawn and left a puddle of mud on your carpet. Your parents will be furious. The curfew will be pulled back to six p.m."

"So I'll wait. I can wait forever if I have to."

He kissed me again and tickled my side. "I'm not so good at waiting, remember?"

"Yeah, that's true." I brushed his hair back from his forehead. "So what are we going to do?"

He wrinkled his nose at me. "I guess we'll just have to break a few rules."

Chapter 24

I can't see Mr. Edelstein. The two cops are standing over him, trying to help him up. Next to me, Rae is taking short, ragged breaths. Deenie is completely silent; she seems to have stopped breathing altogether. I can't look at them; I won't look at them. If I see their faces, I'll understand what's happening in front of me. Mr. Edelstein must be overreacting. That wasn't real grief I saw—it can't be. He's fasting and overwrought. The cops are probably here for something else. Perhaps an elderly relative of his has passed away. Or he was a witness to a crime, and they've come by to collect evidence. Or he has hundreds of unpaid parking tickets and he's in a lot of trouble.

"Do you want to get out of here?" Danny's voice makes me jump.

I turn around and he's standing behind me, a goofy grin on his face. His hands are shoved deep in his pockets. He's wearing his favorite black polo and torn blue jeans.

"Well?" he asks me. "What are you waiting for?"

I motion toward his house.

"That has nothing to do with you," he says. His voice is edged with impatience. "Turn around. Don't look at them."

I do as he says. He nods, pleased, and spreads his arms out wide.

"Come on, Ellie. Let's go. I'll race you."

I stumble toward him. Behind me, Deenie calls my name. I

feel someone grab at my jacket, but I shake them off.

Danny waves at them. "Bye, guys. We're out of here."

We run.

Danny is just a few paces ahead, but my dress shoes are slowing me down, and I can't keep up with him. He disappears over the hilltop, and I shout for him to slow down.

I catch a glimpse of him as I round the corner. He's darted behind some trees and is motioning for me to follow him. "Where are you going?" I gasp.

"We're playing hide-and-seek," he declares. "Starting right—now!"

And he takes off again.

I can't let him get away. So I race after him, tracking him into the shadows, pushing aside branches and stumbling over knotted roots as I go. We run for ages, past the synagogue, the playground, the strip mall, down long winding streets I don't recognize. He never lets me catch him; no matter how hard I push my aching legs, he's always just out of reach. I don't know where he's taking me, but as long as he's in front of me, I have to follow.

At the top of a hill, I pause for a moment to catch my breath and peer into the darkness. He doesn't answer when I shout his name. He's disappeared completely, and I'm scared that I'll be left alone in the middle of this deserted, gloomy street. "Why are you doing this?" I plead. "Can you come out? I don't want to play this game anymore."

"It isn't a game," he says. He's standing next to me, smiling calmly, just like before. I'm shaking and sweating from our sprint, but he's as cool as if he's just woken from a long nap. "We aren't playing. You have to find me."

"What do you mean? You're right here."

He shakes his head. "I've been gone nine months. And you never once looked for me. Why not?"

"I—I don't know," I falter. "I didn't know where to look."

He smiles sadly. "I would have searched for you. I wouldn't have let you go."

"But I didn't," I protest. "Danny, I didn't—"

"It's okay," he interrupts. "Come with me. I'll show you where I've been." He takes off down the street. "It isn't far from here," he calls.

I have no choice. I run after him; my legs are burning, and my lungs are filling with icicles, but I have to follow him. The wait is almost over. God is answering my prayers. I'm going to find Danny. I'm going to succeed where the police have failed.

And when I bring him back, everyone will be so overjoyed that it will wash away what I did. When we're together again, all will be forgiven. We'll start over and make up stories with sweet, forgivable mistakes. Misunderstandings that end in kisses, errors that are painted over by the closing chapter. We'll write ourselves the happy ending we deserve.

I just have to find him and it will be okay.

I only wish that I could run faster. My heart is hammering thunder in my ears, and there are floating kaleidoscope spots dancing in front of me. "Danny, please," I plead between gasps. "Please slow down."

"I can't," he calls over his shoulder. "We're almost out of time. You have to find me before they do."

My side cramps and I double over. "I'm trying," I tell him. "But I haven't eaten anything since yesterday."

He stops suddenly and turns around. Crosses his arms over his chest. "I haven't eaten in nine months, Ellie," he says.

My stomach stabs me, but I bite my lip and swallow the pain. "I'm coming. Please wait."

He doesn't; Danny is pitiless tonight. He pushes me onward, and I stumble blindly after him, following the sound of his beating tennis shoes and the dancing lights before my eyes. I can't see him anymore, but I know that I have to keep going, or he'll never forgive me.

I can't let him go again. This is my last chance to redeem myself. Before they find him.

I'm still running when I collapse onto the grass; I kick my rubber legs to push myself forward. I've almost made it. He promised me. We're almost there.

"Wait for me," I whisper.

He doesn't answer.

"Danny!" I call. "Come back!"

He doesn't. The street is quiet and I'm alone.

"I'm coming."

I close my eyes.

THE MORNING AFTER

I woke up to the blinking of red and blue lights. The pillow next to me was cold; I pushed back the blanket, but there was nobody there but me. He must have slipped away, I thought to myself as I pulled on my robe. He probably went home. It's a good thing he got out before my parents found him there. I didn't want to be grounded at the same time he was.

The acrid smell of burnt toast greeted me as I padded down the stairs. My parents were standing in the kitchen, holding steaming mugs of untouched coffee. Their faces were pinched, distracted. They were listening to a voice I didn't recognize.

"Ellie! I was just about to wake you," my mother said as I came in. "This is Officer Braddock."

A large man in a blue uniform turned to greet me. "Hello, Ellie. I'm afraid I have to ask you a few questions."

I was suddenly scared. The cops were going to take away Danny's license, just as he'd predicted. "Is this about Danny?" I blurted out. "Is he in trouble? Officer, the accident wasn't his fault. It was sleeting."

"I see." The cop and my mother exchanged looks. "You two have been in communication, then?"

I nodded. "Yes. He called me after he crashed the car."

The cop flipped open his notepad. "I see. And what time was this, exactly?"

"Around midnight."

My mother's eyes widened. "What did he say?"

The cop gave her a warning glance. "Did he indicate where he was going?"

I didn't want to answer that question in front of my parents, but something told me that a lie would just make things worse. The cop was staring at me so intently, it was frightening. "Here," I admitted in a low voice. "Danny came here."

They were suddenly all shock and interest. "Danny was here last night?!" My mother gave a huge sigh of relief, and Dad smiled broadly.

I had no idea what was going on. I'd expected anger and shame, maybe a bit of yelling. Why did they look so pleased?

"So he's here right now?" the cop said. He looked suddenly bored.

"No. He left before I woke up."

"And did he say where he was going?"

I shrugged. "I was asleep. Have you asked Mr. Edelstein? Danny must have called him."

My father shook his head. "His dad tried to reach him around twelve thirty, but it went straight to voicemail. So he waited up for him. Danny never came home."

They all blamed me afterward for confusing the case. My mother said that I delayed the investigation by telling the police that Danny had been with me that morning. Because of my story, they didn't file a missing person report until the following day, though they found his wrecked car on the side of the bridge later that afternoon. Danny's phone was half-buried in slush next to the front wheel; his jacket was recovered from the lake a week later. The detectives eventually concluded that Danny went missing right after his last phone call to me. They insisted that he never crawled into my room, that I'd dreamed the whole thing.

I didn't believe them at first. Can you smell and taste your dreams? I never have, and yet Danny's last hug was so vivid and real; it was no more a dream than he was. He'd been there next to me; he'd tasted sweet and warm. He'd even left a trail of mud on my carpet to prove that he had been there.

Except when they searched my room, my rug was white and new, without a trace of dirt. The window that he'd crawled through was frozen shut; the icy branches he had climbed were covered in untouched snow. There was no sign of the boy who'd kissed me good night. There was nothing at all to support my story.

So they came up with a theory based on the facts they had: Danny had indeed called me right after the accident. There is a record of a call beginning at 12:08 a.m. that lasted two minutes and forty-three seconds. He was sitting on the bent guardrail when he spoke to me. One glove, crusted in blood, was found hanging off a jagged piece of metal next to the wreck. After he hung up, Danny attempted to get down from the rail and slipped backward. The phone fell from his hands and slid beneath the car.

And he plummeted off the bridge, down into the icy lake below.

They were puzzled by the lack of a body. They knew where he had fallen in. Poor weather conditions and a delayed search notwithstanding, they should have been able to recover a body. Officer Braddock admitted that he couldn't explain the fact that they had only found Danny's jacket.

Rae and Deenie supported my faith that he would come back. My parents did too; the entire community banded together. They organized prayer vigils and baked a hundred casseroles, which Mr. Edelstein never ate. Dozens of volunteers braved the coldest winter Georgia had ever seen and set out on search expeditions around the scene of the accident.

Everyone believed Danny was coming back. For a week. Two weeks. Then three.

And then their faith slowly melted away with the snow.

Chapter 25

Mr. Edelstein is sitting next to me, holding a book. His eyes are fixed on the page, but his stare is immobile; I think he's only pretending to read.

I don't know where I am. There's a beeping noise over my head and muffled voices just beyond the curtain surrounding us. I want to say something to let him know that I'm awake, but I'm afraid to disturb him. He looks so peaceful with the book in his lap.

I'm lying in a bed that isn't mine. There's a tube taped to my hand and a plastic wristband around my arm. I recognize the logo stamp on my blanket. Above me the beeping sound gets faster. Mr. Edelstein looks up from his book and smiles.

"Ellie. You're awake."

I'm afraid to speak. There's something I needed to say to him, something I'd promised to tell him. But the cops got in the way at the last second, and I never got the chance.

"You ran a long way," he tells me.

I don't know what he's talking about. All I remember is the glare of the porch light over his face. The tall policeman reaching down to him as he fell. And Danny. Danny was there too.

"Nearly five miles," he continues. "While fasting and dehydrated. Unbelievable."

I was searching for something. I was still supposed to be searching. I need to tell him how close I was. He's looking at me and smiling, but there's no hope in his sad eyes anymore. I want to say the right thing and make them light up again. But I owe him the truth, and I still haven't paid my debt.

"Thank God they found you in time," he says. "It was a miracle they did. A true miracle."

A miracle? I've heard that word since I was little. That's what my parents call me. A baby born against all odds. God's answer to their hope. But, as it turned out, their miracle was this man's catastrophe.

"I knew that Danny had been drinking," I whisper.

Mr. Edelstein doesn't react. His expression is unchanged. Did I speak the words out loud, or did I swallow them again?

"I knew," I repeat. My voice wavers but I press on. "But I didn't care. I told Danny to steal the car keys. I told him to do it."

He still doesn't move; it's as if I've paralyzed him with my confession. Maybe he doesn't realize what it means? Maybe that's why he hasn't reacted?

"He wouldn't have done it, if I hadn't pushed him to. He would have stayed back at the house until it was safe. He wouldn't have gotten in the accident. And he wouldn't be missing now."

There's finally a spark of understanding in his eyes. He stirs a little; his lips fall open, but he doesn't speak.

"I should have told you before," I say. "I'm sorry. I'm the reason Danny is missing."

His face clouds over, but there's no anger there, as I expected. He places his hand over mine; his fingers are cold and gray like a ghost's.

"Danny isn't missing," he tells me softly. "They found him last night."

A LOSS OF FAITH

I don't know the exact moment when I lost Deenie and Rae; they probably hid their doubts from me for a while. We were halfway through February before the truth finally came out.

I was feeling under the weather, so Rae and Deenie came over with a giant pot of matzo ball soup. The smell of boiling broth wafted through the house and woke me from my nap. I shuffled downstairs as their voices drifted up toward me.

Rae pointed to a steaming bowl on the counter as I stepped into the room. "There you go. I'm toasting croutons in the oven, if you want to wait a minute."

"Could I freeze a container of this?" I asked as I sipped the broth. "It's fantastic. I want to add it to my collection."

"What do you mean? What collection?"

I pointed to the freezer. "Bottom drawer. So far I have a package of your white chocolate snickerdoodles, three turkey wraps from last week, and a baggie of mushroom pinwheels."

Rae frowned and slowly placed the ladle back into the pot. "What are you saving them for?" But I could tell she already knew the answer to her question. I'd just listed Danny's favorite foods.

"It's for when he comes back. I thought we could have a celebration feast."

She nodded and took a deep breath. "Really. You're planning a feast."

Deenie slid off her seat and put her arm around Rae's shoulders. "Why not? I think it's a nice idea. And it might happen, you know. So we have to be ready."

But her voice gave her away. She was using the placating tone of a mother reasoning with an irrational child. I realized suddenly that she didn't believe Danny was coming back, any more than Rae did.

"Exactly," I said shortly. "We have to be ready for a miracle. You believe in miracles, don't you, Deenie?"

She didn't reply.

I should have let it go, probably. I should have taken her silence as it was intended—a last attempt to spare my feelings. But I'd heard enough statistics and facts from the police, from reporters, and from well-meaning visitors who already spoke of Danny as someone who had "passed." I needed a united front from my best friends.

In this home, at least, Danny was missing, presumed living.

"You don't believe, do you, Deenie?" I demanded.

Rae opened her mouth, but Deenie stopped her before she could speak.

"It doesn't matter what we think," she said. "It's good that you haven't given up hope."

She might as well have punched me in the gut. "What we think?!" I shouted. "So I'm completely alone in this? I always thought you were on my side!"

She glanced down at her feet. "We were. We are."

"What does that mean?" My eyes welled up, and I blinked the tears away. "I'm right here, Deenie. Look at me! You can be honest with me."

"Please don't cry—"

"Just tell me!" I insisted. "Is he coming back?"

"Ellie. I don't know. I'm not God—"

"I'm not asking you to be. Just give me a straight answer, okay? Do you believe that Danny is coming back?"

I didn't breathe through the pause that followed, and by the time she finally answered, my chest hurt from waiting.

"I think he's gone, Ellie," she whispered. Her eyes filled up. "I'm sorry."

I'd lied to her. I didn't want honesty. Nobody really wants that kind of honesty.

"Okay," I said. "Good to know." I picked up the ladle and pulled out a Tupperware container. Dumped spoonfuls of soup until it overflowed and then slammed on the plastic lid. Walked over to the freezer and jammed the bowl into the bottom drawer.

Rae and Deenie watched me without commenting; Deenie was crying silently, without bothering to wipe away the tears staining her collar. Rae's eyes were dry and bloodshot; she kept blinking and sniffing and biting her lips.

"I'm going to my room," I announced, banging the freezer door shut. "Don't follow me."

"Ellie, please," Deenie pleaded. "We didn't mean to hurt you—"

"Don't talk to me," I shot back. "Unless your next words are 'They found Danny,' I don't want to hear anything you have to say."

Chapter 26

"They found Danny," Deenie says.

Mr. Edelstein had told me, and I'd immediately closed my eyes to shut him out. Then my mother and father sat down on my bed and quietly broke the news to me. Each time someone said it, I tried to focus on the words only, and not the grief behind it. They'd found Danny. Surely that was a good thing. It's what I had prayed for. God had finally listened.

But there's no way to shut out Deenie's face.

"They found Danny." She's sobbing.

I don't ask where. Or who found him. I don't want to hear the details that everyone already knows. That story doesn't matter.

Rae comes into view, sits down at the end of the bed. Her cheeks are raw and blistered from crying. "After the funeral we'll be sitting shiva with Danny's father," she tells me.

I nod and close my eyes again. I'm wide awake, but it's easier to pretend weakness at the moment.

"Ellie," Rae says, touching my hand.

I peek at her through heavy lids. "Yeah?"

"After they discharge you, I thought we could all go over to the Edelsteins' together. If you're up to it."

Of course I'm up to it. I ran miles to find Danny. But I'd failed to bring him back. So the least I can do is sit next to his father while he grieves. "I'll go. But I don't think he'll want to see me," I whisper.

Deenie and Rae exchange looks. "Mr. Edelstein told us what you said," Rae says softly. "We didn't know that part of the story. We had no idea you were blaming yourself."

"I was afraid to tell you," I admit. "It's my fault he's gone." It's a relief to say it, even if it means losing them forever. If I truly love my friends, I can't keep lying to them. "I'm so sorry."

Deenie is shaking as she takes my hand; her fingers tremble over mine. "Ellie. Can I talk to you?"

"Not now," Rae urges her, pulling her back. "She's still weak."

"I'm okay." I'm so relieved that they haven't turned their backs on me that I'm ready for whatever they have to say, as long as it's not a rejection. I sit up in the bed to prove my strength. "What's going on?"

Deenie takes a long breath and glances back at Rae, who nods her encouragement. She shudders, grips my hand, and the words tumble from her lips.

"I didn't know you were blaming yourself," she says brokenly. "Or I would have spoken sooner. It isn't your fault, Ellie. It never was."

She pauses a moment and waits for me to speak, but I don't know what to say. How can she think that? She knows what I did. She can't rewrite this story.

"Everyone made mistakes that night," Deenie continues when I don't reply.

"Every one of us," Rae put in.

Deenie waves her hand, dismissing her. "No, Rae. No. Stop protecting me."

"Hold on, what are you saying?" I ask her. "You had nothing to do with it. You weren't even there that night."

Deenie shuts her eyes. "I was," she whispers. Her head is bowed. "I was there."

"I don't understand." I glance between Rae's grave face and Deenie's tortured one.

"I'm so sorry." Her voice is barely audible. There's a breathless pause that lasts too long.

"Sorry for what?" I ask hoarsely.

She slowly raises her eyes to mine. "I was there that night," she tells me. "And it's my fault that he's gone."

MY SHADOW

It was easier to be mad than it was to show them what I was really feeling. So I made a lot of noise heading up to my room; I pushed a chair out of the way, knocked over a plant, slammed my bedroom door. I wanted them to focus on the tantrum. I couldn't let them see what was beneath it.

I was terrified. While Deenie and Rae were behind me, I was on solid ground. I could ignore the news stories that turned morbid less than a week after Danny disappeared. I could handle the looks on the cops' faces when we stopped by to ask about the case. I could deal with my parents' calm reaction to the "facts" as presented by the investigators. I could even accept that his classmates had stopped sharing Danny's missing person photo.

How long could the world hold on? It didn't matter, as long as the three of us did. As long as his friends believed.

But I was alone in this now. I'd been alone for a while, and I hadn't even realized it. I wanted to scream my frustration at Deenie and Rae, but I was afraid of letting them get too close. What if I lost control and let something slip? My guilty secret was right on the tip of my tongue; I was a breath away from letting the truth out, and I just couldn't risk that. If I told them what I'd done, I'd lose everyone.

I banged around my room for a little while, venting my misery on stuffed animals and pillows. The photo of the four of us on a roller coaster got thrown about until the glass cracked. I typed and deleted a hundred angry messages to our friend WhatsApp group.

Then I collapsed on my bed and cried until I fell asleep. I dreamed that the summer had come and the hot Atlanta sun was beating down on me. It was a noisy, sweltering day on the beach, and the spray from the ocean was misting my forehead. I opened my mouth to catch the drops; I was horribly parched, and my skin was burning. I tried to peel the clothes off, but I was wrapped in layers and layers of sheets. Deenie appeared carrying a heavy blanket. "Here you go," she said, tossing the comforter over me. "Now you're completely modest."

"Deenie, I can't breathe," I pleaded.

She smiled. "It's okay. You'll get used to it."

When I woke, the room was pulsing with heat. My face was on fire, my lips chapped with thirst.

I stumbled over to the thermostat and squinted at the dial. Seventy-three degrees. And yet it felt like I was in hell. The room was dense like a sauna; I had to get some air or die. I pulled the curtains open and pushed up the window. A gust of wind made me shiver and cough. I laid my burning forehead against the glass. Gazed into the dark.

And that was when I saw him.

Sitting on a tree branch, just a few inches away from me. Dressed in his black polo and muddy gray tennis shoes. His mop of hair wild and shining white in the moonlight. Grinning at me, as if no time had passed.

"Danny," I gasped.

He didn't answer, just sat there smiling and tapping on the tree branch next to him.

"You want me to come out?" I asked.

He nodded.

"But you know I'm not very good at climbing," I said. One leg was already over the windowsill. "My parents will kill me if they catch me on this tree again. Remember what happened the last time I tried?" I was halfway out already, gripping the shutter with numb fingers.

"You fell," he said.

"Yeah. Almost broke my neck."

"Are you afraid?" he asked.

"No." I eased myself onto the slick bough. "You know what's weird, though?"

"Hmm?"

"It was warm last night. Where did this ice come from?"

He looked away. "From you."

The moonlight was playing tricks with my eyes. Danny was fading into the dark, the shadows shrouding the contours of his face. "Where have you been all this time?" I asked him.

"There," he said, pointing downward. "Look."

I leaned over and peered at the ground. Sure enough, there he was, sitting at the base of the tree, resting his head against the trunk. He was dressed in his winter coat and hat, but one glove was on the ground next to him; he was texting with his bare hand.

"So are you going to answer me?" Danny asked. "I've been waiting a long time."

"I know." It wasn't strange to me that Danny was both next to me and also on the ground. The only thing that mattered was letting him know how much I regretted what I'd done. "I wish I'd answered you that night."

"So do it now. Come down and talk to me."

I took a deep breath and slid back toward the window. "You want me to climb down?"

He shrugged and stood up on the branch. "Or you can jump with me."

I glanced at the ground below. It pitched and swayed beneath me. "It's kind of far." The branch shook, and I threw my arms around it to steady myself.

He leaned over to me and placed an icy hand on my cheek. I shivered under his touch. "So what are you going to do?" he demanded. "How are you going to make this right?"

I glanced at the miserable, snow-covered Danny on the ground and then looked back into the blazing eyes of Danny's demon hovering in front of me.

And suddenly, it was so clear to me. There was only one way to prove my loyalty to him. The rest of the world was trying to bury him alive while I screamed warnings nobody could hear. Danny was counting on me now. So I would do just as he asked. It was the only way to bring him home. And if I was wrong, if Danny wasn't coming back, and this was all just a feverish dream, then I didn't care what happened to me. Either ending worked, because either way, I'd be with him.

I made my mind up to jump. I stood up on the tree branch, reached out for Danny's hand.

He stretched his arm out to me and smiled, but as I grasped for him, he pulled away suddenly and stepped back. "We're not supposed to touch, remember?" he said.

I cried out and clawed the air. Swayed back and forth in the wind. And then I slipped.

I told everyone later that it was an accident. That I'd had a fever and wasn't myself. That I'd made a mistake. Nobody believed me, even though it was true.

My parents found me at the base of the tree, crumpled and bleeding, my leg bent beneath me.

In the ambulance my mother clasped my hand and demanded what I'd been doing on that tree in the middle of the night.

And, out of my mind with fever and pain, I let it all spill out. "I wanted to be with Danny," I sobbed. "And that was the only way."

Problem was, that was also true.

I was introduced to my first psychiatrist while still doped up on painkillers and giddy from fever. I don't remember his name. He had a patchy beard and breath that smelled like pickles.

Dr. Pickle didn't last long. I think he preferred patients who agreed to speak to him.

The next one was a lady with broken glasses. A piece of duct tape held the cracked edge in place. I studied the duct tape for a long time while she talked at me.

When she finally left the room, I readjusted the pillows beneath my cast and stared at the calendar on the desk. A whole week had flown by; I wondered how long they planned to keep me in the hospital. Maybe I should have agreed to talk to Dr. Duct Tape. Asked her to speed the process along.

"Shouldn't a doctor be able to afford a new pair of glasses?"

Danny was sitting on the edge of my bed. He smiled and picked up a pen, then scribbled something on the base of my cast.

"Hey!" I protested. "I can't see what you wrote."

"Get a mirror, genius."

"So why are you here?" I asked him.

"Because you're in a hospital. Surrounded by psychiatrists."

"They think I jumped."

"Didn't you?"

"Yeah. But you told me to."

He frowned and leaned closer to me. "Ellie, you think I want you to hurt yourself?"

I sighed. "No, I guess not. I don't know."

"Do you believe I'm coming back or not?" he demanded.

"Of course I do."

"Good. Then why would you hurt yourself? Don't you want to give me a chance?"

"I do!" I reached out to grab his hand, but he pulled away from me and moved back on the bed. "Danny, I need to know what happened to you," I begged him. "How else am I going to keep believing?"

He told me the story then, the one I'd wanted to hear since he disappeared. The story about the lady and the remote cottage with the padlocked door. The story about how he was actually okay. How he was just waiting to come back to us.

It was a wild story, but of course I had to believe it. Sometimes you have to take a leap of faith for the ones you love.

"Truth or fiction?" I asked him, just to make sure.

He smiled and brought his face close to mine. So close, I could almost feel his breath on my cheek. I thought he was going to whisper the word "truth" in my ear. But instead, he murmured, "Don't try to tell anyone, Ellie; I promise they won't believe you."

Chapter 27

Deenie wraps a hospital blanket around her shoulders and shrinks deep into its folds. Rae puts her arm out to hug her, but Deenie shakes her off. “No, Rae,” she murmurs. “Thank you. But I have to do this on my own. You’ve protected me long enough.”

I’m still trying to process her admission. *I was there that night. It’s my fault—*

“What do you mean?” I ask her. “How was it your fault?”

This had to be some kind of exaggerated guilt. Nothing was ever Deenie’s fault. So she was at the party that night. So were a lot of people. How could she blame herself for what happened to Danny?

Deenie takes a deep breath and squares her shoulders. Her eyes focus on a corner of my pillow, just shy of my face. She’s quiet for a moment; I wait for her to speak, but nothing comes. Finally, I say her name, and she startles hard and with a great effort shifts her gaze to look at me.

“I was like his sister, remember?” she says suddenly.

I’m not sure how to respond, so I just nod.

“I mean, that’s how he thought of me,” she amends. “I was like his sister. Or a first cousin, maybe.” She shakes her head, and a faint smile dawns. “I scolded him too much for a cousin, though. Maybe I was like an aunt to him? A young aunt?”

I shoot Rae a perplexed look, but she seems as baffled as I am.

Is Deenie going to list all the possible ways Danny felt like family?

"Actually, you were more like a sister than I was," Deenie says, glancing at Rae. "I wanted to be like you, do you know that? I tried to imitate how you two were together. God, I was so jealous of your friendship. It was so easy for you."

"Deenie, please—"

"It didn't work," she hurries on, ignoring Rae's pained expression. "I tried to imitate you, but of course it didn't work. How could I have ever hoped it would? You weren't lying to him, Rae. You were honest; even when you shouted and raged at him, you always told the truth. But I was quiet. And so, so righteous." Her face wrinkles in disgust. "Oh, I was a real *tzaddeket*," she says, using the Hebrew word for "pious woman." It sounds like a curse word when she says it. "Such a good girl. And the whole time, I was drowning in my own jealousy."

Rae leans forward and gently takes her hand. "So you're telling Ellie that you were jealous of *me*," she says. It isn't really a question. Her voice challenges her; her eyes are reproachful. "You were jealous of my friendship with Danny?"

Deenie shrinks farther into her blanket and bows her head. "No. No, I wasn't." She sighs and looks back at me. "That's also a lie."

She's struggling to form words now. Her fingers are digging into her knee, turning white. The sentence she gasps out doesn't make sense. It's half apology and half denial. But I know what she's trying to tell me; somehow I think I've known forever, though I've never dared to admit it. "You weren't jealous of Rae," I say quietly. "You were jealous of me."

She doesn't respond, but the tears in her eyes are my answer. They stream down her cheeks and land on my hand.

"Because you loved him too," I finish.

She nods and tries to speak, but a sob cuts her confession short.

I watch her silently for a moment as she cries. I'm not sure how to feel. Am I supposed to resent this revelation? I don't, not even a little bit. I'm so sorry for her, there's no room for any other emotion. How can I blame her for loving Danny? She couldn't control how she felt. And she looks so penitent and miserable, I wish that she'd confided in me sooner. I might have relieved some of her guilt. "It's okay," I assure her. "It doesn't matter now. I realize you couldn't help falling for him—any more than I could. You don't have to apologize. I'm glad you told me."

I wait for the shadow to rise from her face, but there's no relief in her eyes; her tears flow as heavy as before. I reach out to take her hand, to reassure her that I meant what I said. But as I do, I glance over at Rae, and something about her guarded, fearful expression makes me draw back. There's more, I realize. Deenie wasn't just confessing to a feeling. She hasn't finished her story yet.

But I'm scared to press her for the rest. I know I can forgive her for loving him. But what else will I have to forgive? Will I even have a choice? I've just lost my boyfriend forever. I can't lose Deenie, too.

And there's a part of her confession that I can't ignore; I remember it now as I watch her struggle for words. "What were you trying to tell me before?" I ask her finally when she doesn't speak. "Why did you say it was your fault that he's gone?"

"Because it is," she replies. Her voice is hollow and flat, as if she's cried herself empty. "Because I'm the reason Rae called you that night."

I still don't understand what she's telling me. At that moment

I can't even remember why Rae had called me from the party. Danny had been drinking, she'd told me. Danny had been drinking, and he was really out of it. But there was some reason I needed to talk to him right away. Something that had upset me—

"I was the girl," Deenie tells me brokenly. "I was the girl sitting next to him."

It all comes back in a rush. Rae's urgent whisper: *There's this girl here—She's kind of attached herself to him—*

Then my panicked call to Danny. The sound of relief in his voice. *I miss you—*

"*You* were the girl Rae was talking about?" Even as I say it, the words sound incredible to me. Impossible. Not Deenie. Anyone else could have done that. Not my sweet, innocent best friend.

Her shaking has calmed a little, and she takes a deep, shuddering breath, like the first inhale of a person who's drowning. "Rae knew how I felt about Danny, but she never told anyone," she says. "Even when she saw me flirting with him, she protected me, though I didn't deserve it." She gives Rae a grateful look and then drops her eyes again. "She tried to take me aside at the party, to talk to me—but I just brushed her off. So that's why she called you." Deenie doesn't pause to wait for my response now but rushes ahead, as if desperate to finish her confession. "And that's when I did it."

I can't breathe; I can't speak.

"Danny and I were sitting in a dark corner away from everyone," she continues miserably. "But Rae had seen me come in. I never go to parties, and I hadn't told her or anyone else that I was coming, so she was—confused. Suspicious, I think. When I brushed off her questions, she left us alone, but she kept hovering around, keeping an eye on me. And then suddenly she was gone. Danny was checking his phone—for, like, the hundredth time that night. It wasn't fair, I told myself. His heart was broken because you didn't want to be with him anymore. Somehow I convinced myself that he needed to move on, that he deserved to move on. And I just wanted him to look at me the way he used to look at you. I wanted him to stop thinking about you. To think about me just for a moment. So I pushed away his phone—and I kissed him."

There are no words. I know that she is telling the truth. And yet I can't believe her.

"That got his attention," she concludes bitterly. "He was so confused that he didn't do anything at first. He just sat there. So I kissed him again. I kept kissing him, begging him to look at me, to kiss me back—"

"And did he?" My voice is a strangled whisper.

She nods. "Once. But then he stopped and looked at me—just as I hoped he would. But he wasn't really seeing me. His eyes shifted, like he was ashamed of himself. And he said, "Deenie, I love you . . . but—"

She stops, drops her head.

"But—what?"

"He never got a chance to finish. I didn't want to hear the rest, anyway. Thank God he didn't finish the thought."

"You thank God?" I drop her hand and look away. "What is there to thank God for?" The bitterness in my voice sounds fake to my ears. I'm actually totally numb, like after the shock of a blow—just before the pain sets in. I'm trying to picture the scene: a crowd of loud partying kids, the bang of music and the smell of beer, Danny in a secluded corner, hunched over his phone, Deenie inching closer to him, smiling—coaxing him to notice her. But that Deenie is a stranger to me. Her face is grotesque, distorted, unrecognizable. I can't picture the person she's just described.

"I don't understand," I say, looking back at her swollen, pleading eyes. "What did you think was going to happen?"

"I wish I knew," she whispers. "Do you know how many times I've asked myself that question? Deep down, I knew that you still loved each other, Ellie. And I knew that he and I had no future together. I knew all of that, and I did it anyway."

"What were you thinking?" My voice rises. Next to me, Rae reaches out and places a calming hand on my shoulder. I shake it off. "You were *shomer*, for God's sake!" I exclaim. "Were you going to give all that up?" My face flushes and sweat breaks over my brow. And yet, my anger is barely skin-deep. It's an emotion I'm wearing, but beneath it I'm still frozen in denial. I'm displaying anger for her because that's what I'm supposed to be feeling; it's part of the script. But I can't be angry at Deenie. Not until I understand.

"I don't *know*." Her voice breaks and she clasps her hands together. "I know what I dreamed about. Do you want to hear that?"

"No." I shudder and close my eyes. But it's as if I can read her thoughts now, even in the silence. "How far would you have gone?" I whisper. "If he hadn't stopped you?" The darkness fades, and I see their lips coming together, hear her breath quicken, watch their arms intertwine—

My eyes fly open.

"Deenie, please tell me you wouldn't have!"

She doesn't answer me. Her head is bowed before me. "I don't know," she says. "I just don't know how far I would have gone."

Lie to me! I want to scream at her. *You've been lying to me for months. Look me in the eye and lie to me now. Tell me that you would have stopped at the kiss. Tell me you cared too much about our friendship. Tell me something, anything that allows me to forgive you.*

"All I know is, I'm the reason that he's gone," she tells me.

"Deenie, you have to stop saying that—" Rae begins, but I interrupt her.

"Enough," I say sharply. "Deenie, can you please go?" I can't look at either of them right now.

"Ellie, do you want me to—" Rae asks hesitantly.

"Both of you." I slump back against my pillow. "Please. I just really need to be alone."

She nods, as if she'd been expecting that, and they both leave the room without another word.

WHY SHE STOPPED SINGING

The psychiatrist I was seeing couldn't explain my sudden improvement after my discharge from the hospital. "Mourning takes time," she told my parents. "It's a journey with highs and lows. But I'm not sure what's going on with Ellie now. She seems almost—chipper."

The doctor was exaggerating; I wasn't chipper. I'd simply stopped grieving since Danny showed up in my hospital room. Instead, I waited and hoped. And in the meantime, I could talk to him, whenever I wanted. As long I wasn't stupid about it.

Problem was, I was sometimes stupid about it. It was hard to remember that I was the only one seeing him, so I slipped up pretty early on. A couple of weeks after my discharge Rae noticed me laughing at something he'd said. And she completely freaked out.

"Ellie is hallucinating!" she told my parents. "She's talking to a ghost. You have to do something!"

And they tried. They took me to specialists who all had different diagnoses and opinions, ranging from psych ward commitment to vitamin supplements. They chopped down the tree outside my window, as if my ghost required a physical ladder to get into my room. They finally settled on Nina, who assured them that my visions were just a way to cope. Not inherently harmful, as long as they didn't interfere with my life.

So I set about proving that Danny didn't interfere. I attended class and kept up my grades. I took up running every morning, at Nina's suggestion.

And for several months everyone was satisfied. Nina told my parents that I was making progress, and they believed it. Deenie was happy that our group had managed to stay together, even if she couldn't quite see one of its members.

The only one who didn't buy any of it was Rae.

"This isn't right," I overheard her say to Deenie one evening. They were hanging out in my basement and hadn't noticed me coming down the stairs. I crouched quietly behind the banister when I heard her say my name. "Ellie isn't making progress. She's stuck."

"What are you talking about?"

"I've been reading about the five stages of grief," she explained, pulling out her phone. "Denial, anger, bargaining, depression, and acceptance. Ellie's isn't moving past the first stage."

"She seems okay to me," Deenie replied. "She's not depressed anymore. Maybe she's reached acceptance—in her own way."

Rae sighed and shook her head. "And you're stuck in bargaining," she told Deenie.

"What is that supposed to mean?"

She laughed shortly. "I'm just wondering what you're planning to give up this week."

"I'm not giving things up because of Danny," she protested.

"Really?" Rae challenged. "You just gave up your own voice. You won't sing anymore. Tell me that's not about him."

"Why would it be about him?" Deenie asked, but her eyes betrayed her.

Rae shrugged. "You're using religion to kill everything attractive about yourself. Your hair." She waved her hand at the loose dress that fell to Deenie's feet. "Your body. And now your voice. As if it will bring him back."

Deenie shook her head emphatically. "That's not true. I've loved my religion since I was a little girl. But I never needed Judaism to tell me what was right and wrong before. I just knew it, instinctively—and I thought that I could trust myself to always know. But now I realize that I can't. I can't even stray a little. So I'm giving all of it up because I don't have a choice."

"And you think that will help somehow?"

Deenie dropped her head in defeat. "I don't know, Rae. Maybe I'm hoping it will help me," she murmured. "Because no matter what I do, I know I can never bring him back."

Chapter 28

I'm alone with my thoughts for hours, even though I regret sending my friends away almost as soon as they leave the room. But I don't have my phone to call them back, so I have to wait until the doctor comes in to discharge me. My parents bustle around packing up my things, the nurse pulls out my IV and hands my mom a stack of papers, and then somehow I'm standing by my front door, wondering how I got there.

To my surprise, Rae is sitting in the living room when we come in. "Is Deenie here too?" I ask her, glancing around the room.

"No, she's at home. We were going to go visit Mr. Edelstein after you got discharged. So I thought I'd go with you now, and then later with her. Separately."

My parents give me a puzzled look, but I'm too tired to explain. And the truth is, I don't really want to explain. I never want them to find out what Deenie did. Somehow, their knowing about her betrayal would make that story too real to me—and too unforgivable. And I desperately want to forgive.

"Text her to come over," I tell Rae. "We can go together."

Rae nods silently and pulls out her phone while I settle on the couch next to her. I'm exhausted; every muscle in my body feels raw and leaden. I close my eyes for a moment, and when I reopen them, Deenie is sitting curled up in the armchair opposite me. She's listening to Rae talk about the funeral arrangements. I watch

Deenie silently and wait for the feeling of anger to hit. I'm not numb anymore. I should be furious. But I just don't feel it.

I can see my friend disappearing in front of me; she's been slowly drowning herself in thick mourning robes, in rules and rituals and restrictions. She's stifled her own voice in penance, given up everything she's ever loved in a vain attempt to quiet the guilt that's strangling her.

I could turn away from her and nurse my own wounds. I could be resentful—even vengeful, if I wanted. But I could never punish her more harshly than she's already punished herself.

And what's more, I don't want to. I'd shut Danny out when I should have listened to him. I'm not going to repeat that mistake now. I know what he would have wanted me to do.

I sit up and clear my throat to get their attention.

Deenie starts a little and turns to me.

"It's okay," I tell her. "I forgive you."

She stares at me, her eyes wide with disbelief. "You do? Why?"

I consider the question for a moment before answering. "Because, I think, if you were in my place, you would forgive me." There's no doubt in my mind, I realize as I say it. "I'm sure you would."

She nods. "Except that you would never do what I did. I know you wouldn't. Ellie—do you think, maybe—do you think he would forgive me too, if I could ask him?"

Rae's face tenses; she sits up straight and glances around the room. "What do you want Ellie to do?" She's trying to sound understanding, but her question rings with warning. "You want her to ask Danny to forgive you?"

"I can't do that," I tell her. The room is empty. It's just the three of us. "He isn't here."

She flinches when I say it, and I realize for the first time that Deenie had secretly cherished my visions of our friend. It was comforting to her that he was somewhere in the shadows, even if only in my mind. He wasn't truly gone, not while I still believed he was with us. But now he's really vanished, and with him, the hope of his forgiveness, and her salvation.

"Anyway, I can't ask him for you," I add.

She nods wearily and sighs. "No, I guess not."

"But *you* can," I say.

"What do you mean? How?"

"Close your eyes," I instruct her. "As if you're praying."

She looks doubtful, but she does as I ask.

"There. Can you see him now?"

She shakes her head.

"He's wearing that black polo. The gray sneakers with the crack in the sole."

She wrinkles her brows, as if concentrating on a blurry image.

"He needs a haircut," I prompt. "His bangs are practically covering his eyes."

A smile dawns now. Her lips fall open, and she draws a sharp breath. She sees him.

"Talk to him," I say. "Tell him you messed up. Tell him you're sorry."

She speaks. I can't hear what she is telling him, but her expression is pleading, and I know what she is saying, even though she never voices a word. Rae watches her fretfully, irritably, like a scientist who's been forced to attend a séance. She rolls her eyes at me but otherwise doesn't interrupt.

Deenie talks silently for a long time. Rae keeps glancing at the clock. My mom wanders in with a plate of cookies, stares at my friend for a moment, and then wanders out, but Deenie never notices. She sits in the same trance as before, until even I begin to worry.

Perhaps it's too much for her? Maybe she's too fragile to try this experiment. For me Danny was like a guardian angel, but maybe for her he will be different. He could take another form—an accusing demon. I'd met that Danny when my guilt had overwhelmed me at the prayer service. Was that the vision that was speaking to Deenie now?

Suddenly, her peaceful expression changes, and her eyes fly open. She glances at our expectant faces and bites her lip. "I don't want to do that anymore," she tells me hoarsely. "It—it isn't right."

"What do you mean?"

"It isn't real, okay? Danny doesn't live in my mind. Talking to him doesn't mean anything! I'm basically asking myself for forgiveness."

"How is that any different than praying?" Rae mutters.

"Don't start, Rae," Deenie says, turning on her. "God can hear my prayers. But Danny can't hear me—not anymore. And maybe some things can't be forgiven. And maybe you shouldn't forgive me either."

I lean back against a sofa cushion. "But I want to forgive," I say after a moment. "None of this would have happened if I hadn't pushed Danny away, if I'd just forgiven him. I'm not going to do that again."

"But—this is different," Deenie says, her voice sinking to a miserable whisper. "You've been blaming yourself for something that was my fault—"

"It's all of our faults," Rae interrupts.

Deenie looks surprised for a moment and then shakes her head. "You don't have to—" she begins, but Rae cuts her off.

"What? I'm going to let you face the music alone?" Rae asks her bitterly. "I played a part too."

I sigh. "Come on, now. You didn't hide the keys well enough? What did you do?"

Rae looks me in the eye as she confesses. "I was the reason Danny left the party. I saw Deenie flirting with him, so I asked you to call him. When I came back, I found the two of them kissing. So I yelled at him. Screamed at him to get out. That's why he never finished what he wanted to say to Deenie." She doesn't drop her head as Deenie had done. The confession spills from her lips as if she's relieved to finally give it voice. "He ran from the house just as you were calling him. So even if you had told him to go back to the house—to wait until he'd sobered up—I don't think he could have. You may have told him to steal the keys, but I basically pushed him into the car."

I haven't yet recovered from Deenie's confession; this new detail makes my head spin. I'm remembering Danny's last words to me before the accident. *I'll try to sneak into the house. I have to make sure Rae doesn't see me.*

He had to sneak past her to get the keys, because she had just thrown him out.

"But you were just being a good friend," I say to her. "You yelled at him because you were trying to protect me; you were trying to save my relationship with Danny."

She's silent for a moment. "Yeah. Except, deep down, I wasn't really doing it for you—for either of you."

We are both silent, waiting for her to continue. I'm completely lost, but Deenie seems calmer now, as if she knows what is about to come.

"You weren't the only one being hurt by that kiss." Rae's eyes don't waver as she gives me the truth. "It burned me too, Ellie."

It takes me a moment to realize what she's saying. "But you didn't love Danny," I say slowly. "Not like that." About this, at least, I trust my instinct. "I know you didn't."

"You're right," she replies softly. "I didn't love Danny." And for the first time since beginning her confession, her eyes shift. Drop to her hands.

And focus, just for a moment, on Deenie.

THE REST OF RAE'S STORY (transcribed from notes scribbled on a piece of paper that was shoved into my notebook when I wasn't looking)

Danny placed the cookie on Rae's lap. "I just want you to know that you can always have my last cookie," he said.

She wiped her face with her sleeve and gave him a sidelong glance. "You're such a cheeseball," she said. "I don't even know why I told you. It's not going to change anything."

"Exactly." He shrugged. "You told me because you know that it's not going to change anything. I'm not going to look at you any differently."

She hesitated. "But—but the four of us hang out together all the time. It's not like you can forget it. So from now on every time I—I hug Deenie or something, you'll think—" She made a face and shook her head as if to banish the image.

He laughed. "I'll think that you care about your best friend."

She frowned and settled back on the sofa. "Yeah, she's my best friend. And there's so many things I can't tell her."

"It's just one thing." Rae raised her eyebrows, and he waved his hand dismissively. "Okay, okay, I get that it's a big thing. But—still, you can talk to her about everything else."

Rae hesitated again and bit her lip. "Not exactly. I can't tell her anything big, really. I can't tell her about my first time."

Danny sat up a little. "Your first time?"

Rae looked down at her lap, picked up the cookie, and turned it over in her hands. "It was a few months ago. You don't know the guy. I barely knew him myself."

Her fingers tightened on the cookie until it broke apart in her hand.

"Maybe I was trying to prove something to myself? I don't know. So I just decided to do it with some random guy—to get it over with, mostly. Maybe I would be into it? Who knew? Deenie and Ellie treated sex like this amazing life-changing event. But what I was feeling was already life-changing enough. And I guess I wanted to believe that the whole sex thing was no big deal."

Danny hesitated. "So—was it a big deal?"

She grinned. "I don't know. Honestly, it kind of sucked. Neither of us knew what we were doing. And somehow every damn thing he did managed to turn me off." Rae stared glumly at the cookie dust in her hand. "So now I have no idea how I feel. I know I'm in love with a girl. But I've had crushes on guys, too. And I can't tell my family about any of it because I know they won't understand."

"Are you sure about that?" Danny asked. "They've been pretty supportive so far."

Rae shook her head. "Because they understand leaving religion. They won't understand this." She took a deep breath and gave him a tired smile. "A while ago we were watching a movie scene where a bi girl brings home her girlfriend. And my dad said, 'I just don't get it. It's not like she's a lesbian. So if she can be attracted to guys, why doesn't she just date guys?'"

Danny rolled his eyes, but Rae rushed to her father's defense before he could speak.

"But he didn't say it in a mean or hateful way, you know? He really just didn't understand. How could I explain to him that if I could *choose* not to fall in love with my straight best friend, I would?"

"So do you think you'll tell them eventually?"

She nodded. "Yeah, of course. One day."

He put his hand out, and she dumped the cookie crumbs into his palm. "You can talk to Deenie and Ellie, though," he assured her. "I know they'll understand."

She laughed shortly. "You think? Maybe they will. But I guess I'm just not ready for their understanding yet."

Chapter 29

Rae gets up immediately after her confession, before I've had a chance to process what she's just told us. "Don't follow me," she says, her back to us. "I'm going over to visit Mr. Edelstein, and I'll meet you there. But I want to walk alone. Don't run after me and tell me that you love me and you'll support me. I know that already. Don't ask me any questions. Don't ask me what I'm planning to do. I'm not ready to talk about this, not yet. I just wanted the lies to end, that's all. Okay?"

"Yes," Deenie and I whisper in unison. "Okay."

"I love you, Rae," I add—because I just can't help myself.

She sighs, and a little of her usual snark creeps back into her voice. "Jeez, Ellie, I just said—" But I think she's smiling as she leaves the room.

"Did you know?" I ask Deenie after the door closes behind Rae.

"I suspected," Deenie admits. "For a while. But then right after Danny left the party, we had a long talk. And she told me how she felt. How she's felt for a long time."

"What did you say?"

"What could I say? She knew I didn't feel the same way. I told her I loved her and promised her that nothing would change between us."

"And has it?"

She considers for a moment. "No, I don't think so. If anything, the truth brought us closer. I couldn't believe that she stood by me even after what I did." She gives me a wan smile. "And I can't believe you still want to be my friend."

"We all loved Danny," I tell her. "Each in our own way. That's what I'm going to focus on. Not on what divides us."

She doesn't seem reassured. "But my love was selfish."

"So was mine," I tell her. "These last few months I held on to him so tightly that I blocked you and Rae out."

"Maybe sometimes. But you tried to be there for us, as much as you could be." She gets up from the sofa and extends her hand. "And now we have to be there for Danny's father. He doesn't have anybody else now."

Chapter 30

In the Jewish tradition, a funeral takes place as soon as possible after death has been declared, frequently on the same day. The Edelstein case was unusual; an autopsy had to be performed to determine cause of death. So I'm able to attend the funeral because it takes place the day after my discharge from the hospital.

The ceremony passes in a blur; people say nice things about Danny, prayers are recited, and Mr. Edelstein totters at the edge of the grave as he drops the first scoops of earth on the casket. The hollow thud of the clods hitting wood is a sound that will haunt me forever.

The seven-day period of mourning, or shiva, begins shortly afterward. Community members, teachers, and classmates file in and out of the darkened home. Danny's father sits on a low stool in the middle of the room and receives his friends with a dazed, vacant smile. The food they bring sits untouched in piles around him.

Deenie, Rae, and I spend most of the shiva period hovering by his side. We don't talk much except to ask after his needs; he rarely responds, but the buzz of constant visitors keeps the silence from becoming oppressive. By the third day, the strain of receiving comfort is beginning to show. He spends more time in his bedroom and doesn't emerge until noon, then retreats before the sun goes down. People come anyway, sometimes staying for hours.

I know it's considered a sacred tradition and a great kindness to console a mourner, but we've all run out of things to say, and the questions people slip into the conversation are starting to grate on our nerves.

"It was an accident," Rae tells one inquisitive grandmother. "The details don't matter. Anyway, they don't know what happened."

That isn't exactly true, but a shiva is not the place for nosy inquiries. Visitors ask anyway, morbid curiosity seeping through their expressions of concern.

"Why did it take nine months to find him?" my history teacher whispers to his girlfriend over a plate of cinnamon kichel. He doesn't bother lowering his voice. "They used helicopters and dogs and everything."

"I heard that a random jogger found him. Off a side road more than ten miles from where he'd left the wrecked car," the woman whispers. "Ten miles! How did that poor boy walk so far in such awful weather?"

"They say that someone buried him," he informs her, as if this is news. Everybody knows the details, yet no one can stop repeating them. "Those heavy rains and flooding over the holidays uncovered the top layer of dirt—"

"Thank you all for coming," Rae interrupts sharply, jumping up from her chair. "Mr. Edelstein is tired and needs to go lie down."

The shiva period ends finally, and the quiet that descends on the house is worse than the intrusive chatter of well-wishers.

I stay, even after everyone else has left. My parents don't argue; I'm mourning, finally, and they give me my space to do what I need to do.

Mr. Edelstein sits listlessly in the same spot in the middle of the room. The low stool has been replaced with a padded armchair, and the platters of food have been wrapped and placed in the freezer. But he changes nothing else. The mirrors are still draped in dark cloth, the shutters are closed; he makes a murmur of protest when I push open the window to let in some fresh air.

"Not yet, Ellie," he says. "I'm not ready yet."

"What can I do?" I ask him. It's the first time he's addressed me directly. All week he'd been talking through us, as if addressing a roomful of ghosts. "I want to do something for you."

"Do?" His watery eyes focus on mine and wander away. "What is there to do?"

"I don't know," I say desperately. "I know there's nothing I can do—and I know that it's my fault—" He cuts me off with a raised hand.

"None of that, Ellie." His voice is rough with emotion. "There will be no more of that. No more what-ifs. And I don't want to hear the words 'it's my fault.' Do you understand?"

"I don't know how you can stand to be around me," I tell him miserably. "Knowing that it's my—knowing what I did."

"You made a mistake," he replies. "A terrible mistake that will always be with you. There's nothing I can say that will make that go away."

I'm thankful he's finally said it. No one has been that blunt with me, no matter how much I'd begged them to be. My parents blamed themselves when I told them what I'd done. *If we'd only been more understanding*, they said. "Maybe you two wouldn't have gotten into a fight in the first place. And none of this would have happened."

Nina had analyzed my vulnerability on that night; she'd made excuses for my choice. "Teenagers see themselves as invincible; they don't think anything bad can happen to them."

It was a platitude that didn't help me at all. Teenagers hadn't convinced Danny to drink and drive. I had.

"I know there's nothing you can say," I tell Mr. Edelstein. "I wasn't looking for comfort. And I realize this guilt will never go away."

He nods. "At the same time, you aren't the only one responsible."

"You're talking about Deenie and Rae?" I ask him. "They told you what happened that night?"

"They did," he replies. "But I wasn't thinking about them. I was referring to Danny."

I shake my head. "No. It wasn't his fault. I was the one who told him to—"

"Enough," he interrupts. "Danny was free to make his own choices. Remember that."

"But—"

"He made a terrible mistake," he says. "One terrible mistake. But, in the end, that was all it took. It isn't fair, I know. He was a good kid. The best." He looks down at his shaking hands; they're dotted with tears. "My Danny—" He sighs and wipes his wet cheeks. "My Danny could have hurt others that night. I can't let myself forget that. No matter how angry I am at God for taking my boy from me, I still thank Him for that small mercy."

"You thank Him? How? For what?"

He covers his face. "When I pray to God on Danny's behalf, I thank Him that I'm the only one who lost a son that night."

MY GHOST, MY STORY

"Ms. Baker wants me to write a story for this contest," I told him. "I wasn't very nice to her. I told her I didn't want to."

"Why not?" He teetered on my windowsill and then dropped down onto the rug.

I shrugged. "I don't tell stories. That's your job."

"You sure about that?"

"Pretty sure."

"But I haven't told you a story in months," he pointed out.

"Of course you have—"

He grinned. "No. I believe those were yours. You were just using my voice."

I sat down on my bed, picked up our old kissing blanket, and wrapped it around my shoulders. "I hate it when you do that."

"Do what?"

"Turn yourself into a ghost."

His smile vanished. "But I am a ghost. And you're trying to join me."

I plucked at the tattered edge of the blanket. "I don't know what you mean."

"Write the story," he said. "Write all of them. Stop using me as an excuse."

"I'm not. I just don't have anything to write about."

"You sure about that?" he repeats.

"Pretty sure."

"Then you aren't listening to your friends. They've been trying to tell you their stories forever."

Chapter 31

"That's quite a collection," Rae remarks as I slide my manuscript onto the counter between us. It's taken me three months, and I'm finally finished. Rae places a fresh-baked chai-latte muffin in front of me.

I take a bite of it as she flips through the book.

"You have a whole novel here," she remarks. "What are you going to do with it?"

I shrug. "I don't know. I haven't thought about it. It's enough for me if you read it and like it."

She doesn't respond; she's focused on the page in front of her.

"Hey, no fair starting at the middle," I say. I crane my neck to glance over her shoulder. "Why are you reading your part? You know how that goes."

She grunts and peels off a muffin top. "Yeah. I just wanted to check."

"Check what?"

She looks up and shuts the manuscript. "My story—the one about vandalizing the van—it's unfinished."

"I know. But this is all you told me. I wasn't allowed to ask questions, remember?"

She considers for a moment and glances hesitantly around the room.

"Deenie isn't here yet," I say quietly. "And it's okay, I know already. I know Danny interrupted you while you were marking up Rabbi Garner's car." She startles and I raise my hand. "If you read on, you'll see that the rabbi's story is about that day too. But he has no idea it was you. Neither does Deenie."

Rae looks away from me and begins to stack the muffins in a lopsided pyramid between us.

"Rae, you can tell me, if you want," I say. "I promise I'll keep your secret, just like Danny did."

She raises her eyebrows. "You already know it was the rabbi. So what's left to tell?"

I laugh shortly. "Well, for starters—why would you do that? It obviously wasn't random. Why did you pick his car?"

Her hand shakes as she places the last muffin at the pinnacle, and the pyramid collapses suddenly, crumb topping scattering over the counter.

"I was twelve," she says finally. "It was a stupid thing to do."

"True," I agree. "But why did you do it?"

She sighs and picks absentmindedly at a cupcake liner, shredding it between her fingers. "You wouldn't understand," she says finally. "You've always been able to negotiate with your beliefs. Pick and choose. Find a comfortable space for yourself in this religion."

I don't contradict her even though I want to. I've struggled with faith just like anyone else. But my story isn't important now. Rae is finally telling hers, and I need to be open to hear her.

"I could never do that," she continues. "It was all or nothing for me. All good or all evil. There was no middle ground. How could there be? How could God be sometimes wrong?"

She pauses, waiting for my reaction. She appears to expect

a challenge. When I'm silent, she seems surprised—and a little pleased.

"Maybe you remember that I was Rabbi Garner's number-one fan, once upon a time?" she muses, smiling at the memory. "Went to every one of his after-school lectures. Sat at the front of the class. Hand always in the air."

I nod. "I do remember. And then you quit going. None of us could figure out why you stopped showing up. What happened?"

She looks down, embarrassed. "I saw something I wasn't supposed to see. And I could never go back after that."

I don't want to hear what she saw, and yet I'm dying to know. Something tells me that I'm going to regret hearing her next words, but I can't help myself. "What was it? What did you see?" I ask her.

"You can't tell Deenie," she says earnestly. "Promise. It will kill her."

"I swear. I won't say a word." She takes a deep breath, and I have the urge to take back my promise, tell her that she can keep her secret, whatever it is. If it's a confession that will kill Deenie, I'm not sure I'm going to come out of it unscathed.

"I saw Rabbi Garner in a coffee shop just off the highway. Up north, the exit after Dacula," she begins. "I was on a family trip, and my parents pulled over so I could run in to use the bathroom. He was sitting with his back to me. At a booth in the corner." She looks sorry for me, but I have no idea what she's getting at.

"So he was having coffee. So?"

She shakes her head. "He wasn't alone."

The penny drops. She doesn't need to spell it out. But I'm ready to defend him before I've even absorbed what she's trying to tell me.

"You're saying he was with a woman?" I exclaim. "So what? You don't know who she was! How can you jump to conclusions? It could have been a cousin. Or an old congregant. Or—"

"It wasn't a relative, Ellie," she says. "Relatives don't kiss—"

"You don't know!" I interrupt heatedly. I can't bear to hear this. "How can you be so sure?"

The old fighting flame lights up her blue eyes. They blaze at me as she climbs to her feet. "I know what I saw, Ellie. And I knew in that moment that I could never listen to one more word about Torah or *mitzvot* from that man. From any man. But I also couldn't tell anyone what I saw. Especially not Deenie. How could I tell my best friend that her father was a cheater?"

We hear the closing door a second too late. There's a little gasp from the next room, and we freeze in place. The light in Rae's eyes flickers out as she looks past me.

Deenie is standing in the shadows.

No one speaks for a moment; Rae clears her throat over and over as I frantically replay the end of our conversation in my head. How much had Deenie heard? I wonder. What could we deny?

Deenie speaks first, and her composure shocks me as much as her words. "It's okay," she tells us, advancing into the room. "I already know."

"You do?"

She nods and slides in between us at the counter. Picks up a muffin and plucks the top off. Her attitude feels unreal; she's impossibly calm, as if she's practiced her reaction to this exposé and was now delivering a rehearsed act.

I can hardly believe it. How could she be so accepting of the greatest transgression in the Torah? From her own father, of all people. The one whom we looked up to, the person with all the answers. Adultery was a sin that, according to the rabbis, one should die before committing. A revelation this awful should have blown her faith to bits.

She answers our questions before we ask them. "I've known for years," she tells us. "And I've made my peace with it."

She's made her peace with it? How is that possible? Rae's wordless, outraged splutter speaks for both us.

"I don't know what you think my father did," Deenie continues evenly. "But I can tell you the truth, if you're interested in hearing it."

We nod in unison. Rae slowly takes her seat again.

"It was right before my bat mitzvah," she begins. Out of the corner of my eye, I see Rae nod. Their timelines match up, it seems. "I was hoping for a clue about my gift." She smiles at the recollection. "I had my suspicions that they'd bought me the dress I'd been begging for, but I wasn't sure. They were being very coy. So I decided to eavesdrop one night. I knew that it was wrong to spy on my parents." She shrugs and shakes her head. "But I was only twelve, and I told myself that it was such a little sin. Anyway, I was more than punished for it in the end."

She pauses for a moment, and her eyes rest on the manuscript sitting beside me. "This stays between us, right?" she warns, placing her hand on the stack of papers. "My father's story never gets told—do you understand?"

"Obviously!" I say. "I would never do that."

She takes her hand off my manuscript. "You know that he wasn't always religious, right?" she asks us. "That's not a secret. He's always been very open about his journey to Orthodoxy."

I nod. Some of my favorite Rabbi Garner stories were his religious firsts: his first Sabbath. His first week without bacon.

"Five years ago, a girlfriend from his past got in touch with him," Deenie continues. "She was going through a rough time, and she'd heard he was a member of the clergy. She said she was looking for advice. He agreed to see her in his office. For a brief appointment. It turned out to be a mistake. Because once he saw her, he didn't know how to turn her away."

For the first time since beginning the story, Deenie seems uncomfortable. She lowers her head and crushes the muffin crumbs into the counter with her thumb.

"It went too far," she tells us in a low voice. "Not as far as you two seem to think. Not even close. They met several times. With each meeting, he found himself getting emotionally attached. Nothing physical happened, but the old feelings were still there—and it was getting harder to ignore. He knew he couldn't keep telling himself that it was innocent, that their meetings were just counseling sessions. And yet he didn't want to end it."

She sighs and looks up at our faces, as if she's trying to read our reactions. I'm struggling to keep my expression understanding and nonjudgmental. But I'm scared to hear the rest of this story.

"I heard all of this"—she continues—"my father's confession to my mother, as I crouched over the open air vent in my bedroom." She runs a hand over her forehead. "It was a lot for a twelve-year-old to take in. I could hardly stand it. My father was crying, begging my mother for forgiveness. 'It's over,' he swore. 'I asked her to meet me somewhere nobody knew us, and I told her I couldn't continue being her counselor. That I should never have begun in the first place.'"

Rae is shaking her head skeptically. I motion for her to be

patient, but she can't help herself. "But, that can't be it," she insists. "I know what I saw—"

"You saw that she kissed him," Deenie finishes. "I know. He confessed to that, too. That he did nothing to stop it. But then afterward, he stood up and walked away."

Rae doesn't contradict her; she seems to consider the point for a moment. "So, then I was wrong?" she asks doubtfully. "You're telling me I was wrong? Deenie, you don't understand what this meant to me back then! It destroyed me. I was so, so angry. I thought that I'd spent years listening to a hypocrite. But you're telling me I jumped to conclusions. He wasn't actually a cheater?"

Deenie's eyes harden and her jaw tenses. "No, Rae, you were right. He *was* a cheater."

We're both speechless for a moment. "But—but you just said—" Rae stammers.

"Cheating doesn't have to involve seedy motels and hidden credit card charges. In my father's eyes he was a cheater. From the day he agreed to see her. From the moment that he started down a path that only led to one conclusion."

Rae rolls her eyes. "But it doesn't count. He ended it before—"

"That doesn't matter," Deenie says. "He once told me that the decision to place yourself in the way of temptation is just as bad as giving in to that temptation. That in some ways, the first sin is actually worse. When you make that choice, you're still cool-headed. You aren't swayed by emotion or desire. While you're in the heat of the moment, there's at least passion as an excuse. But when you make that initial decision, when you start down a path you know is wrong, you've passed the point of no return. And that's what he's been repenting for."

Rae shakes her head impatiently. "But he *did* turn back. He wasn't the hypocrite I thought he was."

"So?" Deenie demands. "So what?" She seems angry at Rae's understanding, as if she'd been expecting a condemnation from her friend and was disappointed to find forgiveness. "Why is everything so black-and-white to you? Why does everyone have to be either evil or good? Even if my father was everything you thought he was. Let's say he was a serial adulterer." Her face contorts in disgust. "Let's say he'd committed every sin in the book. If he was a liar and a thief—or even a murderer—I'm asking you, *so what?* Why would that destroy your life or your beliefs? He's just one man. He doesn't define our religion. No man does!"

"Well, to me he did—at least when I was twelve—"

"You're not twelve anymore! And if you want to reject our religion, or all religion, then that is your choice and I respect that. And I will love you no matter what."

Rae's eyes fill up, and she shrinks back in her chair. "I love you too—" she whispers.

"But don't you dare blame your decisions on my father or on anyone else," she interrupts. "They're yours. So own them. You have no idea how lucky you are. I wish I could be as self-confident as you are. I wish I could be proud of my choices."

"Deenie, it's okay," I tell her, reaching out to take her hand. "Rae wasn't blaming your father."

"She's right, I wasn't," Rae says. "Back then I did. I don't know, maybe I was just looking for an excuse. I'd been having doubts forever, and this just came to confirm them. And anyway, it doesn't change anything now. I'm not planning to become a 'born-again' Jew or anything."

Deenie settles back on her stool and takes a deep breath. "It's a great responsibility to be the leader of a community," she says. "People look up to you. They expect you to be perfect. I'm sorry that seeing my father with that woman affected you so much. I wish you'd talked to me. I've always known that my dad is imperfect. I still respected and loved him—but I didn't understand how he could know that something was wrong and yet be drawn to it anyway. It just didn't make sense to me—until that New Year's party." She sighs and looks away. "I get it now."

Chapter 32

I decide to introduce Nina to Deenie during winter break. As painful as my own guilt is, I'd managed to soften its impact with months of denial and imagination. I have to learn to deal with it now, and I've started relating to Nina as my helper, instead of the person standing between me and my fantasy. But Deenie has never imagined away her grief as I have. Instead she's been drowning in it—for almost a year—and I've been standing on the edge watching.

I can't watch silently anymore. One afternoon I make an appointment to see Rabbi Garner for a consultation.

He agrees with my suggestion immediately. "I wanted to take her to a therapist from the beginning," he admits. "But Deenie was so resistant. I should have pushed harder, but I was afraid that doing so might backfire and she'd withdraw completely."

"I don't think she was ready before," I tell him. "But I believe she is now. I'll talk to her."

"Thank you." He hesitates for a moment and leans forward across his desk. "It's more than grief over Danny, isn't it? There's something else there, something she doesn't want to tell me. That's what worries me."

I look away and focus on the heavy ledger on his desk. It's hard to meet his eyes; I know too much—about his secret and his daughter's knowledge of it, about the guilt that Deenie has been carrying forever. I know without asking that Deenie never told her father about her role on New Year's Eve.

I wish she had trusted her father with her burden; I think he, of all people, would understand her guilt. But if she isn't ready to share it with him, I can't betray her trust.

"My therapist is pretty good," I tell him. "Let me bring them together."

To my surprise, Deenie agrees to see her. I don't even have to convince her. I wonder if she's suddenly open to the idea because she has nothing to hide from me now. I've listened to her story, and I haven't rejected her. Instead, I want to get closer to her.

The meeting with Nina is casual and relaxed. After a few minutes I leave them alone together and settle on the living room rocking chair where my mother used to sit during my sessions.

The room is quiet and familiar. The curtains are drawn, and the lights are off, but I can make out the same old antiques and bric-a-brac, the dusty bookshelves crowded with ancient books. My mom stayed home to give Deenie and me some space, so it's the first time I've been alone in this room.

It's been a long time since I've been truly alone anywhere.

"I miss you," I say to the shadow in the corner.

Danny emerges from the darkness and stands in the ray of sunlight breaking between the shades.

"I'm not supposed to talk to you anymore," I tell him quietly. "I know that."

He doesn't reply, and I rise from my chair to face him.

"But I never got a chance to say goodbye," I explain. "So I thought that maybe we can break the rules—just one last time."

There's no judgment in his expression; he looks at me, waiting for me to continue.

"I'm trying to do what you want—what you would have wanted. I'm listening now. To Deenie and Rae. I'm listening to your father."

He doesn't respond, but I see gratitude in his eyes.

"Your dad made an appointment for the ECT clinic," I tell him. "It's just an initial meeting; they call it an 'intake and screening.' I'm going to go with him. See what they have to say. And I'll support him, whatever he decides."

He nods silently.

"I'm listening to Nina, too, and to Ms. Baker. I finally chose a submission for the contest. Do you want to know which one I picked?"

He nods his head.

I glance down at my heavy knapsack. The manuscript is bulging from the open pocket. "Some of those are the stories you told me. But I chose one that I wrote myself. About the four of us."

I don't know what to say to bring him to speak, but I'm getting desperate. I want one word from him. Just one. I can't say goodbye like this.

"I've decided to study journalism," I continue. "I just have to find a way to tell my parents. They still think I'm going for premed."

He raises his eyebrows.

"It's just that I'm not finished writing yet," I explain. "I feel like there's more than that—" I motion at the manuscript. "A lot more. Maybe volumes."

There's a flicker of light in his eyes, finally. I've gotten through. I think that maybe he's ready to speak to me.

"Danny," I beg. "Please say something."

His lips part, and I hold my breath—but nothing comes. He steps back into the shadows.

"Just one word," I urge him. "And then I'll say goodbye. I promise."

The curtains rustle as he moves back into the darkness.

"*Please*. Whatever you want, really. It doesn't have to be much. You don't have to say I love you. I just need one word." My voice breaks. "Danny, I'm sorry for what I did. It's too late now, I can't ask you to forgive me, but I want you to know. I know that you can't tell me that it's okay. I just want to hear your voice. Say anything, Danny. It can be stupid or crazy. It can be completely inappropriate. I don't care."

The shadows are silent.

"One word," I plead. *Maybe an old memory will bring him back*, I think. "You can say dildo face," I whisper. "That would be enough for me."

I can barely see him now. His head is down; he's fading into the gray behind the curtains. He raises his eyes for a moment, and I think he's going to speak, but instead a little smile dawns.

I step forward, my goodbye still on my lips, but the darkness closes over him, and he disappears into the shade.

I'm alone in the room.

Chapter 33

"You're in control, Ellie," Nina tells me in one of our therapy sessions. "When you feel that you're losing that control, when you can no longer gain comfort from your talks with Danny, you have to reevaluate. That's where the rules come in."

I don't need the rules now. Moving on isn't just about me any-more. My fantasy world may have comforted me for a while, but my friends had suffered for it. I know that I can't support them in their grief unless I deal with my own. So I can't go back on my goodbye. As hard as it is, I can't keep bringing him back, even for a moment. I'd been through enough to know that it never ended at just five minutes. If I allowed myself, I would spiral again, like an addict.

So that last meeting at Nina's is really our goodbye, though I never got to hear him say it. I suppose that's fair, though. My Danny never got to say goodbye; I didn't get to tell him I loved him one last time; I would never hear him forgive me. No fantasy could ever make up for that.

I may know all of that, but there's hardly a moment that I'm not tempted to break the rules. When the loneliness gets too heavy, when my pillow feels too cold, when the shadows outside my bed-room window claw through the glass, I'm desperate to push them away, if only for a second. I'm in control, I tell myself, but the meaning of those words twists in my mind. *If you're in control, why not?* my demons taunt me. *Just a quick hello. What's the harm?*

So I leave my room when the longing gets too sharp. I talk to my dad about school. I let my mom take me for a haircut and argue about the best style for me. (We settle on a bob.) I go to Rae's house and volunteer as her sous-chef. (I've become an expert onion chopper.) I take long, silent walks with Deenie, or go for short sprints on my own.

Sometimes I try to write my thoughts down, but loneliness blocks me, and I find it hard to speak to a piece of paper.

A few weeks after I submit my story, Ms. Baker has some news for me. I've won second place. The college grant I receive is small, but what I'm really excited about is the writers' retreat in the summer. Two famous authors will be attending and giving seminars to students about their craft. It's an honor that both thrills and terrifies me. How can I go to this retreat when I'm still blocked? What if I'm asked to submit a writing sample and I can't think of anything to say? What if they expose me as a fraud?

I draw out my winning story and copy it just as I had submitted it—but in my own handwriting. Beneath the title I scrawl "by Eliana Merlis, inspired by Danny Edelstein," then wrap the package in foil and ribbon. Deenie and Rae meet me at my door as I head out. We park at the cemetery and follow the path we'd walked the day of his funeral.

I kneel by his grave and place my offering on the fresh earth. "This is really yours," I tell him. "I may have written it, but you inspired it. You inspired all of them."

Rae places a wrapped package of white chocolate chip brownies by the stone; Deenie lays a yellow rose by its side.

"I need to start telling my own stories," I say to him. "I really want to try. But I think I'm still waiting for one last story."

But there are no more stories in this place; the only sound we hear is the rustle of leaves whispering over the tombstones.

"What happened, Danny?" I ask him. "I need to know what happened."

I feel Rae looking at me; I know she's remembering the police version of events, their theories about that night. I'm so thankful that she doesn't say anything. For us, those theories will never be enough. We need to know the truth.

But he doesn't speak to me anymore. He can't comfort Rae and Deenie, can't give us the ending we want.

I have to tell his story, his last one—as best as I can. And it will have to be enough.

It was so cold on that bridge, I begin. Danny's jacket had blown off his shoulders into the lake, and the sweater he was wearing was soaked through with rain. He was desperate to get inside, but he had no idea where he was. So he started to walk down the road, hoping to flag someone down. As he crossed over the bridge, he realized that there was no shelter for miles and that nobody was coming along. So he decided to call his father for help. He knew he'd be in trouble, but there was no point in delaying it anymore.

He felt for his phone and discovered it was gone. He wasn't sure where he'd dropped it, so he started to retrace his steps, hoping it was somewhere in the slush nearby. He was leaning over a black shadow by the guardrail when a pickup truck came roaring around the bend. They saw each other too late.

He didn't feel anything. That was the surprising thing. It didn't hurt, somehow. When he opened his eyes, there were two men leaning over him. The bearded one was swearing. Danny could tell that it was bad, but only by the expressions on their faces. There was a strange metal taste in his mouth, but he felt fine. He couldn't move for some reason, but it was okay, because he didn't really want to. For the first time since the accident he was comfortable, lying in the back seat of their truck.

The two men argued about what to do. The bearded one pointed at his phone. "Hospital's twenty miles from here. I say we take him there. Drop him off."

"And then what?" his companion asked. He wrapped a scarf tighter around his throat. "What if they want to question us?"

"We don't have a choice," Beard replied. "We can't just leave him here."

They kept arguing as Scarf started up the engine. He was freaking out. "I'm screwed, I'm totally screwed," he babbled. "It's a company truck. They're going to fire me."

"Just drive, okay? The kid's not looking so good."

They both glanced back at Danny. "I'm fine," he tried to tell them, but the metal in his mouth was blocking the words.

"Aw, Jesus," Scarf muttered. "He's making noises."

"He'll be all right," Beard snapped. He unbuckled his belt and climbed into the back seat. "We're just a couple of miles out now."

Danny's arms were getting numb, and there was a crushing weight on his chest. He closed his eyes and tried to inhale, but it was like breathing through water. Somebody was shaking him.

"Come on, kid, come on. Wake up."

He wanted to tell them that he was awake. He was suddenly sitting right in between them, watching them; he could smell the whiskey and cigars on Scarf's breath.

"I'm Danny," he told them, but they didn't seem to hear him. "Could you take me home?"

"Oh, fuck," Beard spat out. "Oh, fuck!"

"Do something!" his friend shouted. "Breathe into his mouth."

"I can't," he cried. "Look." He lifted his fingers in the air. They glistened maroon in the moonlight.

Scarf hit the gas hard, and the truck bounced and veered off the road. They came to a halt on a deserted side street.

"What do we do now?" Scarf yelled. "What the hell do we do?"

"This is going to be manslaughter at least," Beard warned. "You stink to high heaven."

"Fuck you, what do we do? Do we just leave him here?"

"Lying out on the road? So some little kid finds him?" Beard swore again and spit out the window. "Jesus, you really are a dick. Get the tools in the trunk."

"I don't have a shovel."

They climbed out, and there was a clatter of metal as they rummaged in the back. "Fine. This will have to do."

"What about his family?"

"Just shut up and dig, will you? Unless you want to go to jail?"

Danny felt suddenly lighter—almost weightless. There was nothing keeping him grounded to the men who grunted and sweated over a small clay hole in the ground.

So he came back to me. It took longer than he expected, but he didn't mind; the rain had stopped and the sun was rising by the time he tapped on my window.

I pushed it open and pulled him into the room.

"How are you so warm?" I asked Danny.

"I think that's you," he said. "I'm freezing." He smiled gratefully as I pulled a blanket off my bed. But even as I wrapped it around his shoulders, I knew that he wasn't cold anymore.

Chapter 34

I arrive at Mr. Edelstein's house more than an hour before I need to. His appointment isn't until later in the evening, but I'm so anxious about it, I head over immediately after school lets out.

He's rummaging through old boxes when I get there, and he points at a pile of old discs on the floor. "I found something for you," he says. "I know that you've finished your collection, but I thought it would interest you anyway."

"I don't know if I'll ever be finished," I remark, picking up a disc labeled *Danny age 10*. "Even if I run out of Danny stories, I'm not going to stop writing. I'm realizing that there are plenty more stories out there."

He passes his laptop over to me, and I balance it on my knees. As I slide the disc in, the screen lights up with static, and then a home video comes into focus. A ten-year-old Danny is sitting on a sofa with a sullen look on his face. He's dressed all in black; a discarded ski mask lies crumpled up next to him. He looks up at the camera and frowns. *"Ema!"* he protests. *"Al titzalmi oti!"*

I realize with a start that Danny has just spoken Hebrew—fluent, unaccented Hebrew. I'd never heard anything from him but a few halting, broken words during Hebrew language class. I'd always assumed he was a beginner. "What did he say?" I ask.

"Mom, don't film me." Mr. Edelstein raises a finger to his lips. "Shhh—Ellie. Just listen."

I pulled him close to me and promised to wait for him forever.

I pause for a moment and study Deenie's and Rae's tear-stained faces. They've been silent through my story, which flows from me like a prayer.

"And I did," I tell them. "I really tried to wait forever. I thought our love was different—I thought it was above the rules."

Rae and Deenie bow their heads, and I know that my prayer is over.

"But it wasn't," I whisper to myself. "Our love wasn't above this rule."

There's a soft chuckle from behind the camera, and Danny waves a hand in front of it. *"Dai, zeh lo matzchik!"*

"Stop it, it's not funny," Mr. Edelstein translates.

A woman's voice interrupts Danny's protest. *"Idan, ma itcha?"* She sounds frustrated—but there's a note of amusement in her reprimand.

Mr. Edelstein reaches out and stops the recording. "She was asking him what his problem was. He was in a lot of trouble that day."

I have so many questions that I can't decide which to ask first. But there is one detail that jumps out at me. "His mother called him Idan!" She had pronounced it Ee-dahn, I noted. I'd never heard anyone call him that. I do a quick search on my phone and pull up my favorite name website. "Idan Noah," I read. "It means 'time of comfort.'"

I shake my head and put my phone down. *Time of comfort.* I think if I had learned its meaning later, I might have smiled at the revelation. But it's too soon, and I'm too raw. Maybe one day I will draw strength from this knowledge. But now it hurts more than it comforts.

"His mom was the only one who used his given name," his father explains. "Dalia was fluent in Hebrew, and she thought it was important to raise him speaking his native tongue." He shrugs resignedly. "I'm afraid my Hebrew wasn't good enough for that. I spoke to him in English and I called him Danny, like everybody else. But he did grow up bilingual."

"I don't understand," I say. "He could have placed out of our language class. Why did he hide that he was fluent? And why didn't he ever tell me his real name?"

His dad laughs and moves to take the computer from me, but I grab on to it and pull it back. There's precious information on that disc.

"I asked him the same thing," he tells me. "Danny could be pretty mysterious when he wanted to be. It wasn't until I met the cute redhead who'd sat next to him on the plane that I figured out why he didn't want to be placed in the advanced Hebrew group."

I can't help smiling at the compliment. "We were in different classes in ninth grade," I said, understanding suddenly. "Hebrew was the only period we had together. I guess he didn't want to give that up."

"As for his name—" He shakes his head. "Who knows? Maybe he was saving it for a last story—in case he ever ran out? Or maybe he was just being a tease. He liked keeping people on their toes."

"Yes, he definitely did," I say. "What was his mother scolding him about—in that video?"

He laughs out loud for the first time in ages. It's a light, crackling sound and reminds me a little of Danny's laugh. "Ah, that was just embarrassing. My boy was the ringleader of a botched break-in. He and a few of his friends dressed up like ninjas and tried to scale the school wall. They were attempting to steal some tests, I believe. They never got past the front gate."

"I remember that story!" I exclaim. "I didn't believe him. It was too ridiculous."

"It was ridiculous!" he says. "He didn't even need the tests; he was a straight A student. Honestly, I think he just did it for the fun. He was really into ninjas for a while. Climbed every tree in the neighborhood."

The alarm on my phone beeps, and I reach into my pocket to

silence it. “We better go or we’ll be late to your appointment.”

He nods and rises from his chair.

“Can I take the disc with me?” I ask him, pulling it out of the laptop. “I want to watch the whole thing. And I think Deenie and Rae will love it.”

“You can keep it,” he says. “But maybe make a copy for me? I want to have the video on my computer—for after the treatment. Just in case I forget some things . . .”

His voice trails off, and he touches the screen.

“Don’t worry,” I tell him. “You won’t lose a single memory, I promise. I’ll make sure you never forget.”

Epilogue

We're sitting around the computer in a circle, a pile of white chocolate chip blondies stacked in a pyramid like a tribute. It's the third playthrough of the fifteen-minute video, and none of us has the heart to take it off repeat.

"Skinniest ninja on Earth," Rae declares after I finally shut it off. "Good old shrimpy boy."

"I wonder how many of those crazy stories were actually true?" Deenie muses.

I reach for a mushroom pinwheel and pluck off the crispy edge. It's my latest contribution to our defrost parties. We've been having one every Sunday morning for the last three months. The freezer of favorite food I'd saved for Danny's homecoming is almost empty—but it's been almost empty for weeks now.

The bottom drawer of my freezer is charmed, it seems. No matter how many times we dig into it, we never come up empty-handed. I strongly suspect that Rae is the magician behind the miracle, but I'm never going to call her on it.

"All the stories were true, I think," I tell her.

"I like the one about the singer," Deenie says quietly. "The one that nobody can hear."

Rae grins at her. "That one is very true."

"I know," she admits. "That's why I brought it up."

I shoot Rae a puzzled look, and she shakes her head. She's obviously as confused as I am. Deenie brushes some crumbs off her skirt and slowly gets to her feet. "I was wondering if you two could be my practice audience," she asks. "Before my audition."

Our baffled expressions speak for us.

"I'm trying out for the spring performance of *Fiddler on the Roof*," she explains.

Rae says something loud and unintelligible.

"It's not a big deal," Deenie insists, raising her hand. "It's just for a part in the chorus. Not a solo role. Anyway, I'm probably not going to get it."

"You're probably not going to get it? *Are you kidding*?"

She looks embarrassed. "They're still pretty mad about my pulling out of the fall production. They weren't going to give me another chance. My father basically had to beg."

"Well, I can't wait to hear you," I say, and Rae nods enthusiastically.

Deenie loads the playback on her phone, clears her throat, and starts her first number. I don't know if it's the fact that I haven't heard Deenie's voice in months, or she's singing with a new passion, but to me it's the most beautiful sound I have ever heard. I barely breathe until she's done.

I forget to clap when she takes a bashful little bow; I just sit openmouthed, grinning from ear to ear. Rae runs over to her and grabs her by the shoulders. "I don't care if you don't get the part," she declares. "That was the best thing that's ever happened to me. Sing another one."

Deenie doesn't respond to the compliment, but her face glows. "What do you want me to sing?"

"I don't care," I tell her. "Your pick."

"How about that song you and Danny liked?" Rae suggests. "'Last Words'? As a tribute to him."

"Really?"

"Yeah," Rae says slyly. "Danny loved it when you sang that one."

"What are you talking about?" I ask. "Danny never heard her sing. She wouldn't let him."

Deenie's face has gone from a pleased pink to bright red. "Well—" She hesitates and glances toward the kitchen window. "Actually—"

"Actually what?"

Deenie looks too embarrassed to answer me, but Rae opens the side door and motions with her hand. "Ellie, why don't you go outside?" she instructs. "Just stand by the trash cans for a moment."

A memory is stirring now, but I'm still not sure what they're getting at. I head out to the patio and walk up to the bins just as Rae pushes open the kitchen window.

There's a faint sound of laughter from inside, and then Deenie's crystal voice floats out to me.

"Oh, I'm dreaming about you, my darling
And what my life would be like if we didn't last the day
Oh, please wake me
From this dream, my darling
So I can tell you I love you
And make sure we leave it that way . . ."

I remember now; the lyrics bring it all back. Deenie sent him out here once, knowing full well that he would be able to hear her if he stood in that spot. I'm standing just where he did that afternoon, and I can hear her as if she's right in front of me.

As she sings, Danny joins me by the window. I can't see him, but I can feel him in the music. I know that he's with me and that he's hearing her again.

"If it's the last words that we say—" she sings. *"If it's the last words that we say—"*

I close my eyes and listen with him.

ACKNOWLEDGMENTS

Though the writing process is often a solitary one, the journey to publication requires a team of dedicated experts and a host of supportive volunteers.

To my amazing team, I'm so grateful that *The Last Words We Said* found a home at Simon & Schuster. Liesa Abrams, you showed me from our very first conversation that you felt for Ellie, Danny, Deenie, and Rae as much as I did. Your editorial suggestions were spot-on; my novel grew so much under your instruction. Kendra Levin, you helped me polish my manuscript and made me say, "Now, why didn't I think of that?" more times than I care to admit. Thank you to Kristie Patterson and Amanda Ramirez, to the sales and marketing team, and to the artists, Laura Eckes and Ana Jarén, who created the gorgeous cover.

To Rena Rossner, my incomparable agent and friend—this is our third novel together, and I hope this is just the beginning of our publication journey. I love that I can always count on you for advice, honest critique, and the best pastries I have ever tasted.

To my volunteers, I would never have had the confidence to write this very personal novel without all your guidance and support. To the Atlanta Jewish community, thank you for welcoming me and my family for the three years we lived in Toco Hills. Though the characters in this novel are entirely fictional, the warmth and hospitality of the congregation is very real. I will always cherish my memories of the *shuls*, the schools, the rabbis, and the teachers that shaped my children's lives. Thank you to my young consultants, who advised me as I wrote the novel. Herschel

Siegel, Shani Weinmann, and Zoie Wittenberg—your insight into high school life in Atlanta was invaluable.

Eliana Megerman, for the hours of book talk over sushi and ice cream, thank you.

To my parents, you encouraged me to write before I even knew I wanted to. I owe everything to you.

To Aviva (better known as the artist Avaya), I have listened to the song "Last Words," which you wrote for the novel, more times than I can count. It makes me cry every time. (I hope everyone goes to Avaya's YouTube channel to hear Deenie's song!)

To Miriam and Talia, you are always my first beta readers and my biggest cheerleaders. I love you more than I can say. Ami and Dani, my twin three-year-old wonders, you keep me young. Literally. I don't have a choice.

To Eric, the best husband and most patient father I have ever met—thank you for pushing me to write, even when the only thing I wanted to do was bake cookies and watch TV. I wouldn't have published a single word without you.

GLOSSARY OF HEBREW AND YIDDISH TERMS

bima: podium (at the front of the synagogue)

daven(ing): pray(ing)

frum: religious

goyish: non-Jewish

kavana: devotion/concentration (here referring to intense concentration during prayer)

kippah: skullcap, a brimless cap, usually made of cloth, traditionally worn by Orthodox Jewish males

kiruv: "to bring one close"—introducing nonpracticing Jews to Jewish customs in order to acquaint them with the faith

mitzvot: commandments (sometimes used to mean "good deeds")

musaf: afternoon prayers

Neilah: the final prayer at the end of the Yom Kippur service

Shabbat: the Jewish Sabbath and a day of rest, observed on Saturday

Shema: a prayer declaring the oneness and sovereignty of God; traditionally the eyes are closed while reciting the first line to increase concentration

shiva: the seven-day mourning period

shofar: a ram's horn which is traditionally blown during Rosh Hashanah services and at the end of Yom Kippur

shul: synagogue

siddur: prayer book